RICHARD BLOMBERG

WARPATH

Warpath, Published August, 2013

Editorial and Proofreading Services: Neysa Jensen, Shannon Miller

Photo Credits:

Shutterstock, *abstract explosion background* #71537224,
© Jiri Vaclavek

Depositphotos, *Game at the soldiers* | Stock Photo #1153826,
© Artem Zamula

Depositphotos, *Silhouettes of American Indians on horseback* | Stock
Vector #7527212, © __akc76

Cover Design: Howard Communigrafix, Inc.
Interior Design and Layout: Howard Communigrafix, Inc.

 **SDP Publishing**

Published by SDP Publishing, an imprint of SDP Publishing
Solutions, LLC.

For more information about this book contact Lisa Akoury-Ross by email at
lross@SDPPublishing.com.

To obtain permission(s) to use material from this work, please submit a written
request to:

SDP Publishing
Permissions Department
36 Captain's Way, East Bridgewater, MA 02333
or email your request to info@SDPPublishing.com.

ISBN-13: 978-0-9889381-6-8

Library of Congress Control Number: 2013946063

Copyright © 2013, Richard Blomberg

Printed in the United States of America

"There can never be peace between nations until it is first known that true peace is within the souls of men."

Black Elk

Glossary

A-10	Thunderbolt Warthog/single-seat jet loaded with Gatling guns and cannons
AA	Assist and Advise (SEALs working with the CIA)
AC-130	Heavily armed gunship flying to support ground troops
Allah Akbar	God is great (part of a Muslim prayer)
ANA	Afghan National Army
BUDS	Basic Underwater Demolition SEAL boot camp
C2	Command and Control (mission control personnel in the field)
CBR	Chemical Biological Radiation (a type of protective suit)
CO	Commanding Officer
COB	Civilians On Base
CTF	Counterterrorism Task Force
DAP	Direct Action Penetrator (a nasty helicopter)
EA-6	Electronic warfare plane launched from aircraft carriers (a jammer)
EKIA	Enemy Killed In Action (a bad guy was killed)
EOD	Explosive Ordinance Disposal unit
F-15	Strike Eagle (fast-moving fighter jet; drops JDAMs)
FKIA	Friendly Killed In Action (a good guy was killed)
frag	Fragmentation grenade
Frog	Term of endearment, from one SEAL to another
gator	Interrogator
HARP	High-Altitude Release Point (where they jump out of the plane)
HCH	High Confidence Hit
HEU	Highly Enriched Uranium
Hooch	SEAL language for private quarters, wherever they are

IED	Improvised Explosive Device (terrorist homemade bomb)
indig	Indigenous Afghanistan soldiers/CIA mercenaries
ISR	Intelligence, Surveillance, and Reconnaissance
Jammer	Electronic jamming device; blocks Internet, radio, and phone signals
JDAM	Joint Direct Attack Munition (2,000-pound, GPS-guided bombs)
JOC	Joint Operations Command Center at Bagram Air Field
MRE	Meal Ready to Eat (military rations)
NAVAID	Navigational Aid (chest-mounted GPS)
MOLLE	Modular Lightweight Load-carrying Equipment (outerwear with lots of pockets)
NOD	Night Observation Device (goggles that see in the dark)
NSOD	Navy Special Ops Desk in JOC
NTRC	Norfolk Trauma and Rehabilitation Center
ORP	Operational Ready Point (mission control point in the field)
Pak Mill	Pakistan Military (good and bad; mostly ineffective)
Pashto	Also known as Afghani, this is the native language of the Pashtun people of South-Central Asia (used by the Taliban)
Pathrai	Pashto word for a CIA electronic transmitter or tracker
Peltor	Noise-cancelling communication headphones
PJ	Air Force Pararescue Jumper (like an EMT)
POTUS	President Of The United States
PUC	Person Under Control (a living prisoner)
RAM	Radar Absorbent Material
RCD	Remote Control Detonation
RECCE	Reconnaissance (snipers)
RPG	Rocket Propelled Grenade

SDV	Swimmer Delivery Vehicle
SOAR	Special Operations Aviation Regiment (The Army's best special operations helicopter aviators.
SSE	Sight Sensitive Exploitation (grab anything with intelligence value)
SWCC	Special Warfare Combatant Craft Crewman (drive SEAL attack boats)
terp	Interpreter
therm	Thermobaric grenade
TNT	Trinitrotoluene (like dynamite)
UAV	Unmanned Aerial Vehicle (drone)
VIP	Very Important Prisoner

1

Near Bamba Kot, Afghanistan

Jack cleared the smoky hut like he'd done a thousand times before. No suicide vests. No trap doors. No one hiding in the shadows waiting to ambush him. Just another desperate mother trying to protect her children.

The Afghan woman facing Jack waved a butcher knife. She had been frying dinner for her family in an iron skillet straddling two flat rocks over a bed of embers. A kerosene lantern flickered on the only table. Soot smeared the mud wall above the poorly vented fireplace. Her kids clutched her robe and cried. The pan of grease caught fire and their only meal of the day burned to a crisp.

"Where is he?" Jack said, and the interpreter repeated. Jack Gunn looked like the one man in a thousand you did not want to mess with. At six foot three, everything about him was massive. He kept a full beard and shaved head to look like an Uzbekistan terrorist instead of a Navy SEAL. His broad nose had been broken and never properly straightened. He moved like he feared nothing. His unwavering gaze missed nothing. He analyzed everything and everybody for threats and weaknesses.

The woman's eyes darted from her kids, to Jack, his gun, the interpreter, and back to her kids. She froze. She said nothing, and looked exhausted.

7

Jack knew she would not give her husband up. He'd had enough. He had learned years ago, if he needed to know quick, ask the kids. He fixed his gaze on the oldest child. The boy started crying. Jack remembered something his Grandpa Joe used to say about catching more flies with honey than vinegar. Without taking his eyes off them, he fished a handful of suckers out of his backpack and held them out to tempt the boy. He stopped crying. When he lunged for the suckers, Jack raised them above his head.

"After you tell me where your father's hiding."

The woman wrapped an arm around her children, pointed the butcher knife at Jack, and screamed some shrill Afghan curse. Grease flames shot to the top of the fireplace. Another day without eating. All those kids could do was cry.

"Man, I hate this God-forsaken place," said Jack.

"Hey Gunner," Jack heard Dewey say in his ear phone, "Sarge's sniffed out something. You'd better get your ass over to Building Five before he chews haji's head off."

Good, bad, or otherwise, the SEALs called every man in Afghanistan, Pakistan, or Iraq "haji." If they wore a robe and turban, kneeled on a prayer rug, or carried a gun, they were haji.

"Check," Jack growled into his microphone. He crouched and backed out the door into the night, sweeping his assault rifle from side to side. He tossed the suckers into the shack, and quickly pulled the rickety door shut without a squeak. In the next instant, her knife slammed between the slats of wood, bounced off Jack's chest plate, and fell to the dirt floor. "Guess it's my lucky day," he said as he jerked the door back open, grabbed the knife, adjusted his grip, and heaved it back at her. It whizzed past her nose and penetrated deep into the hearth above the fire, like a sharp ax chopping soft wood. Jack's rifle laser painted her forehead red. The room went dead quiet. She went dead quiet. Jack took a deep breath, then backed out the door again.

Seeing starving kids trapped in a war by stupid parents drove Jack mad. The bomb-maker Dewey was holding treated his wife and kids like dogs, but she still wouldn't give him up. The woman had made her decision, but the kids had nowhere to go. It was an injustice Jack couldn't fix, but it ate at him like metastatic cancer. Something his wife, Nina, was all too familiar with. But he didn't have time for that right now. He had a job to do.

Jack checked right, and then left. Their target was the Taliban bomb-maker from the previous night's mission in a neighboring village. Images flooded back to Jack of a wailing, desperate Afghan woman running toward him, cradling her flopping, dead son after he had stepped on the bomb trigger buried in their marketplace. His six-year-old legs had been ripped off, leaving mangled stumps. His anemic eyes did not blink. They just stared into eternity. Jack pictured his own son in Virginia. Then the boy in the hut. He was angry enough to rip the bomber's legs off.

Sweat bled from under Jack's helmet, down his neck, into his body armor. He flipped his night vision goggles—NODs—up and rubbed his eyes. He crooked his head to the side, stared into the dark, and listened, like he had done his entire life growing up on the reservation. He heard the wind crooning through pine needles. A baby cried in the night. A boot scuffled in the dirt. There was tension in the air. Someone was about to die.

"The perimeter is secure," Jack heard.

Jack, an eighteen-year SEAL veteran, had quit worrying about what he had become. He hunted terrorists and enemies of the United States of America. He liked his job. The president said he was their best asset. "A perfect combination of Native American bravery and twenty-first-century technology. A warrior's warrior." Many back on the reservation where Jack had grown up, believed white people were half-civilized and had lost their way, lacking spiritual strength and contact with nature's rhythm.

"Why you selling out to join whitey's Navy?" his high school classmates would taunt. "Now you're too good for us? You're a traitor to your own people."

"Well, you're going nowhere except Watering Hole #1," he'd snap back.

Maybe he was a traitor, but he had quit worrying about it. Regardless of his culture, he saw a nation that needed protection.

He didn't know if he loved leading the terrorist-hunting Ghost Team because he was an efficient killer or because he was a patriot. He pictured himself standing in the breach to stop the senseless killing of innocent people. Doing what no one had done for his people a hundred and twenty-five years earlier when they were forced onto reservations. He had given up worrying about that too. If he stopped to think about it, he would be dead. He had a mission to complete, his men to lead and another terrorist plot to foil. He would have plenty of time in his old age, if he survived, to rehash what made him tick.

"Check," said Jack.

He flipped his NODs back down over his eyes. His safety was off. His weapon was hot, and a thirty-round magazine was good to go. He took a drink of water from the sip-tube over his shoulder and listened.

A fire raged inside him like none other, to be the best warrior, the best SEAL, the world had ever known. It came from his Sioux ancestry. His upbringing. His soul. When he was a boy romping over the plains of Montana, Grandpa Joe and the tribal elders taught him the old ways. By the time he was eighteen, he was ready to take on the world.

Warring was in his blood. That's what made the SEALs such a perfect fit for the great, great, great-grandson of Sitting Bull, the Sioux Indian holy man and warrior. If anything, he felt like he had gotten a little payback for his people from the government that had persecuted the Native Americans. Millions of dollars had been invested by the U.S. Navy and others to assure the State Department that Jack remained their weapon for all situations. And Jack was proud of it, even if no one else in his family was.

"We mark you standing outside of Building Three. Nothing but friendlies between you and Five," chirped the voice in Jack's ear.

Jack eased back into the shadows, shivering when his sweaty back touched the wall. The crisp fall air erased the lingering grease-fire smell from the hut, but not his sudden craving for a hamburger and a plateful of fry bread. Damn, he missed his wife, Nina, and six-year-old son, Jake. Thinking of them brought a painful lump to his chest.

He pictured Nina sitting in the chemo chair, and then shook his head to clear away the image. Her voice was in his ear like she was standing right next to him.

"Why can't they find someone else to go? Why is it always you?" She was crying.

Jack hated it when she cried. He did not know what to say without sounding like an emotionless jerk.

"I've got no choice, Nina. They need me."

"And I don't?' she screamed. "I've got *cancer*, Jack."

"I'm really sorry, Nina." Jack wrapped his arms around her, but she shoved him off. "It'll be a quick trip. In and out. I'll get some time off after this one. I promise."

She stood facing Jack, tears streaming down her face. "Jake and I have heard that one before, Jack. It sounds good until the Navy calls and they need you to save their ass again," said Nina. "There'll always be another mission, Jack. The world is falling apart. Hard as you try, you can't save it." said Nina. "You need to decide what and who is more important, the SEALs or me."

He should have found a way to be there instead of halfway around the world in some Afghanistan hellhole. Who was watching Jake? Did he have to go sit in the oncology treatment room and see his mom like that? He slapped himself on the side of the helmet and refocused. Thinking of them could get him killed.

"Check. Light up Five."

A cone of light appeared out of nowhere and miraculously made Building Five, and only Building Five, glow in the dark. Actually, the Air Force strobed down infrared floodlights from planes patiently circling a mile or two off target. The light was visible to the lucky few who wore the NODs.

As he double-timed it across the ink-black compound, he pictured his SEAL snipers stationed on top of other buildings tracking him through their gun scopes, and scanning the compound for threats. ISR (Intelligence, Surveillance, and Reconnaissance) aircraft circled inaudibly above, searching for enemy heat signals. "All clear," called ISR.

Thanks to his ancestors and training, Jack sensed when an enemy gun barrel was pointed at him. It felt like a spider crawling up his neck. He did not have to concentrate or try, it just happened. As he sprinted across the dirt, he felt no spiders.

Jack spotted Dewey as he slid into the barn. "What do ya got?"

Dewey had heard the prisoner talking on a cell phone from outside Building Five. He snuck in from behind, careful not to make a sound. The prisoner about swallowed his tongue when Dewey pressed his rifle barrel against his temple and said in Pashto, "Don't move." The prisoner had been soldering wires to a detonator.

"Sarge started going ape-shit around that wood pile," said Dewey. Sarge, their combat dog, heeled at Dewey's left side, panting and eyeing the pile. Slobber and dirt pooled in the dirt below his dangling tongue. "We checked it for booby traps. Crawl space underneath full of trip wires, fuses, switches, dynamite, and old artillery shells the crazy bastard must've dug up."

"Where is he?" Jack growled. The air stunk of fertilizer and musty oil. There were fifty-gallon barrels of ammonium nitrate along the wall.

Dewey tapped his earpiece. "Bring him in."

Building Five reminded Jack of his grandpa's machine shed where he'd spent summer nights tinkering on lawn mowers and bicycles. Dirt floor, poor light, a mess of tools. Grandpa Joe smoking his pipe, sitting on a three-legged stool, and telling Jack and Travis, Jack's only sibling, stories of growing up on the Montana reservation.

After their parents died, Travis sort of shuffled his way through childhood and left the reservation, abandoning Grandpa Joe, his Sioux heritage, and Jack, as soon as he could. He stopped calling or writing. He might as well have stuck a knife in Grandpa Joe's back. Jack had no idea why Travis ran. Why he gave up. Twenty years later, they rarely talked.

Two SEALs led in the zip-tied bomb-maker, all one hundred and forty pounds of skin and bones on a five-foot-six frame. He bled from the corners of his mouth into his fist-length beard. He walked hunched over.

"The gator's already asked the usual questions. He's not talking," said Dewey as he gave the prisoner a final shove. The prisoner's hands were tied behind his back. He stood in the no-man's land between Jack and Dewey, shooting worried glances from side to side, anticipating the blows to come. He eyed the dog sitting at Dewey's left side. Sarge eyed him like a T-bone steak.

"No big surprise," said Jack. "The Taliban's one big happy family. Only one way to stop them." Jack shouldered his rifle, aimed at the prisoner's head, chambered a round, and clicked the safety off.

The prisoner blabbered something Jack did not need or want the interpreter's help on. It didn't matter. Jack didn't care. The prisoner tried raising his bound hands. Dewey pinned them down. The prisoner pleaded.

Jack exhaled slowly, then moved closer, still aiming at his head. He glared at the prisoner over the gun sights. The prisoner squeezed his eyes shut. Jack paused, then jerked his gun to the side and fired a three-round burst into the dirt beside the prisoner.

The prisoner's knees buckled like he had been shot, but Dewey caught him. He begged Jack not to kill him.

"Fucker's not going to talk," said Dewey. "What you wanna do?"

"Kill him, and there will be three more just like him tomorrow," said Jack.

"He killed that little boy last night," said Dewey. Dewey spit in the prisoner's face and chambered a round.

Jack stared at the prisoner through dark eyes. Killing a terrorist was always better than not killing a terrorist. In Jack's mind, that made one less person he had to worry about. And there were no lack of people trying to kill them, given that Ghost Team had killed hundreds of terrorists over the years.

Jack grabbed the prisoner by the collar. "Start talking, you worthless piece of shit," he yelled. "Who's paying you? Where are they?"

The interpreter did his job. Jack understood bits and pieces of the Pashto dialect. They were getting nowhere.

Jack looked down at the prisoner, and his nose twitched like a snarling dog's. The prisoner went limp when Jack hoisted him off the ground. His feet barely scraped the floor. He kept his eyes down.

"He's wasting our time, and time is something we don't have a lot of," said Jack.

"What do you want to do?" asked Dewey again.

"Let the gators have some fun back at base," said Jack. "Rug him and lug him."

He dropped the prisoner, who cowered in the dirt like a guilty dog expecting to be kicked.

"Blow Five," said Jack. "Leave our food packs for his family."

Jack briefed the team on the evacuation plan. Two men made sure the prisoner had his wrists and ankles zipped, stuck duct tape over his mouth, and rolled him up in a rug from the house—a security blanket against biting and kicking. After a few well-placed kicks, the rug went dead quiet.

"We're ready to rock and roll, Gunner," said Dewey. "Calling in the fast movers to drop a five-hundred pounder on Building Five might have killed his family, so we went with a charge in the crawl space that'll blow when the therm blows." A therm (thermobaric grenade) had so much TNT, it was perfect for collapsing the mud buildings in Afghanistan. It took out the supporting walls and dropped the hammer. Anyone still inside popped like a grape in a mud slam.

The Ghost Team assaulters waited outside the compound wall as the therm exploded. It sounded like a runaway locomotive on the other side, sucking them against the wall, quaking the very ground they stood on. Chips of dried mud clinked off their helmets, but the wall held. Secondary explosions followed as the prisoner's cache of bombs blew.

The team popped smoke to cover their exfiltration and headed back down the same ravine where they'd infiltrated, with their RECCE (reconnaissance) snipers leading the way. They all had the GPS coordinates loaded into their chest units, but they chose the line-of-sight, single-file, Navy SEAL patrol formation. Where one Frog went, they all went, like a Sioux war party.

Most of the SEALs carried fifty pounds of war toys on their backs. On top of that, they had to trade off lugging the prisoner over their shoulder. They double-timed it quickly and quietly, shuffling down the rocky trail toward the extraction point, a mile away.

Jack felt a disturbance to his right. Like his ear was slightly plugged with water. The spider crawled up his neck. He looked up, squinted into the darkness. "Take cover," he growled into his mike.

The team dove for cover. AK-47 bullets sprayed the ravine a split-second later. Jack's RECCE snipers spotted the muzzle flashes and zeroed in on the ridgeline above. Sparks flew as American lead ricocheted off Afghan granite. Enemy fire stopped.

It would have been suicidal for the team to use the ravine in the daytime. It was ambush central, funneling the SEALs right into a Taliban kill zone. Steep canyon walls. One way in. One way out. However, nighttime was different. It was SEAL time. They ruled with technology no Taliban ambusher could imagine. Most of America could not imagine.

"The sneaky bastards must have gotten some night eyes," said Jack. "Probably stole them from us."

The patrol laid low and listened. An explosion rocked the ravine a mile back. A flash in the dark. Distant gunfire too. The team had deployed trailing booby traps. Devious little creations. An explosive core of Semtex with eight trigger wires stretching out twenty feet in all directions, like the world's deadliest daddy longlegs spider. The next unfortunate bastard to snag a wire was cut to pieces, along with his closest friends.

ISR planes marked three bad guys hunkered down behind a cluster of boulders on the ridgeline. "It looks like they've had enough. Move out," said Jack.

They hadn't moved fifty feet when more shots and muzzle flashes came from a different pile of boulders farther down the same ridgeline. The SEAL snipers laced the rocks with 5.56 rounds again while the team dove for cover.

"Get 'em off our ass or we'll die in the crossfire," said Jack into his radio. "We're running out of time. What's the call, Big Daddy?"

"Hold one," said Big Daddy. Big Daddy was Ghost Team's manager, the go-between to keep everyone, from one-star generals all the way up to five stars and beyond, off Jack's back so his men could do what they were paid to do: kill bad guys. Big Daddy trailed along behind Jack's assaulters, with the interpreters, interrogators, medics, and other support staff. He and the combat controllers were the link between the assaulters and the array of Air Force and Army death toys circling their position in the dark Afghan skies. ISR tracked on their radar screens what Jack felt. Over thirty terrorists were quickly scrambling down the ravine, but were still a half-mile behind.

"The drone's marking two groups of three, shadowing your team," said Big Daddy. "We're not screwing around anymore. The A-10 will be on target in thirty seconds."

Jack wedged himself against the back crease of a five-foot-high boulder. He put in a fresh magazine, took a drink, and waited.

The day had begun like most for Jack. He'd rolled out of the rack at 1000 to see what ISR was tracking with their different platforms: drones, satellites, other eavesdropping assets, phone intercepts, and intelligence from local informants.

He'd worked out with his men, showered, eaten, and by noon knew who their target for the night would be. On the current mission, information had come from a local informant and, so far, it had been credible.

He slept during the afternoon, ate again, checked his equipment, and re-checked the intelligence. After dark, Jack held their mission briefing. At 2100, the Chinook helicopter off-loaded the team at their insertion point. They humped three miles uphill, timing it to arrive on target after midnight. ISR and other Air Force assets stalked their every move silently from above. They'd arrived undetected, gotten their man, and destroyed the evidence. Everything had gone flawlessly, but the clock was ticking.

The Warthog growled in from the abyss like an Air Force tsunami, firing thousands of forty-millimeter, mini-tootsie roll sized rounds per minute from Gatling guns, chewing up every inch of ground on the ridgeline above. Jack loved the sound and effect. The ability of his task force to call in such a devastating machine, a game changer. It sounded like a giant man-eating wood-chipper ripping apart everything in its path—trees, homes, terrorists. In the past, he'd combed through the human debris in its wake. Nothing larger than a quarter survived. A human lawn mower. It spared nothing. Forgave nothing. As quickly as it started, it stopped.

"You fucked with the wrong guys tonight," Jack muttered. "Move out."

They patrolled down to the extraction point, well ahead of terrorists chasing them down the ravine. They chucked the rug roll in and climbed aboard their Chinook helicopter for the short hop back to their base.

"Not a bad night. We got to waste a few of Allah's chosen, and we're still in one piece," said Jack.

"Whoop-de-fucking-do! We're putting our lives on the line to nail some bastard making bombs for bread money. When's command going to get their head out of their ass?" asked Dewey. He jabbed the rolled-up prisoner with his rifle. "This guy's a throw away. They're wasting our time."

"I get as pissed as anyone," said Jack. "But something's brewing. I can feel it in my bones."

Jack stared out the open hatch into the dark, felt the

mountain air swirl in their draft, the vibration of the chopper, and the soul of his people. Grandpa Joe had taught him something passed down from one Sioux warrior to the next for hundreds of years. Be faithful toward your friends. Be cruel toward your enemies. The ancients were stirring in Jack's soul. It was time to go on the warpath.

2

Dubai, United Arab Emirates

Dr. Travis Gunn plopped into a rattan love seat on the patio of the Dubai Beach Club Resort. The dry Persian Gulf breeze and a straight-up Bombay Sapphire martini with a twist combined to erase the strain of another day doing anesthesia on the rich and spoiled.

Travis loved Dubai. The City of Gold sat on the shores of the Persian Gulf, where traders from India, Asia, Arabia, Africa, and Europe had passed for centuries. It was born for opulence, luring visitors and seekers into Sheik Mohammad bin Rashid's playground. During the day, Dubai was a permissive, but respectful Muslim city. At night, it was an exotic oasis limited only by one's imagination.

Travis adored peering at the European and Eastern bloc flight attendants around the pool through his Gucci sunglasses. The beach club was a popular oasis for international airlines and patient fly-ins on a combined plastic surgery/holiday package. Either way, the women were adventuresome and eager to take risks in the quest for romance. Like last night, when Bridgett introduced herself to Travis by dirty-dancing him from behind, grinding her breasts and hips into his as she slid up and down. Before he knew her name, they had already made love.

There was something exotic about Travis that attracted women. He had shoulder-length black hair, a broad nose, and a playful smile. He was a thick six foot two with a paunch. But it was his cinnamon-colored skin that intrigued women the most. Once they discovered he was an American Indian, and Travis turned on the old Gunn charm, the game was over. Maybe he wasn't batting a thousand, but good enough to be voted to the all-star team.

"Imagine me a Muslim," Travis said to no one in particular as he held the glass by its stem and took an icy sip of his juniper and licorice flavored elixir. He swallowed slowly and felt the warmth trickle all the way down to his stomach, like a tiny stream breaking through the moat of stress he'd built up during the day. His friend and boss, Dr. Rolf Marques, had grown obnoxious and pushy, trying to recruit Travis to turn Muslim. Staring at the glass in his hand, he said, "I could never give this up. Not for any god." He took another drink. Travis's mind wandered back to a conversation they had an hour earlier, in the office.

"I was thinking about the day we met in medical school," said Rolf, flashing brilliant white teeth at Travis. Rolf wore black scrubs, his favorite color. He leaned back in his chair, feet resting on the corner of his desk. If any Muslim had been in the room, they would have been greatly insulted. To show the bottom of one's feet or throw one's shoe at another was the ultimate sign of disrespect. Since Travis wasn't Muslim, Rolf could relax. He clasped his hands behind his full head of slicked-back black hair. He looked confident. King of his castle in his world-renowned plastic surgery center.

"Yeah, me twitching and you puking your guts out the first time we uncovered our cadaver in freshman anatomy class. What a pair of nitwits."

"We became a hell of a dissecting team, though. Me the brains and you the beast," Rolf said and laughed.

"Your brain's playing tricks on you. If it hadn't been for me taking you under my wing, you'd be roping camels for some Saudi prince," Travis said. "Who introduced you to Red Sox baseball?"

"You did." Rolf pointed at Travis.

"And the weekend trips to Vermont with the sorority girls?"

"Yummy." Rolf licked his lips.

"I was the best thing to ever happen to you, and you know it."

"My wife might argue that one with you," said Rolf. He rubbed his long, delicate fingers together and checked his nails.

Travis fished a cigarette out of a pack in his shirt pocket and dangled it from the corner of his mouth. Rolf shook his head when Travis flicked his lighter.

"You definitely taught me how to have fun," Rolf said. "It was the best time of my life."

"You bet your sweet ass it was." Travis toasted Rolf with his cup of coffee. "The good times are the only ones I care to remember. Fuck the rest." Travis lit up anyway, and shrugged his shoulders at Rolf.

Rolf sighed. "You know old friend . . . you've got to learn to forgive yourself. You can't keep living like this."

"You suck as a psychoanalyst, you know," said Travis. He wiped his nose. "I deal with things in my own way."

Travis stared at his glass, then guzzled the rest. Rolf could do what he wanted, but Travis would never give up the gin. Why should he? Everyone he cared about was either dead or had disowned him, except for Rolf. The only people he knew were strangers. Reality sucked. Gin was good.

Dr. Marques rented an office at the beach club with the adjoining space converted to a plastic surgery exam room. Frequently, Rolf and Travis met patients there for their pre- and post-operative visits. It added a personal touch and showed the patients that the world-famous Dr. Marques really cared.

Travis, the center's one-and-only anesthesiologist, used the office to conduct his own after-hours quality assurance program on Rolf's breast enlargement patients. Were the new ones big enough? Were her nipples erect? Was the bounce perfect? Someone with an open mind had to be first, and he willingly volunteered. They could not have customers going home unsatisfied. They had a reputation to protect.

On non-research nights, the office came in handy for passionate games of "Doctor, Doctor," Travis's favorite. After drinking and grinding with the smooth-talking Dr. Gunn on the dance floor, the lucky ones were invited in for more cocktails from his private stock. At his exam table, their panties slid off, painted toes slipped into the stirrups, they spread their legs, and Travis moved in.

Even Haleema, Dr. Rolf's head nurse from the surgery center, visited Travis's clinic weekly. She arrived and left covered head to foot, as was the Arab custom, but while there, she lived out her fantasy. Behind his doors, there were no Muslim moral police to remind her of a woman's place. Travis's gin flowed, and at least one man in that God-forsaken land let her be a woman the way God intended, free.

When she or any woman was in his arms, Travis's demons rested. He needed women so he could forget his demons. Whether or not killing his cousin had been an accident was immaterial. He was alive. His cousin was dead. And his only living family member, his older brother Jack, Mr. Perfect, was an asshole. His migraine returned. He needed a drink.

Travis made his way into the club bar. Just when he spotted Bridgett, his French lioness from last night, he was interrupted by a text message from Rolf.

> *We need to meet right away.*
> How about tomorrow? I'm kind of busy.
> *Tomorrow's no good. Where are you?*
> I'm with someone.
> *How about the Club office in thirty minutes?*
> I'm with someone!
> *Get rid of her.*

After Travis made arrangements with Bridgett to rendezvous later, he ordered another martini and waited on the Club's veranda for Rolf's black Mercedes to pull into its reserved parking spot. Rolf dressed and acted the part of a world-class surgeon. Armani suits. Mercedes Benz. Arabian colts. Rolf's wife loved Dubai, too. Shopping, golfing, dining, and so much more. They could pay homage to their Islamic faith and still enjoy the benefits of the West. Compared to most of the Middle East, it was Shangri-La.

Travis gave Rolf a slap on the back as he unlocked the club office door, and they went inside.

"I see you're blasted again. Having a good night?" asked Rolf, shaking his head.

"I was until you called. But the night's not over. Bridgett will make it a night to remember. You wouldn't buzz-kill that for me, would you, old buddy?"

"Okay. Okay. Down, boy. Just forget about Bridgett for a minute. Something's come up, something unexpected."

"You look like you could use a drink," said Travis.

"You know I don't do that anymore."

"Maybe the old Rolf needs a drink?"

"Knock it off, Travis. Those days are over. This is serious."

"We just talked a while ago, and everything was fine. What happened?" asked Travis. His erotic fantasy of bareback riding Bridgett started fizzling, and he tried to focus.

"I had a meeting at the office after you left. The imam from my mosque delivered some bad news. A few days ago, there was a terrible accident in a small Pakistani village where many of my father's family live. An 8,000-gallon propane tank exploded and practically wiped out the place," said Rolf as he collapsed into the chair behind his desk.

"No shit, man. That sounds crazy," said Travis. He leaned against the counter to steady himself and lit a cigarette.

"Crazy is an understatement," said Rolf. "A couple of my cousins and an uncle were killed, but that's not the worst of it. The blast ruptured ear drums, the fireball caused second- and third-degree burns, and most of the survivors have penetrating injuries."

"Wow, man. What a mess. How big is your family?"

"Oh, it's hard to say. I think there might be fifteen or twenty still alive in that area," said Rolf. "The imam wants me to help."

"What? Hold on, Rolf. You're no trauma surgeon." Travis took another swig. "What good is a fat-sucking boob doctor going to be in a place like that?"

"Fuck you, Travis. I'm still a surgeon, and a damn good one." He leaned as far back in the chair as possible and put his feet on the corner of the desk. He noticed Travis's two empty martini glasses on the hutch next to a half-full ashtray.

"Why can't you just let the Pakistanis take care of it? I'm sure they're good at it, with all the practice they get," said Travis.

"That's the problem. It's still going to be a week before the Pakistanis get there. Not enough doctors. The war has scared most of them out of the country," said Rolf. "Plus, some of my uncles wouldn't necessarily be welcomed with open arms by the Pakistani troops, if you know what I mean."

Travis never asked a lot of questions about Rolf's family. Rolf always acted a little awkward and didn't really say much except there were too many of them to keep track of. Travis had met some of them when they toured Rolf's surgery center. Seemed like average Arabs to him, and since he didn't want Rolf or anyone else digging into his painful past, he left it at that. "I have no fucking idea what you're talking about."

"Their government is corrupt. They have a lot of enemies." He knew that some of his family was Taliban. Most were fundamentalist. Either way, the Pakistan military would take exception.

"Oh, that's just great. So what? You're just going to jump on a plane, fly up there, and save the world? Now you're Superman?"

"I don't have a choice, Travis. The imam made that perfectly clear. I have to go," said Rolf. "There may be consequences if I don't go. It could affect my family, my business . . . you, here in Dubai. I'm urging you to come with me. I know you're the right person. We did something like it last year, remember?"

"It seems like ten years ago, and we did surgery on one person, not a whole fucking tribe or family or whatever."

"That's right. So we know we can do it. We'd just need to

bring more of everything. They'll be grateful for anything we do. Believe me."

"So, what are we talking about then? What can I do?" asked Travis. He glanced at his watch, and then waved his hand in tight circles. "Can you hurry this up? Bridgett's waiting."

"We're a team, you and me. Despite our differences in just about every way, we work well together. You're my best friend. The patients need anesthesia to have surgery, and a lot of them will need surgery. If I had a better option, I wouldn't be asking you. Wrong place at the wrong time, I'd say."

"No shit," said Travis.

"They have a primitive clinic or hospital that wasn't too badly damaged, but we'll need to bring everything. We can assume they'll have oxygen and a sterilizer, but that's about it."

"It doesn't sound like a five-star trip. More like a no-star shithole. Thanks a lot. It sure as hell messes with my weekend plans with Bridgett," Travis said as he fished another cigarette out of his shirt pocket.

"I don't know where we're going, but I assume it could be dangerous," said Rolf. "They'll tell us once we're in the air. We leave tomorrow night at eight and might be gone a few weeks. You'll get $50,000 for your troubles when we get back. Then you can take Bridgett anywhere she wants. Are you in?"

The thought of a holiday in the south of France with Bridgett stirred some part of Travis that had been dead for years. His shroud of misery lifted momentarily. The sky brightened. He felt his heart skip a beat.

"Look, Rolf, the money's a nice touch, but it doesn't do me much good if I'm dead. You know me. I'm a lover, not a fighter. The only Gunn I like is me. Guns and the people who use them make me real nervous."

"They've assured me we'll be safe. Think of it as a mission trip to a Third World country."

Travis sighed. "These uncles must be pretty special that all they have to do is snap their fingers and the world-famous plastic surgeon, Dr. Rolf Marques, comes running."

"My family is large. I have over fifty aunts and uncles, many I've never told you about. I've never even met most of them. They're involved in all kinds of things, but I don't care. They're family, and that's what's important to me."

"This is sounding worse by the minute." Travis opened the doors of the office bar and filled his glass with more gin. "Are you sure I can't get you one of these?" he said, hoisting his glass toward Rolf.

"Look old friend. Now you're the one worrying too much. The imam in charge guarantees you'll be safe," Rolf said. "Besides, the clinic will be closed while we're gone. You don't want to miss out on all the fun, do you?"

Travis took a long drag on his cigarette, then sighed out smoke. "Okay, I'll go, but only because you're like family, and a brother has to watch out for a brother."

"Thank you! Thank you!" said Rolf as he stood. "I've got to get going. I have a lot to do. Meet me at the clinic at six in the morning to start packing. Oh, I know it's obvious, but don't breathe a word of this to anyone. No one! Not even Bridgett." As Rolf pulled the door open, he said, "Get some sleep. You'll need it."

"Yeah, right," said Travis as the door closed. "Sleep's the last thing I need."

3

Jalalabad, Afghanistan

Jack's base was about a hundred miles to the southeast of Bagram Air Field. It was like most compounds in Afghanistan. Grey mud walls fifteen feet high, surrounding a variety of mud buildings with tin roofs and a large central courtyard big enough to land a Chinook helicopter. The neighboring CIA compound stood a quarter mile of dirt and rocks away. The exterior walls were topped with razor wire, surveillance cameras, and microphones. It was no secret where the Americans were.

The central single-story command building had a variety of antennas, radar-looking dishes, and a swamp cooler on the roof. Surrounding that were ammo bunkers, the mess hall, the "hooch" or SEAL building, and space for support staff. At least one generator always ran.

Ten minutes earlier, Jack had been lifting weights outside a wreck of a garage he had claimed for Ghost Team's. The garage was a dump with three walls and a tin roof, but worked great for housing their pile of iron. With his shirt off, he glistened in the early morning sun. Two hands would not fit around his biceps or his neck. He sat on the end of the bench, catching his breath.

When Jack heard the blast, he quickly jumped up. A flock of honey buzzards bolted from a tree into the afternoon sky above him, startled by the echoing blast, then lazily circled back to their perch in the warm sun to wait for dinner. He held the wet towel above his eyes to block the sun and strained to see. He heard scattered small arms fire, and after a few minutes, another explosion. He gauged it was coming from three to four miles to the north.

He scanned the horizon from side to side, grabbed his rifle that was always nearby, and ran inside his command center. He dialed up Lt. Jaz Johnson on the encrypted satellite phone, Ghost Team's liaison officer in the Bagram command center. Jack liked Jaz. She was as gung-ho Navy as they came.

"What are they coming up with, Jaz?"

"All hell broke loose about five minutes ago," she said. "Looks like a spook convoy went out to meet a source. They haven't been heard from since. GPS trackers are down. We're scrambling assets."

"Sounded like an IED or RPG."

"CO wants you to check it out," said Jaz.

"In the middle of the day? Should I wear a fucking bull's-eye around my neck too?"

"They swept the road today. You'll have Black Hawks for cover. Jammers will block any RCDs (remote control detonations)." Jaz paused and lowered her voice. "They need you there before the trail goes cold, Jack."

"You should get some sleep, Jaz. You sound like shit," said Jack. "Tell the CO we're on it."

They had a lot in common, both having fought their way out of poverty and stereotypes to rise up in the ranks. She was African-American from Minneapolis. The only thing they didn't share were good looks, which made her stand out even more among the officers. Despite her fashion-model appearance— high cheekbones, hazel eyes, and pouty lips—he thought of her like a sister. He wanted to give his protection, even when she clearly didn't need it.

When Jack and Ghost Team rolled on scene, Black Hawks circled the area, providing cover, searching for guilty-looking terrorists to smoke. Jack spotted three craters in the gravel road, and two smoldering CIA Land Rovers. One split in two, the other on its side. A detail of soldiers from a chopper worked to extinguish the fire. Lots of tires, lots of black smoke. A bomb-sniffing dog zigzagged the area sniffing for booby traps. They counted nine dead, two executed by point-blank headshots.

Jack felt a spider on his neck. He quickly turned away from the scene, dropped to a knee, and brought his rifle into firing position. His team followed his lead and did the same, dividing the surrounding area into quadrants, without a word. Jack studied a mud-walled compound through his riflescope at no more than a quarter mile away. Lots of walls and windows and cracks. Heads popped up and down. Some longer than others. One bearded man wearing a turban studied Jack through a pair of binoculars. A rifle leaned against the wall next to him. Jack stared back through his scope. The rifle was an AK-47 for sure. The man wore grey loose-fitting pants under a knee-length shirt, or perahan, worn by ninety percent of Afghan men. It was cold enough; he also wore a dark chapan or type of overcoat. Every man looked the same, good or bad. Jack couldn't tell by looking at someone if they were Taliban or not.

The man didn't move. Jack called it in. The Black Hawks moved over the compound, stirring up enormous clouds of brown dust. Everyone ran for cover, except the man on the wall. He never moved. Just kept watching.

Jack noticed patterns in the tall grass that reminded him of home. Whether they'd run on foot or galloped a horse through a field of Montana wheat, the line of broken and trampled plants was easily tracked. At least it was easy for him. Montana or Afghanistan, grass was grass. Eight to ten separate trails converged on the crime scene like the spokes of a wagon wheel. A couple of them looked like they came from the compound where the man was watching.

Jack turned back to look. The man was gone.

A picture of what had happened started to unfold for Jack. He'd seen it before. Many times before. It had been an IED for sure. Three craters, three separate bombs. Probably unexploded artillery shells recovered from another bombsite by someone like the prisoner they'd captured the previous night. Some Afghan, who gave the CIA information for money, must have called the CIA out for an emergency meeting. Why else would they have come out in the middle of the day? The convoy had been watched from the nearby compound by the triggerman. When the time was right, a remote detonation with a cell phone caught them by surprise.

Jack looked at the compound again. Picked what looked like an ideal observation spot. No binoculars-man watching. After the explosion, the rest of the terrorists charged in from their hiding places in the surrounding grass, guns blazing.

Jack turned his attention to the vehicles for the first time. The first vehicle was torn in two, a twisted flesh and steel inferno. No one could have survived.

Tires burned. Meat sizzled. Heads swelled. Heads burst.

A couple of the bombers had sprayed lead into the dead CIA agents, most likely screaming, "Allah Akbar! Allah Akbar!" at the top of their lungs, until their magazines clicked empty. There were lots of footprints all smeared together in the dirt. Jack moved to the second vehicle. The roof was blown off. The fuel tank had exploded. More dead agents and a young SEAL teammate Jack recognized lay dead.

A wave of nausea and despair hit Jack. Dewey and the rest of Ghost Team stood shoulder to shoulder. When each recognized their buddy Diesel trapped in the wreckage with two bullet holes in his head, the air was sucked out of the whole group.

The destruction and fire flashed Jack back to the night his parents had died. His dad was driving the family home from a friend's house. A party for something. Jack couldn't remember. Only that they had been drinking and it was late. Travis was curled up, sleeping next to Jack on the back bench seat of their old Impala. Jack pretended he was asleep, but listened to his parents argue about something. Jack couldn't remember what. It was the booze talking. It made no sense to a ten-year-old boy.

Things got louder. His mom started screaming. His dad

told her to shut up. She punched him in the arm. He jerked away like he thought she was going to hit him in the face. He must have cranked the steering wheel because the last thing Jack remembered was Travis and he being thrown against the back door, lots of screaming, tires screeching, a weightless feeling, and then rolling. Jack didn't know how long he was out, but the car had landed upright, the front hood was gone, and there was fire. Travis was under him, groaning, so he grabbed him and crawled out a broken window. The fire got bigger. And hotter. Jack put his hand in front of his face to block the heat. He saw his mom. She looked trapped. He planted both feet up on the car door, leaned back, and pulled with all his might. It was jammed. His dad looked dead. She smiled at Jack. The last thing she said before the car exploded was "Take care of Travis."

Jack had replayed that moment a thousand times, searching for ways to save his mom. His dad had been a hard ass. Drank too much. Jack didn't miss him. He had spent years feeling lost without his mom though. He saw her face in the fire. In the face of their dead friend, Diesel. He rubbed the smoke from his eyes and turned from the nightmare.

"Any idea whose detail this was? We count nine," said Jack into his microphone, while he surveyed the charred ground farther from the wreck looking for clues. His radio was linked through satellite to Bagram and Jaz.

"Chief of Base, Agent Keeler," said Jaz.

"Are you shitting me?" Jack stopped searching.

"No sir."

"What the hell was he up to?" Jack returned to the wreck but couldn't find Keeler's body. One of Jack's favorite pictures was of Keeler and his gang along with Jack's team standing in front of a CIA helicopter, weary after a three-day push into Kandahar, the home province of the Taliban. Keeler had one arm around Jack's shoulder and the other extended straight at the camera giving the middle finger salute. That little impromptu celebration was the best laugh Jack had in years. "How many were on this detail?" Out of the corner of his eye, Jack noticed a pair of bloody trails, like somebody had been dragged through the dirt, leading away from the over-turned wreck. He followed them to a small pool of blood, more boot shuffle, and a set of tire marks.

"Including Keeler, ten," reported Jaz.

"Fuck. They got Keeler," said Jack. He crouched down by the pool of blood and tracks, forming a picture of what had happened at that spot a few minutes earlier. The trail was still warm. Jack rubbed some blood between his fingers. Still sticky. They had dragged Keeler from the wreck. Judging by the trail, his legs were broken. They had kicked and beaten him, probably to unconsciousness, thrown him in the car trunk, and hauled ass.

Jack slammed his fist on the ground. He'd seen the same scene play out over and over. Brainwashed Islamic terrorists, kids no more than sixteen to eighteen years old, convinced by the imam that they were doing Allah's will, would do anything, no matter how horrible. And now they had Keeler. What was his poor friend going through right now?

Jack wiped his eyes. His shirt was sweat-wet halfway to his belt. In full combat gear and body armor, Jack sweat year-round. "Maybe Keeler's cell phone survived the blast. Can we get a track on it?"

Everyone lurched into action—the CO, Jaz, and the spooks.

Raven, an airborne cell phone tower and the crown jewel of NSA's fleet of spy planes, had stealth technology, including radar-absorbing wing surfaces, heat shields, and noise suppression. It was stuffed with electronic workstations and headphone-wearing analysts and had a top-secret and highly classified mission.

Every cell phone in the world constantly searched for the nearest service provider. Thousands of new phones were sold each month, swamping service providers. When Raven flew into an area, it took over the service for all cell phones. The NSA cyber geeks on board interrogated the phones and got their positions. They listened to and recorded conversations.

If a phone was powered on, but not in use, it still revealed its position, which was often of more interest than the contents of the call, especially if they knew which terrorist used a particular cell phone. Raven geeks watched and waited as cell phones moved about on an electronic map of Afghanistan. If the signal moved fast, the owner was in a vehicle. If it moved slowly, he was walking. A high confidence hit pinned down the position of the phone to within ten yards.

The terrorists knew cell phones were bad. The late Mullah El-Hashem had banned them in 1998 after the NSA tracked down his phone signal and nearly killed him with a missile. But times were different now, and cell phones had become indispensable, which made Raven crucial to Ghost Team missions in Afghanistan.

"Raven is airborne, but hasn't pinged Keeler's phone," Jaz reported.

"They're heading for Pakistan. If they cross the border, Keeler's fucked. The whole operation is fucked," Jack yelled through the open line to JOC, Jaz, and the CIA.

He winced as he thought of the terrorist-tortured hostage remains he'd recovered on previous missions. Only two had ever been rescued alive. Hundreds of others had suffered horrible deaths at the hands of sadistic and sick Islamic fanatics.

Other ISR assets were quickly airborne and sent to cover the mountainous forty-mile span of Highway A-1 winding to the Pakistan border. Joining the manned-asset Raven were Predator drones controlled remotely through a satellite linkup by pilots sitting at Creech Air Force Base halfway around the world in Nevada. Each drone carried an array of cameras, sensors, and Hellfire missiles.

Jack stayed two steps ahead in his strategizing, never leaving an opening for some spook, or worse yet, some numbnuts politician to tell him how to do his job. Once everyone at JOC was into full-out tracking mode, he hustled his team back to their base to arm up. If they did track down the terrorists, Gunn's team needed to be ready to go wheels-up quickly, to make up the ground they were losing.

Each man methodically went through his equipment checks. Their main weapon was the Heckler and Koch HK416 assault rifle. While every terrorist in the world used the AK-47 or one of its knockoffs, the AK had its weaknesses. Their rounds tumbled through the air, so they lost power, distance, and accuracy.

HK rounds spun. They took a truer, less arcing, more direct course, and as a result, had more killing power when they reached the target. The team religiously cleaned and lubed their guns after returning from missions. Shoved in a full magazine and they were good to go.

Their MOLLE pack pouches strapped over their shirts were stuffed with strip charges, breachers, frags (fragmentation grenade), therms, and bulletproof plates, front and back. Their water packs were full. His NODs had fresh batteries. All they needed was ISR to come up with a target.

After Jack and Travis's parents died in the car accident, the boys lived with Grandpa Joe. Jack and Travis were special boys, even treasures, to the older tribe members, since they were the youngest living relatives of Sitting Bull, their greatest war chief and medicine man. Grandpa Joe led a secret order known as Zuya, Sioux for warpath. Zuya was dedicated to preserving the bloodline and ancient ways of war. Many on the reservation thought the Zuya were a bunch of kooks who were out of touch with the world.

Jack had been taught knife craft, amongst other things, by his Grandpa Joe and the Zuya since he was ten. He could throw his knife through a terrorist's eye socket quicker than he could shoot. He did not like to though, because the bone dulled the blade. Better to bury it in the terrorist's gut or cut his carotid artery. Nice and quiet. Most did not carry a knife. Jack always carried a knife. A good throwing knife.

Jack looked at his watch. Subtracted 8-1/2 hours. Still morning in Virginia. He had been undercover in Yemen the day Nina told him she had breast cancer. The worst day of his life. She was too young. How helpless he felt. He had devoted his life to protecting her and Jake from enemies foreign and domestic, and now she might die from something he could do nothing about. He wondered if Nina had been up puking her guts out all night after the chemo. It hit pretty hard after about eight hours. She had learned to eat right after treatment, because she wouldn't be able to keep anything down for a few days once she got home. Her favorite was banana pancakes at Doc Taylor's, an old beach restaurant in Virginia Beach. Had she gotten her pancakes? Too early to call. Too busy to call.

Jack had no idea if or where Ghost Team would be going, or how many bad guys there would be. He included Sgt. Steve Stackhouse and his two teams of Army Rangers in the mission for extra muscle. They could cut down and repel a force of almost any size with their straight automatic, sixty caliber SAWS machine guns. During down time, just for fun, Stackhouse ordered his men to reduce a terrorist house to rubble with just their SAWS and a thousand rounds of sixty cal. He was a crazy son of a bitch, which was why Jack loved him. Probably a little Apache blood mixed in his past. They'd flat-out covered Gunn's ass many times while Ghost Team was on target.

Jack heard the message as it came in: "Raven has a hit on Keeler's phone in a terrorist safe house in Gerdi, eighteen miles to the east-southeast. The phone's stationary. You're receiving the GPS coordinates now."

"Roger that," said Gunn as he cursed the target-rich town of Gerdi. He did not need GPS coordinates to tell him where that garbage dump was. Ghost Team had operated there before, cutting short the sick lives of future suicide bombers, perverts, and murderers.

After studying the display and getting input from JOC, they decided on a one-mile offset for their insertion point. They would still be far enough away that the helicopters might not be heard, but the team could run the mile to the target quickly once they were on the ground.

"Spin it up," Jack shouted as he circled his index finger in the air.

The rotors turned, the engines whined, and the bird had barely lifted off when they all heard in their noise-cancelling Peltor earphones, "Hold on. Raven just lost the signal."

The pilot turned in his seat, held up his hands, and shrugged. He reached to throttle down.

"Are we just going to sit around here and suck our fucking thumbs?" yelled Jack.

He was ready to throw the pilot out and fly himself when they heard, "Check that. We're back on, Jack. The Gerdi safe house is your target. Haul ass and go get Keeler back."

The Chinooks lifted into the cool, autumn sky and went to full power as they turned east toward the Khyber Pass and Gerdi.

4

Dubai, United Arab Emirates

Travis bolted his condo door and poured another Bombay and tonic. He wondered where he could get some weed. It cleared his head when the walls started closing in, when he was suffocating, when he wished he were dead. How he felt when he let the guilt of his past overwhelm his present, which was most of the time. He could barely hold on during a good day. Now Rolf's surprise threatened to tip him over the edge. He flicked his hands to get some feeling back in his fingertips.

His balcony overlooked the shimmery Dubai Creek, which was lined by palm trees all the way down to the Gulf of Oman. Expensive boats filled the slips below. Travis paced, gulping his drink and chain-smoking to keep the time bomb between his ears from exploding.

The trip into Pakistan with Rolf a year earlier had been horrible, except for the twenty-thousand-dollar bonus. The way Rolf talked about it, they had been on two different trips. Pakistan was nothing like Dubai. Sure, they were both Islamic countries, but that is about all they had in common. Pakistanis were hard-core. Everyone was poor. Barely scraping by. It reminded Travis of the worst parts of the reservation where he'd grown up, but ten times worse. The women wore burkas. The men all carried guns, had beards, and looked at him like he was their sacrificial lamb.

Travis and Rolf had been flown there on what he supposed was some wealthy prince's private jet, to do plastic surgery on a Pakistani man's face disfigured by an accident. The mystery patient did not look injured; he looked about the same as everyone else, but by then Travis was too scared to ask questions. Rolf looked like he was in shock, too. They did what they do, anesthesia and surgery, and by some miracle, they made it back to Dubai in one piece.

Travis sat down at his patio table. He closed his eyes, took a deep breath, and exhaled. His heart throbbed in his ears. He hoped for a clear thought, an answer to his dilemma, anything. It was too much. Panic set in. He needed a Xanax.

He struggled with how Rolf had been so patriotic, so eager to go back to Pakistan when it sounded worse than before. And what was that about he had no choice? Was the imam forcing him to go? Was Rolf's family a bunch of criminals? A barrel of rotten apples?

A hot blast of ocean air hit him in his face, and Travis opened his eyes. He did a search on his computer for propane explosions in Pakistan. Nothing. He searched the Marques name in connection with Pakistan. Nothing. He tried a dozen different ways of wording it. Still nothing.

He felt as alone as he had ever been. Nobody cared about him. Nobody loved him. Nobody to ask for help. It was the way most of his life had been. Lonely.

Life changed forever the day he knocked his cousin under the train. He remembered it as if it were yesterday. Someone or something tripped Travis. His cousin grabbed Travis to save him from falling under the train, but fell backwards himself. Travis had reached out for his hand, but it was too late. He remembered the scream more than anything. And how it instantly stopped. Travis just lay there in shock. Blood splattered everywhere. The screech of the train brakes, metal on metal. It took over a mile for the train to stop.

Ambulances, police, everybody came running. It was the kind of thing a small town or reservation never forgot. Nobody accused him or publically blamed him, but the tribe treated the six-year-old like he had the plague from that point on. Parents would not let their kids play with him. Teachers never called on him. Even his parents were ashamed. But Jack never talked of it and life went on for the two of them.

When their parents died two years later, the boys moved out to the ranch where Grandpa Joe and his Zuya friends taught the boys the old Indian ways. Jack seemed to love anything to do with killing. Guns, arrows, spears, tomahawks, knives. He ate it up. He was a natural.

They steered Travis toward the spiritual side, which he followed so as not to disappoint them. After Jack went off to the Navy, Travis was all alone the last two years of high school. The boys taunted him for having a crazy Grandpa, for being fat, for being whatever. Girls laughed at him. When Travis graduated, he got as far away from Montana as he could. He got a job in a Boston hospital. A year later, he started college. He knew he was embarrassing Grandpa Joe, Grandma Bear Nose, and Jack. He didn't care. He never went back.

Travis checked his watch. The city that never slept bustled ten stories below. All one hundred and sixty floors of the Burj Dubai were lit. It looked like a giant birthday candle. He poured a fresh drink and set it on the table. He put a cigarette in his mouth, but his lighter wouldn't stay lit in the wind. He cupped his hand around it and flicked several times until he got a lung full of smoke.

He had to call Jack. All he had were questions, and his brother always seemed to know the answers. He went to his closet safe and got the phone number Jack had given him to use for emergencies only. Locked up next to the card was the totem Grandpa Joe had carved for him. His was a bird, a crow. Grandpa Joe explained how birds are survivalists.

They choose flight over fight because they know fighting is dangerous, whereas flight is avoiding trouble, injury, and possible death. They teach adaptability and awareness. Not a particularly inspiring totem for Travis to find at that time, unless he was going to fly again.

He took a big swig of his sapphire and tonic, sighed, and dialed his brother's number.

5

Gerdi, Afghanistan

The rotor noise from the twin turbos howled inside the Chinook helicopter. The whine alone was enough to ruin a good set of ears in thirty seconds. It smelled like aircraft fuel, gunpowder, and sweat all stirred up with a spoonful of whoop ass. Jack closed his eyes and took a deep breath. It was the adrenaline surge, their deadliness, and camaraderie before a big mission that Jack would miss the most, if he ever quit. No drug on earth could get him higher than what he felt at that moment. The forty locked-and-loaded members of the Helo Assault Force were itching for payback on the terrorists who ambushed the CIA convoy, killed Diesel, and hijacked Keeler. Even with all the racket, everyone easily heard the mission brief through his Peltor headphones, which blocked out the engine noise. "Listen up," said Jack. "This mission will be a direct action raid on a well-known Taliban IED safe house in Gerdi. The murderers holed up in that rat's nest detonated a roadside bomb in Jalalabad, attacking CIA personnel at 1300 today with nine FKIAs (friendly killed in action) and one hostage, Agent Keeler. Keeler is presumed to be alive at this point." Jack flashed a picture of Keeler.

No one said a word. Danger, dying, nothing but the mission

mattered, Jack presumed. They had their "kill" on. A straight-ahead, unblinking stare. Locked-on like a hungry lion running down a fleeing wildebeest.

Some of the guys' "kill" looks were them being angry and pissed off. Jack's "kill" look communicated one demoralizing truth to the bad guy: your future is in my hands. If I decide to kill you, you're dead, and there's nothing you can do to change that.

Jack had learned from the best. The Zuya were all about bravery in the face of certain death. To maintain one's honor to the end. To embrace death as another step in life, the final step in this world, the first in the next. As a baby SEAL, he had faced death in training and in battle. He had faced overwhelming odds in Afghanistan, Iraq, Croatia, Yemen, and a host of other countries. For him and those like him, death was never far off.

"Some of you lifers knew Keeler's squad. They were good guys. They had families." Jack's voice trailed off. "We've all made mistakes, but not today. I'm not carrying one of you fat fuckers home in a body bag, so there will be no shortcuts and no fuck-ups. Do I make myself clear?"

Jack looked around the helo. There were a few nods or thumbs up, but mostly vacant, pit bull stares. Jack's men trained a hundred hours for every hour they spent in combat. Killing bad guys wasn't an emotional decision. It was the expected outcome if they did everything right. It was a job perk. Ghost Team had taken their share of prisoners over the years. They didn't kill everyone. But the crazy jihadist bastards were usually in a hurry to die, to please their imam, and to get to paradise to claim their promised virgins. If they raised a gun at Jack, they got their wish.

His guys were the tip-of-the-tip of the spear. The level of scrutiny a SEAL went through before he made Jack's Ghost Team was exceeded only by the relentless training he received after he was selected. The expertise required in the constantly evolving, twenty-first century methods of hunt-track-kill deemed that the men had to be smart and meticulous. Jack knew there would be no mistakes. His men were the world's best combat swimmers, high-altitude jumpers, assaulters, and shooters. But most of all, they knew how to finish the job. When the president needed results, Jack got the call.

"ISR had a gold nugget on Agent Keeler's cell phone before they lost the signal thirty minutes ago." Jack passed around fresh reconnaissance photos from a drone circling quietly above the Gerdi compound. The seven buildings inside the compound had been numbered. The primary and secondary target buildings were highlighted.

Big Daddy signaled for Jack to switch to the command channel on his radio. The deafening noise guaranteed no one else could hear them.

"What's up, Big Daddy?" Jack said.

"Twenty minutes ago, two vehicles exited the target compound. Two minutes ago, they crossed over into Pakistan," Big Daddy said as he motioned Jack to the communication console.

"Son of a bitch!" Jack cursed under his breath. "Now I suppose some two star wants to pull the plug. Tuck tail and run."

Both men studied the grainy full motion video trailing across an LCD screen. The video began with a wide-angle shot of two battered Toyotas leaving the Gerdi compound, then hauling ass for the border once they were back on the highway. They fast-forwarded the video to catch up to real time.

Jack chewed on his lower lip, worrying about Agent Keeler. Was he dead? Was he at the compound in Gerdi, or was he already across the border in one of those cars, quickly slipping beyond the reach of Ghost Team?

The team sat along the walls of the flying green tube in web seats that swayed with the helo, applying camouflage face paint. Their weapons were propped between their legs, pointed up at the American flag hanging from the ceiling. As Jack watched them, he had some sort of a vision of his men around a bonfire, all painted up, dancing, whooping, and chanting, feathers instead of helmets, bows and spears instead of assault rifles, and grenade launchers. A Sioux war party. Some part of him wished the vision was real.

Jack stuck a finger in the face paint the men had used to camouflage themselves. He made a green zigzag, "broken arrow" line with the warpaint from under each eye toward his ears, in honor of his people. Something he did before every jump off.

"We're hot on the trail of these pricks, Big Daddy. Let's nail the bastards before it's too late."

Flying in a packed sardine can when Jack went on the warpath was no fun. He could not sit still. Restless legs or something. He had to move. But there was nowhere to go. They'd seen it a thousand times before. This time, though, he sat motionless, staring at the two cars on the screen trying to read the minds of the drivers.

"I've got an idea," said Jack. "Have ISR track both those cars. Let the Pakistani government know what we're up to and that we'll kick their Taliban-hiding asses if they interfere."

"I might reword that before I pass it along to their president," said Big Daddy with a snicker.

"Like I give a shit. As long as they stay the hell out of my way," said Jack.

"Is there any more, or am I just supposed to call the Pakistani president and tell him to piss off?"

"Look. We've no idea who's in those cars. But we do have the last known location of Keeler's phone," said Jack. "We have to assume he's alive and a prisoner where we pinged his phone. That safe house is where the trail leads, and that's where we have to go. Just get us on the ground."

The Chinook banked hard right and flared to begin its descent to the helo-landing zone, thumping like an army of pounding hammers. Big Daddy got off the radio with Jaz at JOC and gave Jack two thumbs up.

"The mission is a go. You're clear to kill."

6

Gerdi, Afghanistan

For a town the size of Gerdi, it was far too quiet.

Jack and his seven-man Delta squad, along with Sarge, pressed their backs against the cold, twenty-foot high mud wall. Their breaths made fog in the still night. Sarge's panting made three times the fog of a man. His mahogany and black ears were alert. Jack tried the gate. It was unlocked.

"We're in soft, Big Daddy," Jack whispered into his microphone boom. Everyone on Ghost Team heard.

Alpha and Echo squads held their positions while the RECCE snipers climbed the walls and signaled back to Big Daddy with one click on the radio. From their orbit two miles out and two miles up, the ISR plane confirmed RECCE was in position and there were no enemy heat signals.

Jack heard laughter from inside building number one, Delta's target. Dull yellow light leaked through an open window. A small generator putted and popped in the dark. A generator was the only way locals could have electricity in Afghanistan. Otherwise it was fires, lanterns, and flashlights.

He peeked around the corner. No threats. He backed around outside the gate and signaled to Big Daddy they were set.

"Three, two, one. Execute! Execute!" Big Daddy commanded.

Delta squad bolted through the gate and crossed the

45

courtyard to the maintenance garage. Sarge did not make a sound. The metal garage door was locked. Jack slid along the wall and hid in the shadows outside a shadeless window. He sent two assaulters around the building in opposite directions, searching for other windows or angles to get a count of bad guys and a fix on their positions.

The garage was the type of place Jack half-expected to see Grandpa Joe sitting on his stool, whittling a totem out of a little chunk of wood. Animal totems gave insight and direction to the holder. Jack's free hand slid into his pocket and he wrapped his fingers around the cougar totem Grandpa Joe had carved for him before he left for the Navy. Cats are nimble, have keen eyesight, and curious instincts. People with cat medicine tend to be prowlers and hunters who silently stalk their prey. Grandpa Joe said it would bring Jack luck. Remind him of whom he was.

They counted six men who acted drunk. None of them held weapons. They looked like the same jihadist crazies Jack had been watching for years doing unspeakable things to Americans, NATO troops, and even their own people. If everyone saw what Jack had seen, they would understand why he hated anyone with a turban and beard. He'd seen informants or Afghan Army types who worked side by side with American troops and the CIA, turn into suicide bombers or back stabbers once they had earned the trust of the Americans. Their friend one minute, their killer the next. He'd recovered countless mutilated remains of Americans who were victims of their jihad attacks. They were sick. None could be trusted. Keeler had learned that the hard way.

There was no sign of Keeler. The terrorists were yapping loud enough that Jack flipped on his mike so the interpreter could listen to their conversation from the safety of Ghost Team's operational ready point outside the compound wall.

"They're talking about an IED, a hostage, Mohammed, and someone named Ahmed," the interpreter said.

"This is the place," whispered Jack. "Let's nail the bastards."

Jack rammed his left shoulder into the wooden side door,

and it crashed to the dirt floor. He sidestepped into the room with his rifle pressed hard against his right shoulder. The six turbaned partiers, haggard and sloppy, instantly stopped jabbering. Some ducked. Others whipped around toward the racket. They squinted to see who stood in the shadows on the far side of the garage.

In the next instant, to Jack's relief, two of the captives lunged for their rifles leaning against a table. Four precise and silenced spurts from Jack's rifle and the two men flipped backward and fell against the wall.

The four remaining terrorists turned sniveling cowards, held up their hands, and screamed some gibberish. They backed away from Jack. The other SEALs spread out, aiming red laser dots at the terrorists' foreheads.

With the prisoners secured, Jack called for the interpreters and interrogators to be sent in from the ORP (operational ready point). Dewey unleashed Sarge to work the garage. Jack had two of his guys make sure the rest of the building was secure in case some stupid bastard was hiding in the shadows, sleeping it off or taking a dump. There were plenty of explosives and IED-making supplies, but no sign of Keeler. Jack noticed two beat-up Toyotas in the dim light. He never saw new cars in Afghanistan, always pieced together, black-smoke junkers with different colored fenders and doors in place of the originals.

Sarge worked the greasy junkers for explosives, then Jack searched the greasy junkers. He found a forgotten video camera tucked under the seat. He rewound it and pressed play.

On the video screen he saw a couple of the turbaned bombers spray lead into the dead CIA agents, screaming, "Allah Akbar! Allah Akbar!" until their magazines clicked empty.

The terrorist leader, who Jack supposed was either Ahmed or Mohammed, paused and squinted through the smoke. Standing in front of the wreck, he ripped a pistol from its holster, muttered "No Mercy" in English, extended his arm, and fired one bullet through the forehead. Another through the chest. The American jerked, then slumped forward, still restrained by his safety belts. The scrawny shooter smiled. The leader's face burned with jihad. His beard looked ablaze. He was on fire. As if his time had come, he chambered another round.

The first Land Rover was crackling. Fire not getting bigger. Not getting smaller. Just burning to the ground. The sky was blue. The buzzards circled; they were in no hurry. Their time would come. There were no sirens, gunships, or gunfire. It was eerily quiet. The fuel-tank fuse was burning.

In the back seat, flanked by the last two dead agents, the corpse in the middle started screaming and clawing at the car. He went berserk. His legs were pinned. The first vehicle roared like a blowtorch a few feet away. Keeler screamed. His face covered in blood. His clothes smoking, maybe on fire. Jack held a hand over his mouth watching his friend suffer.

The lead jihadist scrambled around the fizzling SUV for a good headshot. He probably wanted the infidel to see his executioner.

The others backed away. A sixth sense seemed to be warning them that time was up. Although the gas tank could blow any second, their bearded leader didn't appear to care.

Before he pulled the trigger, what appeared to be his second-in-command grabbed his arm and said with urgency, "Wait Ahmed. Mullah Mohammed Abdul trained us to be ruthless and cunning. You've learned his ways, and he'll be proud. But could this last American be of more value to us alive?"

Jack knew all about Mullah "The Hatchet" Mohammed Abdul. He was as sick as they came. Liked to carve up people, friend or foe, with his hatchet. He had become the Taliban's spiritual leader, the head of the ruling security council after Mullah El-Hashem was killed. Who was this Ahmed? That's what Jack needed to know.

They dragged the screaming Keeler by the armpits, his broken legs trailing awkwardly behind. A head-kick by Ahmed snapped him into unconsciousness. They swung him into the trunk and were gone in less than ten minutes since the attack had started.

Jack stuck the camera into the pocket of his MOLLE pack. He popped the trunk of the Toyota open to find pools of Keeler's clotted blood. His gut twisted. He studied the blood tracks in the dirt and another pool around a chair. He searched the trunk of the other car, but found nothing.

"Hey, Gunner. Sarge found something," said Dewey. Sarge stood, nose down, sniffing under the chair.

Jack walked over as Dewey shined his flashlight. A mangled human ear lay in a pool of blood.

"Bag it," mumbled Jack. "Fucking bastards." He crouched down and grabbed a handful of dirt. He worked it back and forth, letting the dirt fall between his fingers. Sometimes the terrorists got it over with fast. Other times they drug it out. Keeler was losing one piece at a time. Ghost Team needed to move fast.

He took a deep breath and laid his rifle on the table. His eyes narrowed.

"Time for a little TQ," he said as he cracked his knuckles and sized up the terrorists. The interpreter and interrogator had arrived.

"Tell me what I want to know or I'll splatter your brains on these walls, just like your friends. Understand?" Jack eyed each and every one of them with such insanity, that they had to look away.

No response from the prisoners, only bloodshot glances back and forth at one another.

"Where's the American?"

Again, no response.

Jack stood six inches taller than them with a hundred pounds more of muscle. The veins in his bull neck were the size of night crawlers. He clenched his jaw, grabbed the first man's shirt, and lifted him off the ground until they were face to face. The man stared at him and looked like he was about to spit. Jack drove his right knee up with a crushing blow to the man's balls. He let go and numbnuts crumpled in a heap, moaning and writhing.

The second man started to move away, but Jack caught him with a leg sweep, sending him crashing onto his back. When he tried to sit up, Jack crushed his nose with a full-face elbow smash. Candidates three and four were holding their hands up, pleading, "No! No! Not me."

"You're out of time. Start talking," Jack hollered. His spit pelted the men. The first two rolled and groaned in the dirt, in no hurry to come up for more.

"We just got here! We don't know what you're talking about," claimed prisoners three and four.

"They're lying," said the interpreter.

"No shit," said Jack sarcastically.

Jack pulled his knife from its sheath and laid it on the table. He picked up his HK416 with its ten-inch barrel, a precise twenty-first century instrument of death. Since Jack had to pick one weapon to trust his life with, the HK was his baby. He turned to the interrogator, who was Afghani, and asked, "Are we good?"

The interrogator nodded. He knew what came next. He'd been there before.

Jack jammed his gun barrel into the forehead of dipshit number three, grabbing the man's neck with the other hand. Jack wrapped the fingers around number three's windpipe and squeezed, cutting off his air supply. His eyes bulged.

"You have until I count to three. Start talking." Jack glowered into his eyes. "One! Two!"

"I don't know!" number three squeaked.

"Three!" Jack pulled the rifle trigger. Three's head exploded, spraying blood and grey globs of brain matter and bone fragments onto Jack's face and the other three suspects. The startling sound and smoke sent number four into a hysterical panic. Jack stepped in front of him and pressed the gun into his forehead.

"I oughta break your neck, you murdering fuck. Now, where's the American?"

Jack nailed the gun barrel against the man's forehead.

Four was quiet, hyperventilating, eyes closed. Tears rolled down his cheeks.

"One! Two!"

"Stop! Stop! Okay! Okay! Yes, the prisoner was here, but they're gone."

"I can see that, asshole. Where is he?" Jack demanded.

"They were told to bring the prisoner back across the border into Pakistan. I don't know where they were going, only that they were heading north of Peshawar. I've never seen their leader, Ahmed, before. That's all I know."

"Who told them?" asked Jack.

"I don't know. Someone on the phone."

"Is the prisoner alive?" Jack asked.

"I think so."

Jack thought of Agent Keeler. His family. The overwhelming sense of urgency to find his comrade returned.

"How did they get to Pakistan?"

"They took two cars," said four.

"Son of a bitch," Jack said.

He looked into the faces of the three men before him. Imagined them pulling off the attack earlier that day that had ended the life of some honorable men. He remembered them on the video, laughing and screaming "Allah Akbar," while celebrating the murder of nine Americans.

Without hesitation, he pulled the trigger and double tapped each one of them between the eyes before they had time to blink.

The clock ticked. It was time to go.

7

Gerdi, Afghanistan

"Six EKIAs (enemy killed in action), no PUCs," Jack radioed Big Daddy. A prisoner had to at least be breathing to be considered a PUC (prisoner under control). Their prisoners were the non-breathing type.

"Check. Hold on," replied Big Daddy.

"You guys okay?" Jack asked his team as the smoke cleared. He wiped haji's blood from his face and hands with a skullcap he carried in his MOLLE pack for cold weather. The team was busy field-checking their gear. Fresh magazines could be heard locking into place and they took up positions guarding the perimeter of the garage. The eye-in-the-sky reported locals in the streets, moving on their position. Ghost Team snipers and Stackhouse's rangers checked in and were ready for action.

"Okay, Jack. What did we learn?" interrupted Big Daddy over the radio.

"One EKIA admitted that the attackers bugged out in the two cars ISR is tracking, headed north of Peshawar, Pakistan. Leader's name is Ahmed."

"Well, that's a big fucking help," radioed Big Daddy. "Everyone and his brother are named Ahmed."

"Sounds like that prick Mullah Mohammed Abdul is calling the shots."

"Any clues on where to find him?" asked Big Daddy.

"Those getaway cars should lead us right to him."

"I'll pass it on to JOC. Complete your SSE (sight sensitive exploitation) and get ready to launch."

SSE meant grabbing anything for the intelligence geeks to analyze. They took pictures of the dead terrorists. They went through pockets, taking everything: matches, cigarettes, identifications, money, and cell phones. They took pictures of the two cars, the chair, the blood, the ear.

They used their Leatherman tools to cut the index finger off each of the EKIAs at the knuckle so the FBI could use the prints and DNA. A bunch of dead guys missing their nose-picking fingers sent a message to the enemy: The United States of America had come calling. Dead guys with their heads missing were the Taliban's signature.

Out of the many failed rescue missions of Americans taken prisoner by the Taliban, Jack remembered the most recent. They'd tried to save regular Army Private Winston, but by the time they got on target, it was a ghoulish, bloody nightmare. Besides both ears, they'd cut off his arms, penis, and finally his head. They'd scattered Winston's body parts for the crows and jackals to eat.

After that, Jack burned with intense hatred for the Taliban. Tormented by nightmares, he hunted twenty-four hours a day. If haji didn't talk, he died. If haji talked, he died. The team made an oath to annihilate the terrorist cell, preferably ripping them apart limb by limb, just like they'd done to Private Winston. It took two weeks, but they finally tracked down the cell and called in a salvo of six HIMAR missiles.

The HIMAR was a wonderfully creative and unique invention. Each HIMAR missile was packed with over six hundred armor-piercing bomblets. Each bomblet was the size of a soda can. The bomblets ejected from the back of the missile. Jack and the team watched the "steel rain," as it was known, cut the unsuspecting butchers to pieces with over 3,600 bomblets. Justice had been served, but there'd been no sweetness in revenge. Jack knew there wouldn't be. Winston's mother and father had lost a young son in the most atrocious, unimaginable way. No amount of Indian medicine could put Winston back together.

Visions of his six-year-old cousin, split in two by the train, came to mind. How he had jerked Travis back before he was sucked under the steel wheels, too, and then dragged the upper-half of his cousin off the tracks. In all his years of combat and witnessing countless horrible atrocities, it was the worst. As hard as Jack tried, there were just some things no man could fix.

Maybe Nina was right. Odds were in favor of the bad guys. They vastly outnumbered the good guys and they were vicious. For an instant, Jack wished he were home. Then he pictured his six-year-old son, Jake, carrying an assault rifle, twenty years down the road, trying to complete the job Jack had failed to do. Keeler, Diesel, and the others CIA agents killed in the attack now had families without daddies and husbands. Those were the people Jack answered to. He had a job to do and the clock in his head kept ticking.

After they gathered all the explosives and IED-making supplies into a pile, they photographed and documented the entire ordinance, then wired a strip charge to a remote detonator and shoved it under the pile. They did not want to risk taking black-market explosives back into the helicopter, and they sure as shit did not want to leave it for haji junior.

Jack's team dragged the six dead Talibs across the garage and swung them onto the funeral pyre. To the casual observer, it would look like six rookie bomb-makers had gotten a little sloppy. To the other IED cells in Gerdi and beyond, it would send a warning that they did not want to mess with Jack "Boom Boom" Gunn's Ghost Team.

"This is just great," said Jack. "Another shithole building in a shithole country." He kicked an oil drum over onto the dead hajis.

"I've got good news and bad news," Big Daddy said into their headphones. "The good news is JOC confirmed the two cars that fled across the border split up; car number one skirted north around Peshawar. Car number two went straight into the city. ISR burned an infrared tracking beacon into the roof of car number two, then broke off surveillance over the city, after taking on fire. We continued tracking the northbound vehicle, and now we've picked up the scent of car number two again. It emerged from Peshawar heading north, probably for the same location."

"What's the fucking bad news?" asked Jack.

"Keeler's alive."

Jack didn't like word games. He never had. People getting cute with him pissed him off. They had a job to do. He had a job to do. Time was critical. Lives were at stake. He was interested in one thing and one thing only. Find Keeler, go get him and kill every haji responsible. "Either shit or get off the pot, Big Daddy. If you got something to say then spit it the fuck out."

"Easy does it, Jack. JOC just picked up a broadcast from the Al Jazeera web site," said Big Daddy.

Jack's blood started to boil. Usually killing the perpetrators of a heinous crime soothed his nerves, and he'd just whacked six of them. But he was starting to fidget again. The entire assault force standing in the garage turned and stared at the Toyota junker a few feet away with the open trunk and pool of drying blood. Jack picked up the bloody chair and smashed the windshield. "Fucking assholes."

"That's not the worst of it," continued Big Daddy over their headsets. "The video showed Keeler strapped to a chair, with two terrorists at his side holding a jihad flag."

"Bottom line," growled Jack. "You said he was fucking alive."

"Keeler was alive, but looked closer to dead. They tried to get him to denounce the U.S., but he spit in this Ahmed's face. There was a lot of blood and screaming, and in the end, Ahmed slashed his ear off."

They looked at one another, all thinking the same thing. Too bad Jack had killed all six of the bastards, because it would have felt pretty righteous to kill them again. Dewey picked up Keeler's ear that looked more like a dog treat, and stuck it in a bag.

"Once they start cutting shit off, it's about over," said Jack. His instincts were kicking in again, like the Zuya had taught him. Hunting, tracking, and killing was what he was put on earth to do. His ancestors hunted buffalo. He hunted sick perverted insane men. He had learned to follow the trail of a wounded animal by studying the twigs and mud and grass. That wouldn't help him save Keeler, who was across the border in Pakistan. He had a few hours at most. He needed every twenty-first-century asset available to Ghost Team to track Ahmed down.

"Tell the pilots not to lose them. Especially the car that went north first, since that's probably the one Keeler's in," Jack said.

"Sounds good, Jack, but it's like trying to track a turd floating down a shit river," said Big Daddy.

"I don't need any of their bullshit excuses. It's time to get the job done. Now let's get back to base, gear up, and be ready to roll when those cars stop moving," Jack said.

When their helo was airborne and a half a mile from the compound, Jack leaned toward the open door and pressed the remote detonator. The Gerdi night lit up like a Roman candle. Jack felt the heat flash against his cheek.

"Have a nice flight to paradise, assholes," he said in eulogy and threw the detonator out the door.

The helicopter formation came around to the west and put the pedal to the metal. The pilots, JOC, and Big Daddy, along with the CIA, NSA, FBI, Navy, Defense Department, anyone with a card in the game, anyone aware of the situation, was scrambling assets to gather information and formulate a rescue plan.

On the other hand, Jack and his Ghost Team rested in their bulkhead sling seats for the forty-five minute flight back to base. They all did quick equipment checks again, ate energy

bars, drank, pissed, and took catnaps. Whatever it took to be
ready to crank it up again. They'd done it night after night for
so long, it was automatic.

Jack let the brain wizards at command do their thing and
he shut down, too. He imagined Nina was home in bed by
then. The chemotherapy drugs would be kicking in, and so
would the vomiting. No matter how much Zofran they gave
her, she puked her guts out for a couple days after every round
of chemo. Only six more rounds to go. The chopper made Jack
vibrate in his seat like he was sitting on a blender set for puree.
His stomach was churning.

Breast cancer at thirty-five years old. Jack still had a hard
time believing it. A friend of the SEALs had let Jack and Nina
use his beach house at Cape Hatteras six months earlier. They
drank too much, ate too little, and spent most of the night
wrapped in each other's arms and legs, making up for lost time.
Jack took himself for quite the man when it came to such things,
but Nina pushed him to the limit. The lavishly tiled, dual-
headed, his-and-hers, steam room-shower combo was where
she went on the attack. By morning, they were wonderfully
exhausted and famished. Jack made his breakfast specialty:
eggs, bacon, toast, and strong coffee. They ate in bed, propped
up on pillows against the headboard, watching sandpipers run
up and down the beach, just ahead of the sea foam, snagging
crustaceans and insects with their pencil-long beaks.

Jack and Nina didn't talk for the longest time. A moment
they didn't want to end. Nina was naked from the waist up. Jack
lay on his side, stroking her thigh, taking her all in with the
ocean as the backdrop. He noticed some dimpling on her left
breast and touched it. Nina jumped, like she had been pinched.
They hoped the lump underneath was from their rough sex.

The biopsy of the two-centimeter mass proved differently.
Nina crumpled to the floor, phone still in her hand, the day the
diagnosis came in. Jack was already back overseas in Yemen.

He managed to get back home a couple weeks later for
her mastectomy. She stayed upbeat and positive, but Jack saw

something in her eyes that brought him as close to tears as he had ever been. His wife, a woman who'd never given up on anything since Jack knew her, a Sioux warrior in every sense of the word, shrugged her shoulders and surrendered for the first time in her life. She smiled at Jack and Jake as they took her away to the OR.

8

Dubai, United Arab Emirates

The sound of screeching tires from the street below his condo balcony startled Travis. He opened his eyes. He was slouched back in a chair, drenched in sweat. He pushed himself upright, still halfway between asleep and awake.

Fragments of his dream came back to him, of his fourteen-year-old self sprinting down a winding dirt path along a stream, totem in hand, then across a meadow under a full moon to the sweat lodge or Temescal. He hung his towel on a branch, the smell of burning sage everywhere. He laid his crow totem on the ground under the beaded power staff stuck in the ground, to allow it to purify for a moment. He also placed a couple of cigarettes near the staff, as tobacco was the herb of unification. The sacred purification was about to begin.

He gazed into the bonfire outside the lodge, calming his mind, while a pile of lava rocks glowed in the middle of the blaze where they had been heating for hours. The fire tender sprinkled tobacco in four directions, calling the spirits of the North, South, East, and West to purify Travis as he entered the lodge to face his demons.

The ten-by-twenty-foot, dome-shaped skeleton of willow branches was covered by thick tarps. The lodge is a metaphor for the loving, healing womb of Gaia, the Earth Mother. As Travis crouched and entered the tarp door facing east, he was "smudged." An eagle feather was used to waft smoke from a can of burning sage, around his face to purify himself of negative energy. He found a place in the dark to sit cross-legged in the dirt, returned to his mother's womb. The air was cool. He smelled the earth and woodsy sage. He rested both open palms on his knees, facing up, holding his totem. He reflected on what he would ask the Creator to purify him of.

A stooped old man soon started carrying in fiery, glowing rocks with deer antlers, one by one, until there were seven stones in the fire pit. These first stones represented Travis's ancestors, who came to share their energy and wisdom. The old man carried in a bucket of water infused with sage and pulled the canvas flap shut.

The old man started a quiet chant. A drum beat slowly and softly. It soothed Travis and he swayed slightly back and forth, eyes closed. The old man dipped a ladle of cool water and poured it over the stones. Steam permeated every pore of the Temescal, turning it into a sauna in seconds. Travis sprinkled tobacco on the rocks as a gift, so the spirits would come hear his prayers and pleas. He was immersed in the four basic elements of the Native American sweat lodge: air, earth, fire, and water.

After fifteen minutes, seven more glowing stones were carried in by the old man with the deer antler. More sage vapor. Travis stripped off his shirt. After two more rounds, twenty-eight rocks were piled into the fire pit, and the heat became unbearable. Travis gasped. It was the fourth round that burned away the last of his impurities. The steam burned his lungs all the way in and out. He rolled onto his belly in the dirt, to let his skin soak up the earth's coolness. His lips were next to the ground, where the air wasn't boiling, but he didn't quit.

His mother's spirit came to him, and with her, peace. She cooed to him like a mother to a newborn. Comforting him and coaxing Travis to be brave. Be strong. Always trust the Great Spirit.

When the door opened and cool air washed in, Travis felt like a baby coming into the world for the first time. His clothes sodden with steam and sweat. Tears streamed down his cheeks. He stood and walked back outside where the crisp night air enveloped and chilled him. The old man threw a woven blanket over his shoulders. Travis rinsed his face and hands with sage water. He felt as cleansed and alive as he had ever felt. He was reborn.

He remembered his totem and fetched it from his pocket, except the crow was no longer a crow, but had been transformed into a bear totem. Bear medicine taught him to slow down and reserve his energy. It had something to do with an awakening inside. Bears were climbers and reached for new heights. They loved honey and appreciated the sweetness life offered.

The clarity and energy of his dream started to fade and his memory quickly returned. He grabbed his cell phone. No missed calls from his brother Jack. He lit a cigarette and watched the smoke wisps slowly make their way to the sliding door.

Travis hadn't thought of the sweat lodge or any of the old Indian mystic stuff in years. Once off the reservation and on his own, he started a new life and forgot the old. He didn't have time for the past. So why the sweat lodge dream? Was it a warning? A premonition? Was he going crazy? He needed answers, not questions. Why the hell hadn't Jack called him back yet?

9

Jalalabad, Afghanistan

Back at base, someone from the intel shack knocked on Jack's hooch door. Jack paused the Al Jazeera video as a man stuck his head in and said, "A note here to call your brother at this number, Jack."

"I don't have time for this shit," Jack said and flicked the post-it onto the desk like a piece of trash. "Thanks, though," he said to the man and hit the play button again.

He heard Keeler's leg bones crunch back and forth. The splintered end of the tibia sticking through a hole in his khakis looked like a snapped tree branch. The bleeding from his ears had stopped and crusted over. He looked like a rag used to scrub a slaughterhouse floor.

Keeler's color was more yellow than red. The color of raw chicken skin. The color of death.

Ahmed poured cold water on Keeler's face and blood-caked hair.

With his first full breath, Keeler screamed a full fifteen seconds, writhing into the fetal position.

They spit on him. Jabbed him with their boots. Pissed in his face. A dozen AK gun barrels pointed at him. Fingers on triggers.

"Stop. Stop," he mumbled. He struggled up onto an elbow.

"I know who you are, Agent Keeler, you son of a bitch." He spit in Keeler's face.

"Go to hell, you murdering prick!" Keeler managed to say.

Ahmed smacked Keeler across his mouth with the back of his hand and spit again. "Tell us everything you know, you son of a bitch. Everything! Or else . . ."

The men in the room yelled, "Kill the infidel. Do it. Do it!"

Ahmed said something, and the men jerked Keeler off the ground and bound him to a chair. They tied his head back, high and tight, so his face could be seen. Two black-hooded terrorists stretched a jihad flag behind him. Another video camera started filming.

Keeler's primal screams were so horrible, the jihadists stopped laughing. Ahmed stepped into the picture.

"Silence, you sniveling coward!" Ahmed yelled. He pulled out his knife and held it an inch from Keeler's eye before settling it into the groove between his skull and the top of his left ear. He sawed it back and forth ever so slightly, just enough to start a fresh leak of blood down the side of Keeler's neck.

"Unless you want to lose everything, piece by piece, you'll look into the camera and admit the truth," Ahmed said in slow, deliberate English as he rocked the knife back and forth. "Choose your words carefully, Agent Keeler."

Keeler breathed in and spit a mouthful of blood into Ahmed's eyes.

Ahmed hesitated a moment, then sliced straight down in one quick slash as he screamed something in Pashto. Keeler's ear fell to the dirt.

Keeler screamed. Blood spurted down his neck. The Taliban soldiers twisted his broken legs. He lost consciousness again.

They cut the prisoner down and in doing so, discovered Keeler's cell phone. Ahmed studied the screen for a minute, pushing buttons, then turned it off and stuck it in his pocket. The video stopped.

When Ahmed sliced Keeler's ear off, Jack kicked the desk. "That must be when we lost his signal." The folds of his scowl deepened. He rubbed his forehead and his scalp with both hands, locked his fingers behind his neck, arched his back, and closed his eyes, dreading what the prick would do next. He had watched his own men die before. Held them in his arms. Heard their last wishes. He always felt the same—helpless, small, and angry for not being able to stop it from happening.

After all the years, the thought of talking to Travis still conjured memories of that terrible moment when they were kids. Jack had watched his cousin die in slow motion. Saw one of the boys trip and bump into Travis, who knocked their cousin under the train. He saw it happen, but reacted way too slowly. He watched his parents die and always wondered what would have happened if he had yelled at them to stop arguing, maybe they would still be alive. He was only ten, but a big ten. He could have driven them home.

"It's the middle of the night, Travis," he said into the phone. "You'd better be dying."

"How are you doing, Jack? How's Nina?" He sounded like someone trying to breathe through a paper bag and talk at the same time.

"I'm busy. What do you want?"

"Well, uh, I'm not sure where to start. It's a long story and, uh, well . . ."

"What the hell's the matter with you? Give me the short version or I'm gone." Jack drummed his fingers on the desk while running the video again.

"Well, I'm caught up in something here that scares the shit out of me, and I need your advice."

"Make it quick," Jack sighed.

"Rolf needs me to go back to Pakistan with him to do surgery. A propane explosion injured or killed a bunch of his family."

"Good."

"What?"

"You heard me." Jack was watching the terrorists kick and torture Keeler on the monitor while he researched the said propane explosion on the adjacent computer screen.

"Whatever. Rolf wants to leave tomorrow at six. He didn't know exactly where we're flying," said Travis.

Travis explained for a few more minutes the details of Rolf's imam putting the screws to Rolf to help and that some of Rolf's family were enemies of the Pakistani government.

"I searched the NSA and CIA data banks while you were babbling. We've got nothing on the Marques family or any propane explosions in Pakistan," said Jack. "But whether or not there was some catastrophe, you're probably a dead man if you go flying off to Pakistan with your goat-roping, raghead friend."

"That's not exactly what I wanted to hear," said Travis.

"I deal with these fuckers every day. What did you think I'd say?"

"You're the expert. You tell me."

"When are you going to wake up, Travis? Any one of those sons of bitches could be the next Taliban whack job." Jack had paused the video on Ahmed studying Keeler's cell phone.

"Just forget about it, Mr. High and Mighty. I don't need this shit," said Travis.

"No. *You* forget about it, fuck face," interrupted Jack. "These men you seem so determined to help will hide behind their families and shoot at me from between their kids' legs. Their fucking jihad holy war is all that matters."

"Whatever."

"Listen, Travis, these guys might be lunatics." Jack used a gentler tone. He rocked back in his chair.

"Or they might not be, and it could be like Rolf says," said Travis.

"You're still a glass-half-full guy, after everything you've been through, huh?" asked Jack.

"I don't know what I am, Jack. But I don't think Rolf is one of the crazies."

"I assume every Muslim over here is an asshole, including your surgeon friend. One minute they're your best friend, the next they stab you in the back. I'm not making this shit up." Jack was quiet for a moment.

"You still there?" said Travis.

"Yeah. Just thinking." Jack didn't speak for a while as he stared at Ahmed on the screen. "This could be the perfect way to sneak in the back door on these son of a bitches. Maybe Rolf's family is an offshoot group we've never heard of, and you'd be the guy to help us out and get a foot in the door. They're not going to suspect you. Just be yourself. Act scared shitless."

"Great. That's your advice? Act scared shitless," said Travis. "I could've figured that one out on my own."

There was no response. Jack clicked a couple of screens and read.

"Can you hear me? Are you still there? Jack?"

"Calm down, will you? I was just re-checking something. The CIA has nothing on Rolf Marques, or anyone else with that last name, so that's a good sign. Just keep your eyes and ears open and, when you get back, we'll have somebody debrief you."

"A minute ago you said I was a dead man and now you think I should go?" asked Travis. "What the hell kind of advice is that?"

"Your call. But if you do, we should always know where you are. We'll set you up with a tracking device so we can pinpoint your exact location 24/7. We'll watch you every step of the way. Then if these guys turn out to be assholes, I'll know right where to find you." Jack pulled up the secure phone number for the station chief in Dubai.

"Listen, Jack, I'm a love 'em or leave 'em kind of guy," said Travis. "I don't know anything about this warrior, secret-agent bullshit. I'm a doctor, remember? First of all, do no harm."

"You're still an American, better yet, a Native American, whether you like it or not! The Zuya trained you, too. You know more about this stuff than you think."

"That's bullshit."

"You sure work hard to forget. Bad things happen to everyone, Travis. The Zuya used to preach what's past and cannot be prevented should not be grieved for. It's what you do with it that determines who you are." Jack had pulled out his cougar totem and studied Grandpa Joe's carving as he rolled it in his fingers. He felt the cougar's power.

Travis was silent. Jack continued, "Remember how Grandpa Joe used to say we will be known forever by the tracks we leave. I want the last thing I do to be the noblest thing I ever did. I want to leave a mark. I want people to know I stood for something good. That I died with honor."

"Okay, brother, I'm in," he said more confidently than he felt.

"That a boy," said Jack. "Maybe it'll be all for nothing."

"I hope it is."

"I've got a lot of work to do on this end. After we hang up, don't use this phone except to call your surgeon. Go out and buy a disposable prepaid international cell phone. You'll receive a text message on this phone with a phone number. Call it with your new phone to arrange a rendezvous to get a tracking beacon."

"What tracking beacon? What if they find it?" Travis asked.

"Trust me. This is what I do," said Jack. "Focus on getting ready. Don't say a word to anyone, and be on your guard. They'll be suspicious of an American, even a drunk expat. But you've helped them before, so maybe they won't watch you so close. Don't worry, just let us handle it."

"Now I'm definitely getting scared."

"Remember what I told you to do. Remember Grandpa Joe. And for God's sake, stop drinking," said Jack. "You're doing the honorable thing. I'll see you soon."

Jack had promised his mom he'd always take care of Travis, but his brother sure didn't make it easy.

Jack was a natural protector. He tried to protect the innocent, the poor, those who couldn't protect themselves. It's what he devoted his life to. He lived every day in fear of failing to protect. Sure he had failed plenty, but he didn't want to fail when he was needed most. He didn't want to fail Nina. He didn't want to fail Keeler. He didn't want to fail his country, his people or himself. He would rather die than lose to the Islamic extremists who seemed hell-bent on turning the entire world into mass chaos. Failure was not an option.

Ghost Team wasn't accustomed to arriving back at base so early. Their missions usually took till dawn. The fourteen-hour nights of autumn allowed them to carry out ambitious missions deep into the Taliban-controlled mountains. Enough dark time to climb over mountains and blindside the unsuspecting terrorists from above, fly deep into Taliban country to shut down a madrassa, or dress up in robes and turbans and drive around in beat-up Afghani pickups armed with roof-mounted Mark 19 grenade launchers, leveling terrorist cell headquarters. Every night was a different problem and different plan of attack.

Jack wandered across their compound to the Operations Command Center to eavesdrop on the speakerphone communications link with the spooks at Bagram. The Air Force had lost track of the two cars and returned to base. No surprise to Jack. Probably some General pulled the plug to cover his or her ass. While the U.S. military rarely flew over Pakistan, the CIA birds patrolled across the border whenever and wherever they wanted. So while the Air Force was grounded, the CIA was still hot on the trail of the cars and Ahmed.

A CIA had their Sentinel drone and Liberty, a stealth aircraft, working the area. In the region north of Peshawar, where they'd lost track of the bombers around midnight, Sentinel and Liberty searched for clues.

Finally at 0030, all three command centers simultaneously heard a report from Liberty.

"Keeler's phone signal just switched on!"

The good news jolted Jack like a full-power shock from a defibrillator. He dialed the secure line to Jaz at NSOD. "Keeler must've got them to turn it on. He knows the drill. We're his only hope. What's it looking like, Lieutenant?"

"Too early to tell," she said. "Stay on the line."

Liberty quickly began orbiting the signal, but stayed six miles out. The quieter drone circled to within a mile and climbed to 20,000 feet. Between the two of them, they nailed down the signal to a remote compound near Tangy, Pakistan. The compound sat thirty miles north of Peshawar and thirty-six miles inside of Pakistan's western border.

Both platforms transmitted emerald and white infrared video of the target compound onto the command center monitors. They clearly marked a fire burning in the courtyard and heat rising from a central building's chimney.

Suddenly, on the infrared video, a crowd spilled out of the central building. They bounced and banged into one another, more like they were drunk than fighting. They headed toward the courtyard fire, while four marks went into a different building. Soon, six men came back out carrying something rectangular.

"What do you make of that?" asked Jaz.

"There's heat in the middle. It's Keeler," said Jack. He ground his teeth, hunched over the desk, and looked back and forth between the two video feeds, searching for clues.

The stretcher was dropped near the fire, and the crowd of fanatics surrounded it. Everyone watching their monitors—Jaz, the spooks, and Jack—clearly saw the person on the stretcher move his arms. The crowd on the screen started jumping and celebrating. Someone stood addressing the crowd, waving his arms. Another stood next to him. With the figures on the grainy video shaded green and the background a weird mixture of white and black shapes, it was very different from daytime, high-definition video. Not close to the same degree of clarity, but far better than nothing.

"Looks like either Ahmed or Mohammed is getting them worked up," said Jack. "My guess is Mohammed, now that they're back on his turf. Besides, it looks like he may be waving that fucking hatchet of his."

"We should have neutralized that son of a bitch when we had the chance," said Jaz.

"Neutralize? Are you going politically correct on me, Jaz?"

"Sorry. We should have blown his haji ass to hell and back when we had the chance."

"That's better. Has to be Keeler. We have his phone pinging at that compound, and his legs were broken," Jack said.

"JOC concurs, Jack," Jaz answered.

"We have proof-of-life," said Jack. "Rescuing him just became our highest priority."

Proof-of-life was paramount in any rescue mission before troops could be put in harm's way. Once they proved the target was alive, everyone wanted a piece of the action. Generals, admirals, spooks, and politicians made suggestions, handed out blame, and took credit, while the real warriors risked their lives.

Jack's team had done previous mission planning into the area north of Tangy. It was a Taliban cesspool where mutant terrorists were trained and brainwashed. Hundreds of madrassas flourished. The Taliban ruled. The Pakistan government stayed clear.

Jaz and Jack studied contingency plans from their encrypted files. Different command centers, same screens, while they talked on a secure line.

"A HAHO jump is the only option to avoid alerting the Pak Mill and Taliban checkpoints along the border. We get in, get our man, and get the hell out. We'll need POTUS approval," Jack said.

"Not a problem," Jaz replied. "Even politicians do the right and honorable thing once in a while. When the president sees the torture video and our proof-of-life footage, you'll get your green light, but something tells me that wouldn't stop you, anyway."

"Me disobey orders? I'm crushed," said Jack.

"That's what I thought. Same old Boom Boom."

"Find me a target, smart-ass, I mean Ma'am. Is that too much to ask?"

"You forgot to say please."

"Please do your job, sir."

Jack heard Jaz laugh.

"There's not enough time to put this together before dawn."

They couldn't risk a daytime assault. "We'll gear up and get some payback later tonight," Jack said.

"Roger that," said Jaz.

Back in his hooch, Jack video-conferenced his wife, Nina, and four-year-old son, Jake. Nina was lying in bed and Jake was beside her watching cartoons on TV.

"Keeping anything down yet?"

"Was a bad day, but I'll survive." She looked pale and gaunt. Not her usual beauty, but not even cancer could take that away.

Jack was already at a loss for words. "Did any of the wives stop by?"

"They've been showing the video of Keeler on the news, so the wives have been calling," said Nina. "Keeler was one of yours, right?"

Jack nodded.

"I really want to be there for the next round," said Jack. "What'd the doctor say?"

"She said everything looks good. Stop worrying about me and stay focused on saving Keeler."

"Nina. What did the doctor say?"

"Jake. Go get in bed. I'll come read to you when we're done talking."

Jake did as he was told.

"With five positive lymph nodes, the mastectomy and chemo should put it into remission," said Nina. She looked away to see if Jake was in his room and looked back. A mixing bowl lay next to her pillow. Jack could see pill bottles on the bedside tables. His picture too. "Don't worry. Once my hair grows back and reconstruction is done, Doctor says I'll be as good as new."

"You're a fighter, just like the old man. A couple of days and you'll feel a lot better."

"I don't know, Jack. I feel worse this time around. What if I don't get better? What if the chemo doesn't work?"

"It's going to work, Nina. I know it."

"Well what if it doesn't? I didn't want cancer and I got it. I don't want the cancer to come back, but it might. I don't want to die." She choked up, put her hand over her mouth, leaned over the bowl, and threw up.

Jack was coming apart watching Nina suffer. He knew he should do something, say something, anything to make her feel better. But he just sat, waiting for her to recover and turn back toward the screen.

"What will happen to Jake if something happens to me?" She could barely get the words out before she choked up again. "That's all I can think about, Jack. What will happen to our little boy?"

"Nothing is going to happen, Nina. Remember the doctors said to take it one day at a time. If you try to take it all in at once, you'll be overwhelmed."

"I don't care what the doctors said, Jack. How would you raise Jake by yourself? You're never home."

"I don't want to talk about it right now, Nina. Nothing's going to happen."

"I have to talk about it, Jack. It's all I think about. What if you're killed over there and I die? What would happen to Jake? Who would take care of him?"

That hit Jack like a sledgehammer in his gut. Him and Nina dead? Jake would grow up without parents, just like Jack and Travis. A thousand images of his life without parents and the things he had gone through raced through his brain.

Jake walked back into the room, clutching his blanket. "Who's going to take care of me? Where are you and Daddy going, Mommy?" He was crying. He looked stricken.

Nina looked away from the screen with a troubled expression. "Jake, go back to bed, honey."

"I forgot to say goodbye to Daddy."

"Let him come here," Jack said. He tried to smile with confidence into the computer at his little boy when he said, "Nothing bad is going to happen to Mommy or Daddy, okay?"

Nina hugged Jake and held him for a long time, until his tears stopped, while Jack watched on his computer screen.

A little happier, Jake went back to his room.

"I don't know what to say, except that I know in my heart that nothing bad is going to happen to you or me." Jack smiled at the computer. "Do you trust me?"

"There's no one in the world I trust more. I'm sorry for laying this on you, but glad you listened."

"I want to be there for you. I'm going to be there, soon. I love you."

"I love you too."

Jack kissed his hand and pressed it to Nina's lips on the computer screen. "Call you in a couple days. Hang in there."

10

Dubai, United Arab Emirates

Travis paused at the threshold of Rolf's Dubai Center for Cosmetic Surgery. Spokes of sunlight fanned from under the horizon, up into the Persian Gulf sky. From where he stood, the peak of the tallest building in the world, the 2,684-foot Burj Dubai, looked like a stepping-stone to the rising Middle Eastern sun. He heard the muezzin's morning call to prayer summoning believers throughout the city. It happened five times a day, which meant everyone but Travis took a prayer break.

He walked through the empty surgery center to Rolf's office and groaned as he plopped into the overstuffed armchair in front of Rolf's desk and stretched his weary legs.

In the prayer room connected to Rolf's office, Travis heard Rolf reciting his Salat prayers in unison with a billion Muslims around the world.

> *God is Great and Transcendent.*
> *There is no God but God.*
> *Muhammad is the messenger of God.*
> *Arise and Pray.*
> *Arise and do good works.*
> *God is Great and Transcendent.*
> *There is no God but God.*

Rolf finished with "Prayer is better than sleep. Prayer is better than sleep." He had renewed his commitment to Islam after straying during his seven years of plastic surgery training in Boston and Paris. He had not missed a morning in five years. Travis was skeptical. Rolf used to be a party animal and now all he wanted to do was pray.

Rolf walked back into his office, "Travis, you look like hell."

"I feel worse," said Travis. "How about two aspirin and a shot of Starbucks?"

"Just made it. One cup of coffee coming right up. Two sugars, no cream."

Travis sported the same wrinkled Hawaiian shirt as the day before and had a cigarette tucked behind his ear. He wore sunglasses even though the office was dim. He cradled the cup, softly blew across the top, and sipped the steaming Arabica, Rolf's favorite blend, then rested his head back on the cool leather.

"That bad, huh?"

"Let's just say Bridgett isn't into quick goodbyes," said Travis. "I'm exhausted."

"You told her you were leaving? What the hell! You promised not to say anything." Rolf let his arms flop at his side like he had been deflated.

"Relax. Relax, and stop yelling, for God's sake. My head's killing me," said Travis as he held a hand over his ear. "Bridgett's flying home to Paris today. She wanted to leave a good taste in my mouth, if you know what I mean." Travis smacked his lips. "Or have you forgotten?"

"Damn it, Travis, stop screwing around," said Rolf. "Are you sure you weren't too drunk to remember?"

"Of course I'm sure. I haven't breathed a word to anyone. Cross my heart and hope to die," said Travis as he traced a cross on his chest. A bead of sweat trickled down his temple.

Travis couldn't tell if Rolf believed him or not. He was a terrible liar. If Rolf had looked him straight in the eye and said, "Come, Travis, tell me the truth," he would have spilled his guts, but Rolf never asked.

"Okay," Rolf said, easing back into his chair. "I've been thinking. Maybe you're right and I should try to find one of our own anesthesiologists to go on this trip."

Travis had been thinking that very thing himself. Rolf was his friend and all, but there was a limit. He wanted to bolt and keep running until he was sitting in his favorite chair on the club veranda, drink in hand, but he said "Hey, I'm here, aren't I? I'm good to go." He sat up straighter and took another sip of coffee.

They both looked out the window at a dust devil twirling and whipping the sugar sand back and forth. A second twister whirled into view. Their tails wrapped around one another, tangled like two writhing snakes stirring the same spot of desert for a moment, then parted again and went their separate directions.

"It's another perfect Dubai sunrise. Hot and windy," said Rolf. They kept staring out the window. "This trip is something I must do for my family," Rolf continued. "But you don't have to do this. Why don't you just stay here?"

"And leave you high and dry? What about your family and the explosion?" said Travis. "I've been doing some thinking too. You have a chance to help your family before it's too late. I never had that chance"

Rolf nodded.

"So what's the big deal?"

"Last night I had to beg you to come. Now you're anxious to go. What's changed?"

Travis sipped his coffee. "Listen. We've been doing this a lot of years, you and me. But if you're worried about me, forget it. I don't have anywhere to go except this surgery center and the beach club veranda. I know I freaked out last year, but it'll be easier the second time around. We'll get in, do our thing, and get out."

"Well, I do worry about you. And it might not be as simple as last year."

"We'll handle it like we always have. With style." He smiled and acted like he was tipping his top hat.

"The truth is, I really do need you. It's a big job and short notice. I don't have a problem with your anesthesia. It's your drinking, smoking, and screwing around that bothers me." Rolf looked straight into Travis's sunglasses and pointed. "You mess around where we're going, and you'll end up dickless. These people are serious about Islam. Promise to keep your zipper up, your mouth shut? No camel jockey jokes?"

"For you, old buddy, and fifty thousand smackers, I'll swear celibacy. Although women in burqas drive me crazy," Travis said with his disarming smile.

"Well, don't say that I didn't warn you," said Rolf.

"There's just one thing I need to know. Last year you looked like you were just as scared as I was," said Travis, his voice quivering slightly. "This sounds worse. Do you know what you're getting us into?"

"We have an old saying in Islam: 'Show mercy toward those on earth so that Allah will show mercy to you.' Allah is calling me to be merciful. To put my fear aside and follow him. It is his will."

"That's it? That's why you're not afraid?"

The employee door chimed again. They both jumped to greet Haleema. Rolf held a finger up to his lips to signal Travis to keep their conversation between them.

Haleema squeezed Rolf's hand and gave him a wink. She kissed Travis on the cheek, lifted his glasses, saw Travis's bloodshot eyes, and let them fall back down.

"You're hopeless, Travis. Who was it this time?"

"I don't know what you're talking about. I was getting ready for the trip."

"How? By drinking all the gin in Dubai?"

"Somebody has to. Besides, I couldn't sleep."

"Likely story." She gave Travis a wink.

When Rolf had asked her to go on the trip, she said yes without hesitation. Travis guessed it was the money, and wondered how much she got compared to him. Rolf couldn't do anything without both of them.

Travis chugged the rest of his coffee and focused on packing enough drugs to anesthetize an army. All he needed were a couple of battery-powered pumps and monitors, plus an assortment of breathing tubes, and he'd be ready to perform backpack anesthesia. He packed a shoulder bag with every anesthetic drug imaginable. Besides Propofol, he packed plenty of Fentanyl, his past drug of choice, Midazolam for anxiety, and Anectine for paralysis. Once they took off, he would not let the medicine bag out of his sight. Without it, people would die.

Travis said, "I've got to run home and get my things. I'll be back by six. I need to pick up a couple of extra cartons of cigarettes. Your Pakistani brothers may hate my guts, but they love a good American smoke."

"Take a shower while you're at it. You reek," Rolf said. "And don't be late."

Travis drove north on the expressway for his rendezvous with the CIA agent Jack had arranged. Travis was impressed that Jack could make one phone call and things went down. He wished he knew Jack better. Maybe they would start over when he got back. He wondered if they would give him a gun. He hated guns. The Zuya had taught him to use guns, spears, knives, you name it. Travis had tried to forget it all. He wasn't going to shoot anyone anyway.

He exited the freeway after five miles, constantly checking his rearview mirror, paranoid of a tail. He had seen plenty of movies; he knew what to look for. He pulled into the underground parking lot beneath Spinneys Supermarket, near the International Trade Center, and parked next to a white Mercedes. He left the trunk unlocked and went upstairs, as the text message had instructed.

Travis bought two large bags of snacks and junk food, two cases of Diet Coke, and four cartons of Marlboros. When he got back to his car, the trunk was closed, and the Mercedes was gone.

He cautiously drove back to his condo but was so concerned about being followed that his hands started going numb again. His nerves were shot.

After he pulled into the underground parking of his condo building, and was sure he was alone, Travis popped the trunk open to retrieve the other carton of Marlboros and checked for the tiny identifying mark.

The tracking device concealed inside one of the cigarette packs made the carton feel heavier. Or was he imagining that? His sweaty shirt clung to his belly. Travis held the carton to his ear, but heard nothing. He looked over his shoulder, and then hurried upstairs to pack.

11

Over the Northern Tribal Area, Pakistan

At 2200 that night, Jack and the thirty-four men of his Ghost Team rode in the belly of the Air Force MC-130 Combat Talon. They'd crossed from Afghanistan to Pakistan and were twenty minutes from their high-altitude release point.

The Sentinel drone had kept the Taliban compound under constant surveillance since the previous night. Around dawn, a robed man carrying a shiny aluminum-looking suitcase got into a waiting vehicle and headed north.

"We got a runner. Do we follow him or stay on target?" the drone driver asked JOC.

"Let him go. We can't afford to lose Keeler," replied JOC. "We'll hand him off to NSA."

The terrorists inside the compound appeared casual and complacent. They ate and slept, seeming to savor their victorious week of jihad.

JOC analyzed data flowing in from all levels of the intelligence community. NSA satellites provided photos of the compound and everything else within a five-mile radius. Combined with live video feeds and infrared images, they discerned every possible detail of the two buildings.

Agent Keeler's phone signal had died at 0100, then come back on for thirty minutes in the middle of the morning. No calls were made, but its blip on the ISR screen on-board Liberty encouraged the rescuers. Proof of life.

HAHO parachute jumps by the Special Forces were extremely dangerous. Jumping out of the back of an aircraft into the subzero abyss 30,000 feet over enemy territory was only for the bravest of the brave. More SEALs died training for war than in war, and HAHO jumps had claimed its share of the young.

Jack had made hundreds of jumps. He loved HALOs for the long free fall before opening a thousand feet from the ground. Ghost Team spent two weeks a year jumping at The Ranch in Arizona, and flying at the indoor skydiving wind tunnel in Eloy. Free-falling gave him a rare sense of peace and tranquility. It never got old.

HAHO jumps were more challenging in that they glided laterally, sometimes twenty miles, instead of going straight down. It took a lot of adjusting and coordinating to get the whole team to make their mark, especially in the dark. Throw in weather, mountains, terrorists, illegal entry into a foreign nation. A thousand things could go wrong on a HAHO.

The men had their warpaint on and, since going wheels up, they had been breathing one-hundred-percent oxygen through parachutist oxygen masks. Any time they jumped from above 18,000 feet, they pre-oxygenated for thirty minutes. If they jumped from over 25,000 feet, protocol required them to pre-oxygenate for an hour. Then if their oxygen masks failed at 30,000 feet, pre-oxygenating gave them a chance to survive until they fell to the thicker, oxygen-rich air below. They were jumping from an altitude higher than Mt. Everest, and every SEAL knew the perils that prowl the thin air.

Jack had his broken arrows painted on his cheeks. His cougar totem in his pocket. He'd checked and rechecked everything. The plan of attack was solid. He knew computer screens in some of the most secure places in the world would be following the live video feed of their attack. Perhaps the president himself would steal away from the Oval Office to watch Jack's men operate.

He hoped so. People needed to know the degree of sacrifice his men made to protect the president and people of the free world. Ghost Team would be putting on a show tonight.

The men sat in webbed seats strapped to the bulkheads and were tethered to the plane's oxygen supply hoses. Everything had been cleared out of the cargo area except for the Air Force personnel tracking the position of their aircraft.

Sarge slept next to Dewey, both of them breathing through masks. He was an experienced canine HAHO jumper and was game for anything.

Jack drank an energy drink, sipped water from his hydration backpack, took a piss, and rechecked his gear.

Peltor headphones covered their ears, allowing Jack to hear his comrades talk, even in this deafening place. The Peltor's reception and noise-cancelling ability was far superior to the tiny ear buds worn by other special ops teams.

Jack's Kevlar helmet fit snugly over his stocking-capped, shaved head, the brim resting on his brow. He wore a fourth-generation flip-down NOD for night vision. The boys in the metal shop had shaped a weight for the back of Jack's helmet to counter the weight from the NODs and video camera, so his helmet wasn't always tipping forward. Jack swung the boom mike to the side and connected the microphone cable directly to his oxygen mask.

The interior lights went off, the IR lights on, and Ghost Team switched to NODs.

Gunn's HK416 was loaded with a thirty-round magazine. He had three backup mags. He'd rarely used all hundred and twenty rounds, even in a four-hour firefight. SEALs believed precision was far more important than a lucky shot. But if they did run out of ammo, helos flew in and dropped "GO" bags with more ammo or whatever they needed.

Jack tightened the straps of his parachute system. His chest-mounted NAVAID functioned as a global positioning system, wireless communication device, and computer all rolled into one.

The jumpmaster gave the ten minute to HARP signal. The plane bucked from turbulence. Jack checked their position on the monitor then turned to his men.

"Ready?"

They gave him thumbs ups.

"We release at 30,000 on oxygen with a ten-mile offset. We've glided a lot farther before, so no big deal," said Jack. "The winds here can be tricky as hell, so stay with your NAVAID and follow my lead. Once we form up, it's a three-mile hump to the target. Find Keeler and kick haji's ass."

"Hooyah."

Jack loved his men. They were as eager as bloodhounds to get on the ground to do what they all loved to do—hunt, track, and kill.

Dewey loaded Sarge into an insulated jump bag with his furry head sticking out. He covered Sarge's snout back up with his canine oxygen mask. Jack strapped Sarge to Dewey's chest, like a momma with a papoose.

Two other operators had four foot-long collapsible ladders strapped across their backs. Ladders were worth their weight in gold when it came time to climb over compound walls, but a pain in the ass to HAHO with. That honor usually went to the rookies.

They switched over to the bottles of oxygen secured in the parachute rigs. They finally got the one minute to HARP. The dive ramp dropped. The men formed two equal columns behind Jack with the heavies, the guys weighted up with ladders and equipment, at the head of the line.

Jack went first. His boots gripped the end of the ramp when the thirty-second signal came. The roar of the death-zone air screaming by at one hundred and twenty knots energized and dared them. They counted down three, two, one, and got the "go" finger.

Jack dove out headfirst. He counted a six-second delay before he opened his chute to get lower and out in front of the team. The other thirty-four men followed, alternating between the two lines. They waddled out one after another as fast as they could, getting good separation with their air speed.

Jack checked his NAVAID and corrected his direction, speed, and altitude to the target as he dangled. He radioed the teammates above and gave the heading, altitude, and glide ratio to the landing zone. Unless there was a problem, there'd be radio silence.

He illuminated his chute with his IR laser. To the men above watching through their NODs, his chute would glow like a firefly and give a point of reference. To the Taliban eyes on the ground, it would be another pitch-black night in paradise. Jack turned on the IR strobe on the back of his helmet for the boys to follow. It would be forty-five minutes of sitting in the saddle, before touchdown. As a form of meditation, he allowed his mind to drift.

Jack wondered what Keeler was going through. Maybe they had taken the other ear, or worse. With the crowd of crazies Jack had watched surround his stretcher from the satellite video, anything bad was possible. CNN had Keeler's name all over the news, so Mohammed and Ahmed would use that against Keeler. They were professionals at keeping victims alive with tourniquets while they tortured them to death. Somehow Keeler had gotten them to switch on his phone again, which was a good sign. At least he was still alive. He must have known Ghost Team was watching.

It would be tricky for his team to get to the madrassa without being detected. The area was full of madrassas, so lots of Taliban eyes and ears. Double-tapping Mohammed "The Hatchet" and Ahmed the bomber. That would be the perfect ending.

He hoped Nina was doing better on Day Two. Some day soon, he planned to put her in her favorite chair, and give her a glass of their favorite Markham cabernet. He would sit on the floor and rub her feet with eucalyptus oil. After a while, he would rub her shoulders too, kneading her stress away with his strong fingers. Nina said a good foot rub was better than sex, which disappointed Jack a little, since he always hoped that was where things were headed. But he understood.

He also hoped Travis had gotten the phone and connected with his guy. He felt unsettled about Rolf Marques and why nothing popped on the background checks. The CIA had something on everybody. Something wasn't right, but it was too late. Travis was already on his way to Pakistan. Perhaps he would save the world. Jack smiled at the irony.

On the ground, they rolled-up their chutes, O2 bottles, and masks, and booby-trapped the pile as a little payback for Diesel, compliments of Jack Gunn. Nothing extravagant. Just a couple of frags.

After an equipment and radio check, they formed up with RECCE out front as usual, laying down the route to the target three miles away.

Liberty confirmed the assault team was alone.

The Air Force was ready to rain down fire. Ghost Team wanted blood. They all wanted revenge.

12

Northern Tribal Area, Pakistan

Four hundred yards from the compound gate, Ghost Team readied to launch the attack. Arriving undetected on the cold moonless night, Ghost Team's approach was monitored from above. ISR marked heat coming from the two target buildings, but no sentries or outside activity.

The combat controllers on the ground got a status report from the Storm, the whirling dervish of deadly American aircraft circling Ghost Team's position. The Storm included a variety of Air Force attack planes and Army helicopters orbiting Jack's position: the F-15 Strike Eagle, the A-10 Thunderbolt Warthog, the AC-130 gunship, the Black Hawk helicopters, the drones, and Liberty. The Night Stalkers, Army special operation pilots from the 160th SOAR (Special Operations Aviation Regiment), were the best combat helicopter aviators in the world.

The Pakistanis had been notified to stay away. If they interfered, it was at their own risk. The Storm had POTUS authorization to shoot first, and the Pakistanis knew it.

Storm aircraft stayed five to fifteen miles away and at different altitudes, depending on the type of aircraft and mission, so the noise did not alert the terrorists of their presence. But those same planes could be on target in a flash with their lethal cannons, howitzers, Gatling guns, or bombs to crash the party.

Alpha, Delta, and Echo squads, plus the RECCE snipers, were all business. They were ready to do what SEALs do. Finish the job.

"Move to set," Jack whispered into his microphone. "Delta's on Building Eleven and Echo on Twelve. Alpha's providing support and securing the perimeter. RECCE gets over the wall and on the roofs to provide cover before we ring the doorbell. We'll breach the gates, front and back. Move fast on this one, boys. It's go-time."

Ghost Team had operated against similar compounds in Afghanistan many times, but they weren't in Afghanistan anymore. Other than the Storm swirling above, they'd be up a shit creek without a paddle if things went south.

RECCE guys assembled the twenty-foot tactical ladders at the ORP. The two assault teams got their seven-foot strip charges ready and bumped knuckles. RECCE moved out across the clearing first. Command and Control stayed back at ORP, concealed by the pine trees.

The assault groups fanned out and headed toward their set points. Sarge and Dewey led, Sarge sniffing for booby traps and pressure plates.

Stealth was critical during the approach to set point. Each step and movement had to be precise. The slightest noise might alert a guard or dog and, in an instant, their surprise party could turn into a firefight.

When Delta arrived at set point the main gate would not budge. They stuck a seven-foot strip charge of C-12 to the wood. The blasting cap had already been connected to the initiator, which Jack held in his right hand.

The rest of the team lined up behind him and pressed their backs against the mud wall. When he got the signal, all he had to do was squeeze.

RECCE got to high ground and solid sniper positions. Alpha climbed over the wall and took up designated positions to cover the assaulters' flanks. The Air Force tracked all the jumpers' IR movement from above. The only signals Liberty saw were friendlies.

Jack called, "Light up Eleven and Twelve."

Within seconds, infrared floodlights strobed the two buildings, which glowed like high noon.

"Delta team's set," radioed Jack.

"Echo team's set."

"Three, two, one, execute. Execute," said Big Daddy.

On the first "execute," Jack squeezed the initiator, and the gate roared, landing in pieces about thirty feet inside the courtyard. On the second "execute," the Echo team leader squeezed his initiator and another distinct explosion and flash shocked the Taliban stronghold.

Jack peeked around the corner. The courtyard filled with dust and smoke.

If the mission weren't a hostage rescue, Jack would have called for Combat Clearance. They would have taken their time, clearing the corners and letting the dust settle before advancing, maintaining the tactical advantage of seeing in the dark. Most of the time, haji did not have night vision.

A hostage rescue, on the other hand, was a full out "GO! GO! GO!" The hostage's life was considered more important than the assaulters' lives, more important than anything.

The assaulters took off running, searching for doors. Liberty and Sentinel picked up four hajis running out of Building Eleven, dragging their AK-47s by the slings, as if it were a fire drill. The Air Force strobed them, and the RECCE snipers plugged them before they'd taken three steps.

Two more sneaky bastards tried to squirt out a back alley window. Instantly, the floodlight strobed them.

"Smoke two more," they all heard in their radios.

Building Eleven, Jack's target, was the building the fanatics had come out of pushing and shoving the previous night. Echo's Building Twelve was the maintenance garage from which the stretcher had been carried.

Sarge rushed into Building Eleven first, sniffing for booby traps. Jack crammed through the small door with Delta close behind. The haji doorways, as usual, were low and narrow, a real pain in the ass to squat and squeeze through quickly. Especially at six foot three and loaded for war.

They were trying to move fast, but it was pitch black. Even with NODs, they never knew where one of the deadly pricks was hiding. Hajis hid behind doors, furniture, on shelves, or even inside the thick, mud walls. They built narrow passageways inside the walls and concealed the gun holes to make them next to impossible to detect on the fly.

Jack heard scraping from behind him. His spider-on-the-neck instincts told him exactly where the gun barrel was. The instant he dove for cover, machine gun flames erupted from a hole in the wall. The rounds laced a line of sparks across the opposite wall.

Jack lay on his right side, on top of his rifle. He rolled farther over onto his back, brought the rifle barrel up with his gloved left hand, and pulled the trigger. He was dead on target, and the enemy gunfire stopped.

Jack practiced firing from all kinds of positions at their training facilities in Virginia. Standing, sitting, lying down, hanging upside down, between his legs. He was deadly with whatever weapon happened to be near at hand, although he preferred his H & K.

He was pissed more than anything that the prick tried to gut shoot him from a rat hole. That was how he had lost one of his best men. At that instant, all his fury for that murder turned him instantly savage.

He scrambled to the wall in a crawl, just below the gun hole, making himself an impossible target. He heard rustling inside the wall, but he wasn't sure if the shooter was injured, getting ready for round two, or moving out.

The hole had grown bigger since he'd blasted it. He grabbed a frag. Yelled at his team to get down. Popped the pin. Stuffed it through the hole, and dove back through the little door.

The ground quaked. Chunks of wall obliterated the door. An opening the size of a door replaced the spy hole. The shooter lay broken on the rock pile. He gurgled. His eyes stared straight ahead, not blinking. Bubbles and blood frothed out a flap ripped in the side of his neck. Jack stomped on the man's AK, bending it in half. Sarge climbed on top of the dying haji, sniffing his dying breath.

"Let's move," said Jack. He didn't look back.

He continued working the back hallway with Sarge and Dewey, slightly aware that his headache was back. As a baby SEAL, the first concussion had been a surprise. Even scared him until the old timers explained it came with the territory. He grew to expect them near heavy explosions. That one was minor. He didn't even throw up.

The door to the next room was jammed.

"Most likely barricaded and booby trapped," said Jack.

He quietly stuck a charge on the door, a twelve inch long strip of putty that looked like caulking. It created a pushing charge that worked perfectly for interior doors.

The door disappeared in a bright flash. His Peltors muffled the noise. There were no secondary explosions from a booby trap. After debris settled, Dewey sent Sarge in, who quickly got hold of a live one. Jack heard him screaming.

All men begged for mercy when threatened with a large, angry dog. Once Sarge sank his teeth in, he never let go, unless Dewey ordered him or the guy was dead.

"Let's go," Jack said. "The clock's ticking."

They peeked around the corner a couple of times, then crouched and bolted in, angling toward Sarge's snarls behind a barricade at the far end of the room. Jack's IR flashlight shone on a dark-skinned man bleeding from shrapnel wounds, soaking his shredded robe with blood. He slumped against the wall.

"Where's the American?" Jack fumed as he grabbed him by the collar.

With great effort, the man fished his still-smoldering cigarette from the dirt with his shaking hand, and stuck it between his blue lips, staring at Jack.

Jack let go and stood up.

The man inhaled deeply. The head of his cigarette glowed white. He smiled. Exhaled smoke through his gapped teeth and said, "Fuck y—"

Before he could finish, Jack put two 5.56 holes through the middle of his forehead.

"Have a nice day, asshole," said Jack. The only emotion he had at that moment was urgency. He wasn't sad or remorseful or energized or celebrating. He was locked down and mission focused.

They took pictures of the EKIA, then Jack and Dewey quickly did their SSE. They found a knife, rifle, lighter, and some other garbage. They stuffed the booty into the back pouches of their MOLLE packs and moved on to the next room.

Jack heard movement, shouts, and gunfire from other parts of the building. No one was finding the hostage. Chatter sounded increasingly frustrated. "Where the hell is Keeler?"

Jack, Dewey, and Sarge set up on either side of the next doorjamb. Jack pushed on the door, but it didn't move. He rapped on it harder with his gun butt, and automatic gunfire erupted from inside, shredding the door. Sarge jumped but did not make a sound. There was no way they wanted to peek around the corner and get face-shot.

Jack popped the pin on another frag and threw it.

"Grenade in. Frag out!"

Three seconds later, the door lit up and splintered, along with hundreds of metal missiles from the grenade. Jack and Dewey rushed through the door.

The shooter had barricaded himself behind a wooden table turned on its side. He moaned and bled through his white robe, but still groped for his gun.

Jack gave him a quick butt stroke with his rifle in the side of the head. His annoying whining stopped as he went limp.

Sarge barked. Jack and Dewey crouched, pivoted, and panned their IR flashlights. Through the dust and the eerie green light of their NODs, they saw the lifeless body of Agent Keeler.

"Fucking barbaric son of a bitches," Dewey said.

Keeler's legs had been cleanly chopped off, rope tourniquets twisted around his thighs to keep him alive and screaming for the grand finale. His head lay against the wall six feet away, along with an arm. A bloody machete lay in the dirt.

"We found Keeler's body," Jack said into his radio. He let it sink in for a few seconds. He knew what they were thinking. Too late to save him, again.

"The gig's up. Bring the 47s in for exfiltration."

They no longer had a hostage to rescue. It was time to blow. They could stop pussyfooting around and nail any Taliban stragglers still in the neighborhood.

"Finish clearing the compound. Do your SSE, and let's take Agent Keeler home. We'll need a body bag."

Those last few words struck at the souls of all SEALs. Never leave a teammate behind, even if Keeler wasn't a SEAL. It was a code they'd die for.

Jack and Dewey returned to their still-breathing, but unconscious, captive. After Jack studied the man's face a few moments, he recognized him from the video.

He radioed Big Daddy. "I have a PUC. Looks like that Arab fuck, Ahmed, from the video."

While Jack waited for Big Daddy to verify, he did their SSE. Dewey collected Agent Keeler's body parts for transport back home. Dewey found Keeler's tongue and other ear and put them in the bag, too.

Jack collected Ahmed's knife, rifle, and handgun with some Arabic engraving on it. In his pocket, he found a handwritten note. A little unusual for haji, since they were mostly illiterate. Jack had survived four months of Arabic language school. He wasn't fluent by any means, but he knew enough.

Half a dozen aluminum suitcases, mostly shredded by the grenade, lay in one corner. Jack checked, but they were empty. "Pretty fancy for a bunch of douche bags." There was no sign of Mohammed "The Hatchet," except for Keeler's chopped-up body. He had slipped out through the cracks.

"Holy shit, Big Daddy! I found a note on the PUC. If I

didn't know better, I think it says this asshole is the brother of Mullah El-Hashem."

"No shit! Cuff him, stuff him, and let's get the hell out of here," said Big Daddy. "The terp will check it. The 47s are twenty minutes out. Let's rock and roll. Over and out."

Liberty watched their backs while they humped it back to their ORP. One man lugged Keeler's body bag. Another jogged with the unconscious and bleeding Ahmed over his shoulder. They heard the rotor noise as the Chinook drew close. Jack's men knew better than to drop their guard so far from home. The luggers dropped their loads and caught their breath while the others searched the dark for haji heat signals.

Jack handed the note to the interpreter. "I'll be damned! You're right, Jack. It definitely says, 'Your brother Mullah El-Hashem would have been proud.'" A frigid swirl of cold air rushed through the treetops above.

"Roger that," said Jack. "I guess that language school wasn't a complete waste of the taxpayers' money."

Jack rocked back on his heels and grabbed Big Daddy's arm. "What's up, Jack?"

"Wait one damn minute," said Jack. "No one knows we have El-Hashem's brother, right?"

Big Daddy and the C2 (Command and Control) guys nodded.

"Let's call in Strike Eagle and drop a couple of two-thousand pounders," said Jack. "There won't be anything left. The Taliban will think he's dead, along with all the other sick bastards. He'll be a gold mine of information, and no one will know he even exists. It'll be our own dirty little secret."

"You're a sneaky bastard, Jack. Let's get the hell out of here and blow this fucker," said Big Daddy.

The Chinook lifted off with the Black Hawks and rest of the Storm covering. Strike Eagle dropped two JDAM GPS-guided bombs and obliterated the compound.

The olive green body bag in the middle of the helo deck gnawed Jack's nerves raw. He wanted to punch a hole, break a chair, and kill the son of a bitch responsible. Worse yet, the terrorist responsible lay at his feet in the chopper, on a stretcher with the PJs working to keep him alive.

Nothing would have felt more righteous to Jack than to put a couple of bullets in his brain and throw him out the hatch. Jack knew he wasn't alone.

"Relax, boys. It's out of our hands for now." Jack looked each man in the eye. "Just be patient. We're not done with this son of a bitch yet."

The unconscious prisoner twitched, jerked, and started foaming at the mouth. The PJs checked his pupils with their flashlights, and then administered IV Valium to stop the seizure. They intubated and ventilated him to protect his airway. They wrapped the bleeding leg wounds, put anti-shock pants on, and gave him plasma.

The Chinook flew back across the border into Afghanistan.

Jack couldn't believe Keeler was dead, but he knew there had been little chance of saving him. All the way back to base, Jack thought about Keeler's wife and kids and the horrible news some staffer was going to have to dress up and deliver to their home. Nina's worries about both of them dying started to reside in a small corner of his subconscious. He didn't think about it when he was working, but it was there as soon as he powered down.

SEALs did things every day of their lives that could get them killed. It was all dangerous. That was part of what made it so cool to be a SEAL. They feared nothing, especially death. Jack was indestructible. And while bullets whizzed around him constantly, he was pretty sure his spider would give him the edge he needed to stay alive for Nina and Jake.

Being a Sioux warrior, he wasn't afraid to die. He just didn't think some punk Taliban terrorist would be the one to get the job done.

After they landed back at base, several of the CIA operatives from the base stuck their heads in the hatch to look at the bastard who'd killed their friends.

Jack guarded the PUC in case anyone decided to take matters into their own hands.

After a brief layover, they took off to fly Jack and the prisoner to the CIA's covert one-room Pakistani hospital where Ahmed's secrets could be exhumed.

13

Chitral, Pakistan

As Travis and Rolf climbed out of the sheik's new jet onto Pakistani soil, a pair of ten-wheeled cargo trucks charged toward them from the far end of the paved runway. Diesel smoke boiled from their exhaust pipes, looking like two angry bulls' horns jabbing above the cab roofs. A sedan sandwiched in the cradle of the approaching convoy cruised below the greasy smear trailing behind in the crisp air. Imam Rashid hurried down the stairs to greet the convoy. Haleema followed once the men had deplaned and stood off to the side.

"What the hell, Rolf. I suppose that's the welcoming committee hurrying over here with the red carpet," said Travis, glancing over his shoulder to see if they were alone. "I've had long nights in the operating room, but that was the worst night I've ever had. Weren't you worried, even a little?" Travis still lugged his shoulder bag full of medicine and cigarettes.

"No. You just make them nervous. It's not like I didn't warn you," Rolf said with a smirk. "You're probably the first American they've been ordered *not* to kill. Consider yourself lucky."

"That's a great comfort," said Travis. "Make sure you remind the crazy bastards why I'm here. I'm not the enemy."

Travis stretched his throbbing back and took his first breath of fresh air since leaving Dubai the previous night. Trapped for twelve terrifying hours onboard the luxurious tri-engine Dassault, he realized he had made a big mistake, and Rolf was going to be no help at all.

The flight from Dubai into Peshawar had been a cakewalk for Haleema. She stayed up front with the pilots. It was horrible for Travis. When one of the guards insisted on watching Travis take a piss with his finger resting on his rifle trigger, Travis realized they weren't on any ordinary mission trip. Had Rolf not been there, Travis feared they would have banged his virgin American ass and killed him.

The first leg of the trip could not have ended worse. Peshawar International Airport never turned on the landing lights at night. The local idiots enjoyed shooting at them or the airplanes they were guiding, from the surrounding hills. Their instrument-only landing came up a little short. They touched down on a set of railroad tracks crossing the end of the runway.

The guards refused to buckle up, so they bounced around the cabin like popcorn seeds in a pan of sizzling oil. After the plane rolled to a stop, one of the guards grabbed Travis by the hair, shoved him back in the leather seat, and pinned him with the butt of his rifle, as if Travis were trying to escape. If it hadn't been for Rolf calming the guards down, Travis feared what the morons would have done next.

The imam in charge said they could not risk detection or inspection in Peshawar, but the landing at their final destination could only be accomplished in the light of day. They'd sleep on the plane and take off at first light for the final leg of the trip.

With the window shades drawn and the interior lights dimmed, the ever-wary guards sat one bullet away, cursing Travis in their native tongue. Rolf spoke to them in Pashto, pointing at the cockpit. They laughed, eased back in their chairs, and laid their rifles on the floor.

"For whatever you just said, thanks," said Travis.

"I said if the pilots didn't kill us, they don't need to worry about some American doctor. Besides, with the way you look, they're not too worried," said Rolf, as he looked Travis over. "You sure have let yourself go."

"You know, I'm here to help you," said Travis. "I don't need this bullshit."

"Nothing personal, but they hate Americans around here, remember?" said Rolf.

"No shit. That part I've got."

"They've hated Americans since Gary Powers took off from Peshawar in his U-2 spy plane back in 1960 to fly over the Soviet Union," said Rolf.

"Yeah, well I'm not flying a spy plane, and these assholes are still assholes," said Travis. "What I'd like to know is whose side are you on?"

"Come on, Travis. What do you think?" Rolf said as he rolled his eyes and shook his head. "Now be quiet and get some sleep. You'll need it." Rolf leaned back and closed his eyes.

Travis flopped back in his chair and mumbled again, "Fucking assholes."

Grandpa Joe and the Zuya thought he was such a deep thinker. And he had been at one point. He made it through medical school. Yet, he always felt cursed, ever since the day his cousin died. After his parents died, he had no one who cared. Especially not his brother, Jack. No one loved him. So, he did what he wanted. Went where he wanted. Bought what he wanted. Fucked who he wanted. His life was a disaster. Travis needed to wake up and start thinking again.

The jet roared back into fresh air at first light.

From 35,000 feet, they watched the sun rise over the highest mountain range on the planet, the Himalayas. Mount Everest and K2 lurked somewhere beyond the curve of the dandelion-colored horizon to the east. For generations, the fifteen hundred miles of granite had served to preserve and separate billions of Chinese, Indians, Buddhist, Hindus, and Muslims.

The Himalayas were undefeated by those who'd died trying to conquer them. They stood without remorse or concern, poised for another hundred thousand years.

The plane descended into a valley surrounded by the high peaks of the Hindu Kush in the Northwest Frontier province of Pakistan. Travis watched out the side window as the plane snaked north and touched down in the morning fog, just feet beyond the Chitral River.

They taxied to the only hangar, where Rolf and Travis stood, stretching in the cool morning shadows. Chitral lay at the foot of Tirich Mir. At 25,289 feet, it was the highest peak of the Hindu Kush. With the jet engines silent, they heard river waters trickling, goat bells clanging, and the squealing brakes of two cargo trucks and a weathered Mercedes sedan pulling up beside them.

Eight bearded men climbed down from the trucks with a commander growling orders to establish a perimeter guard. Six of them surrounded and faced away from the plane, shouldering their machine guns. The remaining two had rocket-propelled grenade launchers and were scanning for threats. The gunpowder-charged air crackled with so much testosterone that the coos of a mourning dove snapped their heads around, ready to annihilate the bird.

The commander opened the rear door of the Mercedes. One boot, then the other, tested the footing, then a white-robed and turbaned man, a smile etched across his worn face, emerged.

"Mullah Nabir, what an honor," said Imam Rashid as he walked to the limo to greet him. "It's good to see you again."

"Welcome to Chitral, my friend, and to you, too, Dr. Marques. We've been waiting for this day," said Mullah Nabir. "The world knows Chitral as the home of the snow leopard, and the home of Allah's beloved Taliban."

He shook hands with Rolf, pulled him aside and said, "You've some important work to do here, Doctor. Praises be to Allah."

Rolf bowed and said, "Thank you, Mullah Nabir. It is indeed my honor to be at your service. Please let me introduce my—"

"That won't be necessary, Doctor. Outsiders aren't welcome, especially him," the mullah said. "We'll tolerate him as long as we must, for the good of the security council. I don't approve of his kind being here. We know your Mr. Gunn is more than he appears. He'll do what he's told. Do you understand?"

"I assure you he will," said Rolf. "But what do you mean?"

"In good time, Doctor. Now get these trucks loaded, and let's get the hell out of here. I get nervous being out in the open like this," said Mullah Nabir as he glanced up at the cloudless sky.

After the medical supplies were transferred to the trucks, they escorted Rolf and Haleema to the Mercedes to ride with the mullah. The guards pulled a black hood over Travis's head and led him to a truck. The biggest guard shoved him as he climbed in. Travis clunked his head on something metal. They laughed and jabbed him in the ass with their rifles to keep him moving. A little dizzy and sleep deprived, he settled in for a diesel-stinking, dusty ride.

Travis clutched his shoulder bag, confident that his brother Jack was tracking his every move. He knew Jack would follow through on his promise, but he was not sure about the U.S. Travis got nervous around military types. They had a bad reputation among Native Americans, given their history.

14

The Catacombs, Afghanistan

The Catacombs included over two miles of underground corridors, rooms, and hangars beneath the runways of Bagram Air Field. A variety of checkpoints and security doors sealed off the CIA's section, making it as impenetrable as Langley itself. Highly classified information and personnel blew through its hallways like a black wind. Assets, targets, and missions were blended and sanctioned without a trace.

Jack knew his way around its passageways better than his own home. He had loved caves and tunnels since conquering his fear of the dark on his eleven-year-old Vision Quest, the Sioux rite of passage to manhood.

A hundred years earlier, boys were expected to endure hardship without complaining. They learned to go without food for days without showing weakness. They had to run for a sun and moon without rest. They traversed wild country without getting lost, both day and night. An aspiring Sioux warrior could not refuse any of those challenges.

Grandpa Joe started Jack on his Quest by leaving him in a cave, blindfolded, sitting on a boulder overnight until the sun's rays shined upon him in the morning. He could not remove the blindfold. He could not yell for help. Jack heard all kinds of terrifying noises. What were they doing?

Would they attack a blindfolded child? The cave howled. A thunderstorm crashed against the mountain outside. Jack flinched, but he never took his blindfold off until the sun warmed his face. It was then that he discovered Grandpa Joe had been sitting on the rock next to him all night, protecting his grandson from harm. At the ceremony after breakfast, Jack was given the Indian name Raging Bull, and his training in the ways of the Sioux warrior began.

Jack studied the concrete Quonset hut from the doorway. It was a replica of a Taliban hospital room his team discovered on a previous mission into Pakistan. The CIA recreated it in their underground base to trick terrorists into thinking they were safely tucked away in a Pakistani hospital, while Preacher used his revolutionary interrogation technique. In that part of the world, the terrorists and Americans alike built underground if they wanted to survive attacks and escape detection. Electrical conduits ran from side to side, curving across the top of the nine-foot dome. Floodlights dangled from the conduits, spraying out a dim, yellow light. It smelled like a moldy basement.

Three rusty, metal-framed beds lined one wall. The mattresses looked like squished slices of bread. An aluminum hospital chart hung from the foot of each bed, notes written in Pashto. Microphones and video cameras hidden in the room sent info to the CIA observation room on the other side of the wall.

Two bearded, bandaged CIA freedom fighters from Pakistan sat on their beds performing a sound check on the earpieces hidden under their white gauze turbans. They'd been briefed on Ahmed's medications and how to adjust them. Asylum in the U.S. for themselves and their families awaited them if they convinced the prisoner he was in a Taliban hospital.

Preacher walked beside Ahmed's gurney, dutifully squeezing the breathing bag twelve times a minute. Four medics slid the prisoner from the gurney onto the squeaky bed. The springs, probably the originals, sagged halfway to the floor. He was casted in plaster from the hips down as a precaution to keep him from running, nothing more. The IV bag hung from a hook on the wall. The Propofol pump sat on a stainless steel cart. It infused at a rate sufficient to maintain unconsciousness.

"When can I talk to him, Preach?" Jack asked from the doorway.

"No internal injuries that we can detect," said Preacher. The prisoner had been scanned, stitched, and run through the mill. He had received some of the best healthcare America had to offer. Preach handed the ambu-bag-squeezing responsibilities to someone else. "He's been pretty stable. I think it's time to wake this little prick up and find out what he knows. We've added Versed to the IV bag, so he'll have amnesia after we stop the Propofol. Even though he'll be awake and talking, he won't remember shit. Nothing."

"Sounds good," said Jack. "So I could beat him senseless, maybe rip his nuts off, poke an eye out, and he wouldn't remember a thing?"

"Yeah, you could, but we're trying something different here, remember?"

"How's this any different?" asked Jack. "Every other drug we've tried in interrogations has been a bust. The best and easiest way to make him talk is to make him think he's going to die. Why don't you do your experimenting on someone else and let me do what's worked since the beginning of time?" Jack cracked his knuckles.

"Just shut the fuck up for a minute, Jack. You know, you can be a real pain in the ass," said Preach.

"You're sounding more like my wife every day."

"You're about to learn something new here, pretty boy, so listen up," said Preach. "What makes people all stupid and happy and willing to blab their dirty little secrets to complete strangers? What drug compels people to make complete jackasses out of themselves, without remembering a thing? I'm sure you've been there."

Jack shrugged, raised his hands, and sheepishly confessed, "Alcohol?"

"You bet your sweet ass, alcohol!" said Preacher. "But the problem is that our guest bomber is a teetotaler because of certain religious convictions. Ahmed right?"

Jack nodded and motioned for Preach to hurry it up.

"Ahmed has probably never tasted booze. So how am I going to force him to drink alcohol?"

"Stick a hose down his throat? Pump it up his ass? I don't know."

"I'm not," said Preacher, with a smile.

"Cut the bullshit," said Jack. "I'm tired, I'm hungry, and I'm pissed off. I want to put a bullet between his eyes and go home. Spill your guts."

"I'm going to run pure alcohol in his IV," Preacher said, pointing at the IV bag dripping from the hook. "Once I turn off the Propofol and he regains consciousness, one of our 'patients' will switch his IV over to a Versed/alcohol bag. When he starts acting drunk, they'll play up how he defeated the Americans. They'll say they were the only Taliban who were hurt and brought to this secret hospital across the border in Pakistan."

"He's supposed to believe that? I hope your actors are convincing," said Jack.

"They are. Their lives depend on it. If he responds like most drunks, he'll start bragging, blabbing, and gushing information. We'll listen and prompt our guys with any question you'd like. In the end, he'll wake up the next day with a headache and that's about it. He won't remember a thing."

"Sounds too good to be true," said Jack. "Think it'll work?"

"I know it will," said Preach. "I'm the only one on the entire base who's permitted to have alcohol. Finding volunteers to practice on was no problem."

"Hear any good secrets?" asked Jack.

"You wouldn't believe some of the shit I heard," said Preach.

"Well, let's get the show on the road. I'll buy the first round," said Jack.

"Hold on, Jack. It'll take a while to wake him up and make sure he's okay before we hit the booze button."

Jack slammed his fist into a cabinet. He turned back and blocked the doorway, a hand gripping each side of the frame. His smile vanished.

On the way down to the interrogation hospital room, Jack learned that Travis had spent the night parked off the side of the runway in Peshawar, Pakistan. The plane had taken off again and Travis's beacon had disappeared. Jack was kicking himself for letting Travis go. He knew what they did to Americans in Taliban land. While Travis was probably freaking out, Jack knew it was more important than ever to stay calm and keep thinking.

"Look, Preach, you're a good guy, but now you're starting to piss me off. That son of a bitch massacred our friends, so pardon me if I don't give a shit how he feels. You boys do what you got to do, but if it's all the same to you, how about you get this fucking dog-and-pony show moving before they kill my brother, too?"

15

Chitral, Pakistan

Travis had stopped riding roller coasters at eleven years old, after he vomited a hot dog and cherry snow cone all over himself, Jack, and Jack's girlfriend during a ride on Twister. He thought about that as he bounced and jostled around in the back of the truck, breathing diesel fumes through the hood, sitting shoulder to shoulder with two stinking thugs. Sweat ran down his face. His stomach contracted. He drooled and swallowed hard. Travis knew he could keep his breakfast down for five, maybe ten more seconds.

He ripped off the hood, lunged for the back of the truck, jerked the oiled tarp to the side, and puked his guts out onto a dusty city street filled with Pakistanis.

In the next instant, a hand grabbed his collar and yanked him back onto the floor of the truck so hard he choked and gagged on bread chunks. One guard yelled and stuck his gun in Travis's face while the other pulled him back up to his seat and put the hood back on.

The truck continued to bounce, swerve, and brake for what seemed like an eternity before screeching to a halt. Someone outside yelled, and the guards beside Travis flung back the greasy rear tarp. Bright sun and a cool swoosh of air washed through the hold where Travis still slouched, his vomit-tangled hair covering his eyes. He held the black hood, now converted to a dripping barf bag.

"Isn't this the most incredible place on earth?" Rolf said as he came into view. "Ugh. What's that awful smell?"

"Take one guess," Travis groaned. "Let's trade places next time. I'll ride in the Mercedes while you sit back here with the garbage."

"Were you being a nuisance again?" said Rolf. "I tried to warn you."

"I don't know what's come over you, but I didn't sign up for this bullshit. Maybe you're having a grand old time chitchatting with your mullahs, but I feel like I'm a hiccup away from dying," said Travis, climbing out of the truck. "And I don't see anything that looks like a propane explosion."

"Relax! There are just a few formalities I need to take care of. Then we'll get down to business. We don't want to offend anyone."

"Oh, by all means. We can't have any hurt feelings," said Travis. "Your family is supposedly desperate for our help and I'm being kicked around like some stray dog, but why don't you take your fucking time and sit down for a nice hot cup of tea?"

"It's a little more complicated than that," said Rolf. "The mullahs, soldiers, everyone's definitely on edge with an American along. Are you sure you didn't tell anyone where you were going?"

"Who would I tell? I didn't have any idea where we were going," said Travis.

"These are not the kind of people who like surprises. You don't want to fuck around."

"Well, if it's all the same to you, I don't want to die," said Travis. "They need me a lot more than I need them."

"You're getting yourself worked up for no reason," said Rolf. "No one's going to die. We're here for a week or two, and then back to Dubai. Back to your beach club and Bridgett. Why don't you just relax and stretch out here in the truck? Catch up on your sleep."

"Like I can sleep with them around," said Travis, nodding toward the guards. "As soon as you're gone, who knows what'll happen?"

"I'll tell the guards to take it easy on you," said Rolf. "I'm going to a meeting with Mullah Mohammed Abdul, who's familiar with the village where we're going. I'm told he heads their security council and is their spiritual leader. Now my stomach is churning. How do I look?" Rolf asked, combing his fingers through his thick hair.

"Cleanliness isn't a high priority around here, from what I've seen. You look fine," said Travis. "Why don't I come along?"

"You'll be safer here," said Rolf. "No infidels are allowed near our spiritual leaders."

"You mean *their* leaders. Right?" said Travis.

"Exactly," said Rolf. He cupped his hand around the corner of his mouth so the two guards wouldn't hear. "I'm just playing along. You know, when in Rome, do as the Romans do. Now you just relax and get some sleep. I won't be long."

Rolf tapped Travis on the foot, turned, said something to the guards, and left. The guards looked inside at Travis, and then stepped around the side of the truck and out of sight. Travis heard them talking and saw clouds of cigarette smoke wafting past. A couple of pine trees, the only things visible, shaded the back of the truck.

Travis did not dare get up to look around, so he stretched out on the floor between two shipping crates and rested his head on the medicine bag. He had a dreaded feeling that the bag and its special pack of cigarettes were his only hope.

He never felt more alone than he did at that moment. Even on his Vision Quest, when Grandpa Joe took him into the forest, blindfolded him and left him sitting on a stump overnight, he was at peace. When Travis turned eleven, he was the Spirit Keeper of his parents' spirits, in order to learn as much as he could from their wisdom. The Sioux considered it the ultimate expression of love. Their spirits became his personal totem that continued to teach him throughout his life. That is, until he decided he did not need totems and spirits and the Zuya anymore. It was the twenty-first century. That stuff was for a world that didn't exist anymore.

"Travis! Wake up." The truck rattled and barked a huge plume of smoke out the back.

"What the hell! What's the matter?" He bolted straight up, grabbing a couple of crates, eyes wide open. The two guards climbed in.

"Meeting's over. We're going to the hospital to set up. We'll start doing surgery tomorrow," Rolf said, as he turned to walk back to the Mercedes.

Travis rubbed his eyes. "How'd the meeting go?"

"Mullah Mohammed's the most passionate man I've ever met. He's a prophet of Allah's and a disciple of Mullah El-Hashem, with a plan to save the world."

"Are you shitting me? You're playing the part again, right?" Travis said into Rolf's ear, so no one could hear.

"I'm serious," said Rolf out loud. "If people would keep an open mind, it's as if Allah is speaking directly though him."

Travis pulled himself up onto his crate, rolling his eyes. He heard the other two vehicles start up. "Come on, Rolf. Mohammed, mullah, and Allah all rolled up into one big bullshit burrito with this mullah spreading the good news. Annihilate all of the infidels, and the world will be safe again. Give me a fucking break. El-Hashem was a terrorist and a mass murderer."

"That's about how I figured you'd respond, but then what should I expect from a lying, spying son of a bitch?" Rolf shouted as he leaned inside the truck, spit flying and his eyes bugging out.

Travis jumped back up on his seat like he'd been poked in the ass. His eyes darted back and forth. A guard pressed in on each side. He drummed his fingers. His feet twitched. "What'd they say in there? You're not turning into one of them are you?"

"I trusted you when no one else would, not even your Navy SEAL brother, Jack Gunn."

Travis exhaled, his shoulders sagged, and he stared out of the back of the truck, beyond Rolf. He thought that would have been a perfect time for Jack and the SEALs to make a grand entrance.

"So I've got a brother. So what? Just because he's in the Navy doesn't make me a spy."

"In the Navy! He's a little more than just in the Navy!" said Rolf. "A SEAL? Are you fucking kidding me? You made contact with him before last year's trip. Mullah Mohammed filled me in on everything. Your CIA is not the only one with wire taps."

"Don't go crazy on me, Rolf. Let's keep it in perspective," said Travis. He started to hyperventilate. "I wanted someone to know, just in case something happened. Do I look like a spy?"

"You swore to me you hadn't told anyone. Now I don't know what to think." Rolf climbed up on the bumper, face-to-face with Travis. "If there is anything else you need to tell me, this is your last chance."

"I'm sorry I didn't tell you about my brother, but you're starting to scare me with your ultimatums. What? Are you one of *them* now?" said Travis, glancing at the guards.

"Let's just say my eyes have been opened," said Rolf. "Mullah Mohammed showed me a video that aired on Al Jazeera last night. My father, Ahmed El-Hashem, led a Taliban attack into Afghanistan, attacked the CIA, killed nine spies, and took their leader as prisoner. Plans are underway for the Grand Jihad. That's why we're here."

Travis's jaw hung open. "Your father is an El-Hashem? You're a fucking El-Hashem?"

"You guessed it. There was no propane explosion and no family tragedy," said Rolf. "That part I made up. But we *are* here to do surgery. For me to fulfill my obligation to Imam Rashid. It's my cost of keeping the surgery center open. Over the next three days, we'll be doing facial identity-changing surgery on the twelve members of the Taliban's security council, including Mullah Mohammed Abdul."

Travis was numb. He couldn't feel his hands. His eyes glazed over.

"Didn't you think it a little odd they allowed an American into Pakistan?" asked Rolf. "I did."

"I always trusted you. Always," whispered Travis, wiping his mouth with his sleeve. "How can you do this to me?"

"Don't blame me. You think everything's a big joke. Well, the joke's on you," said Rolf.

"I don't understand. Why me?"

"Imam Rashid laid it all out. You jeopardized last year's mission when we changed the face of Mustafa, who was on Pakistan's most-wanted list, into a man free to come and go anywhere in the world. You notified your spy Navy SEAL brother, who works for the CIA, but Mohammed kept you alive knowing they'd need your services one more time, once they saw how easily Mustafa walked through airport security. They've kept you under constant surveillance. They've kept an eye on your brother, too."

"Rolf, you're making a big mistake. I didn't do any of that."

"You're a liar, Travis. The CIA agent my father captured told Mohammed everything. You and your brother will both be dead soon. There's nothing I can do to change that. But first, you've got one last job to do."

"They're making this up as they go, and you're eating it up hook, line, and sinker. Don't do it Rolf. You're not one of them."

"My hands are tied."

One of the guards, with a smoldering Marlboro hanging out the corner of his mouth, shook an empty Marlboro box upside down.

"By the way, the guards thank you for the cigarettes."

Travis snatched his bag. It had been cut open. "Shit." His heart pounded in his ears. He scanned the remaining cartons and quickly inventoried the drugs. The Marlboro carton with the secret mark on it was still there. He zipped the bag and hugged it in his lap.

Travis couldn't breathe. His chest burned. He was dizzy. He checked his pulse. The truck sped back down the mountain road toward Chitral. The burning turned to pressure. His left arm ached. He was sure he was going to have a heart attack.

How had he been talked into this? What was he thinking? They were all fucking insane. And now Rolf?

16

The Catacombs, Afghanistan

The operation to locate Travis frustrated Jack to no end. The bigger problem was Chitral, Pakistan, where Travis's tracker had popped up after being off the grid for half a day. It was a nasty place; ripe with the type of targets Jack always had the green light on. But the U.S. wasn't officially at war in Pakistan; so American troops weren't permitted to go there.

Jack had expected Rolf and Travis's mission trip, if that's what it was, to be somewhere in the southern part of the country, where they had gone the previous year. It wasn't a hundred percent safe, but it wasn't a war zone. He sure didn't expect him to end up in Chitral, the unofficial home of the Taliban. Jack was wringing his hands and irritating the hell out of everyone in the Catacombs to find out what was going on in Chitral.

Even Pakistan's military treaded softly in Chitral. They knew where the Taliban permitted them to go and not go. Bad things happened to them or their families if they forgot who ran the show.

Until they had a reason to go in, Jack could do nothing more than watch Travis's light blink on the locator map and wait for something to happen.

17

Chitral, Pakistan

The Taliban staged a sewer break, forcing the evacuation of all patients and staff from District Headquarters Hospital. Several buckets of human diarrhea from local outhouses were dumped on the hallway floors as evidence.

Trucks, jeeps, and machine-gun toting Taliban security blocked all hospital entrances and would continue to do so until the supposed sewer repairs and cleanup were complete, which could take weeks in Pakistan. The Taliban had taken control, and no one could stop them.

Once they arrived at the quarantined hospital, Travis wasn't allowed outside again. Even though the operating room smelled like a shit factory, he took in a deep, pungent breath and tried to relax. His hands were tied behind his back and a noose wrapped around his neck with one of the guards holding the other end. He gave it a jerk every few minutes just to throw off Travis.

There were only two places in the world Travis loved to be. The OR, because patients trusted him with their life, and Happy Hour because drinking Bombay Sapphire martinis cured everything that ailed him. The rest of the time, Travis ran. He'd been running so long; sometimes he couldn't remember what he was running from or where he was going.

He tried to dredge up anything useful from his years of Zuya training. Grandpa Joe had taught Travis that his best weapon was his mind. But Travis never completely bought into the old remedies. He learned many secrets and saw more than his share of miracle healing, but he was embarrassed to talk about it with doctors and scientists once he left home. He saw what happened to Grandpa Joe. Even his own people stopped listening. Like throwing a blanket over an antique Victrola music machine, and turning it into a TV stand. He became an irrelevant relic. Travis did not want to become like Grandpa Joe.

Complex thinker. What a joke. He tried to focus his mind on Jack to send a signal, but it had been too long. His mind was gone. He clung to the medicine/cigarette tote strapped over his shoulder and hoped Jack could follow the tracking signal, if it was even working. Old school, new school, something had to work.

Rolf did not even look up when the guards jerked Travis into the operating room by his noose. Rolf leaned over a table under the surgical lights, sketching on photos of the twelve council members' faces, planning their new identities. The two wary guards corralled Travis and kept him at bay. So Rolf was serious. They really were going to do surgery on a bunch of crazy bastards intent on who knew what.

The operating room was surprisingly clean and well equipped. Even the sewer smell was less noticeable. There was an OR table and lights, an instrument sterilizer, tanks of oxygen, and a humming ice machine. Far more than Travis had expected. A copper-kettle anesthesia machine, which had been common in 1960, sat near the head of the table. The world of anesthesia had advanced ten generations since copper-kettle machines.

"This place is anesthesia machine purgatory. No one would believe this back in Boston," said Travis, hoping to break the ice.

"Could you please be quiet?" Rolf stopped drawing. "Even a dipshit like you should be able to read the handwriting on the wall. We're not in Boston anymore." He didn't wait for a reply, but went right back to creating.

Travis turned away from the table, but there was nowhere to go.

The blood pressure cuff and EKG machine looked older than the anesthesia machine. Inside the drawer of a supply cart he found a flashlight, an old laryngoscope, and several endotracheal tubes. Judging by the yellow, crusty sputum flakes falling from the crevices of the rubber breathing tubes, they were passing from throat to throat, with no cleaning.

"Disgusting," said Travis as he slammed the drawer shut.

"I told you once. Shut the fuck up. I need to concentrate," Rolf said, as he leaned on the table with both hands, exhaled, and gave a sideways stare at Travis. "No one here is going to put up with your whining and bullshit anymore. No one . . . including me. I have a big job to do, and that's my only focus. They would have killed you already, except I need you to do anesthesia. So what's it going to be? Are you in or out?"

"So that's what it's come to? You'll kill me if I don't help you create a dozen mass murderers?" said Travis.

"Of course not. What kind of animal do you think I am?" Rolf smirked at Travis. "I wouldn't kill you. They would." Rolf tilted his head toward the guards, who smiled back a most devious and rotten smile. "And they'd enjoy it. You know they would." The guard jerked Travis's noose.

"Okay. Okay. I get it," said Travis as he raised a palm. "Just tell them to put their guns down. Please!"

"You're sure?" asked Rolf. "Because I don't want any more of your fucking games. If you're in, then do your job and quit your bitching and moaning. Can you do that?"

Travis nodded with an eye on the guards.

"Good. Now get out and leave me alone," said Rolf. "Morning is going to come fast, and you'd better be ready. And remember. One slip-up and you're done."

Rolf again tilted his head toward the two stooges. "Believe it or not, you *are* expendable. It would be harder for me to do both surgery and anesthesia, but I can and I will. So don't get any funny fucking ideas. Understood?"

Rolf waved a hand at the guards who led Travis across the hall to the storeroom where the monitors, pumps, and other anesthesia supplies were still packed in crates. They took the noose off, untied his hands, and retired to a pile of boxes to smoke. Next to them were a couple aluminum suitcases that stood out like two-carat diamond earrings at a homeless shelter.

There was equipment to unpack, and medications to draw up. He plopped on top of a stack of crates and lit up. His two goat-stinking guards, who looked like they'd rather enjoy snuffing him, followed.

Later, with everything set, Travis worried as he tried to doze off on the floor, his head resting on the medicine bag turned zipper-side down. He felt completely abandoned and alone. A feeling he'd grown used to over the years. He had never been popular like Jack. When the tribe decided Travis could not be trusted, Travis was not trusted. Although it was too late, he wondered what would have happened if he had admitted to being the one who knocked his cousin under the train, whether he actually had or not. Would they have trusted him then? Everything that happened in his life since was affected by that one moment. Had someone put a curse on him? He wondered. Had the gods turned their backs on him? Who could blame them? Wherever he went, whatever he did, he never escaped.

Jack had been right. Rolf fit right in with all the other Islamic crazies. Travis's plan was shit. He was screwed. The American cigarettes he'd brought to bridge the gap with the barbarians were going fast. They might cut his throat just to get the rest of the smokes and discover the tracking device that obviously wasn't doing shit. He felt like a harbor seal being lowered into a great white shark tank. They killed for sport. It was only a matter of time before the Taliban sharks tore him to shreds.

↗ ↗ ↗

"Wake up," said Rolf, kicking him on the foot.

Travis jerked out of his restless sleep, rubbed his eyes, and looked up at Rolf and his two guards. He felt he had better odds of surviving the sharks in his nightmares than the next twenty-four hours.

He wondered, after all their years partying in Boston and working together, how Rolf had kept secret that he was an El-Hashem. Maybe they were threatening to kill his wife and kids if he didn't do what they wanted. Travis could understand that. But to think Rolf was voluntarily helping the Taliban pull off their "Grand Jihad" felt like Travis was being pulled under by a rogue wave.

Travis got up off the floor and made a guard understand with sign language that he needed to go to the bathroom. From the smell and look of the hallway, he could have pissed on the floor and nobody would have noticed, but they took him to a bathroom lit only by the rising sun. When they got back to the storeroom, Haleema was standing there with a tray of food and water. Travis had completely forgotten about her. She looked like a Saudi princess in her white robe and hijab headscarf. Her dark eyes were a dichotomy of tenderness and sorrow. She mouthed the words, "How could you?" as she handed Travis the tray. Then Haleema bowed, turned, and walked away. Travis called to her, but she kept walking. The guards' mouths hung open, like they'd never seen anything so beautiful.

Twelve surgeries in two to three days. He thought about injecting their IVs with a nasty infection, say with some of the shit water from the hall floor. An E. coli infection took a couple of days to turn septic, so maybe Rolf would not figure it out until it was too late. But even if he managed to kill all twelve of the patients, he was still lost in the evil empire.

He had to face the facts. He was surrounded, trapped, outnumbered, outgunned, and outsmarted. He was out of luck. If all the surgeries went perfectly and all twelve security council members were ecstatic with their new identities, maybe they'd let him go back to Dubai and live happily ever after. As eternally optimistic as he was, that did not seem too likely.

He was down to his last option: Jack "Boom Boom" Gunn and the Navy SEALs. If they were tracking him and got there soon, they could catch all the bad guys, stop the Grand Jihad, and save him. He just had to play along and stay alive until the cavalry came. That was it then. Wait for Jack to save his ass. It sounded like the same solution he'd used growing up. Bullies would pick on little Travis and big brother Jack kicked their asses.

They walked across the diarrhea hall to the operating room. No one seemed the least bit concerned that much of the corridor was smeared in a teeming pool of sewage. The guards tied masks over their gangly beards and put shoe covers over their shitty boots. Otherwise, they were in street clothes, one stationed on either side of Travis, AK-47s ready.

From the thunder-like vibrations he'd felt in the early morning hours, he expected a garrison of Taliban jihadists had arrived by truck and had locked down the hospital. No one was getting in or out. His queasy stomach returned.

Haleema had scrubbed the walls and tacked sheets over the windows. She stood gowned, gloved, and had the back table instruments organized. Normally chatty, even flirty in Dubai, she gave a nod, and then shook her head slowly. Her eyes looked tired or sad. He couldn't quite tell. Was she trying to tell him something? She turned away and took a surgical sponge to dab her eyes.

Travis had seen hundreds of fundamentalist Muslim men with their fist-length beards, turbaned heads, and strife-etched faces. Not so much in permissive Dubai, but anywhere else in the Middle East, especially on his trip to Pakistan the previous year, and on the current disaster. But all twelve of the Taliban leaders who paraded into the OR, one by one over the next three days, looked entirely different.

They were lean, handsome men in floor-length gowns who were beardless for the first time in their adult lives. Normally, shaving would have been forbidden and an insult to Islam and Allah, but it was their duty. They were part of the plan. Shaving, then changing their faces with surgery, would allow them unrestricted travel to carry out jihad anywhere on the globe. Their time was coming.

Mohammed Abdul's surgery was saved for last. As he walked into the OR, he recited prayers barely audible to Travis. He rubbed the jagged scar stretching across his throat where American shrapnel had nearly severed his jugular. Travis knew nothing of Mohammed except the brief comments by Rolf claiming him to be a prophet. When Mohammed pulled a hatchet from beneath his robe and pointed its finely honed edge at Travis, for the first time Travis truly felt he would die. The OR lights reflected off the polished steel and danced across the ceiling as Mohammed tilted the hatchet back and forth. A wry smile twitched the corner of his mouth, and he shook his head as if he were looking at the most despicable slime on the face of the earth.

For most of the last five years, Travis wished he were dead. He remembered many nights of leaning on his condo balcony rail, staring at the blur of Dubai's night lights. He had wished he could stop breathing. He'd wanted to jump. He'd wanted it to be over. Now all he could think about was how much he wanted to live.

When Mohammed lay down on the surgery table, he was so tall that his black, scarf-wound head lay at one end of the table and his feet hung over the other. Rolf had already asked Mohammed everything Travis needed to know so the infidel doctor would not need to speak.

Travis placed the blood pressure cuff, EKG pads, and pulse oximeter. Mohammed's vital signs were those of a twenty-year-old. Good, clean living. Travis's hands shook. There was a bullet with his name on it just inches away if he screwed up. But he slid the IV in easily and injected Versed, Fentanyl, and Propofol to put Mohammed to sleep. Twenty seconds later, he paralyzed him.

Travis and Rolf both knew Travis could inflict serious brain damage or worse if he "forgot" to breathe for the patient. Rolf watched Travis with the eyes of a hawk. The chest rose and fell. Travis didn't feel like dying, so he kept squeezing the bag.

Travis lubed a nasal breathing tube the diameter of Mohammed's little finger and snaked it down his right nostril. The guards shouted to stop, and a cold gun barrel jammed into the back of Travis's neck.

He froze and said nervously to Rolf, "The patient's not being ventilated, Rolf. What do you want me to do?"

Rolf quickly jumped in, hands up, explaining in Pashto that everything was under control.

As the wide-eyed roomful of guards watched, Travis shoved the rest of the twelve-inch tube down Mohammed's nose. One of the guards fainted. His head bounced off the concrete. While the circus of observers dragged him out by the ankles, Travis ignored them, secured the airway, and started the Propofol infusion to keep Mohammed asleep.

Travis put the breathing tube down his nose so Rolf could work on the lip reduction first. A crescent-shaped chunk of tissue was excised from behind each lip, inside the mouth. By sewing the edges together, each lip pulled in, reducing its overall size.

For the second stage, Travis changed to a mouth tube so Rolf could work on the nose and eyes. Mohammed had a long hanging nose tip. The plan was to shorten his nose and give him a "Mr. Piggy" nose. The nose was flipped up, like looking under a lady's skirt, and its cartilaginous structure filed and reshaped.

Finally, Rolf worked on the eyes so they would appear more open and gave Mohammed a cat-eye look.

By mid-afternoon, finally satisfied, Rolf bowed to the entourage. They applauded. Rolf and Haleema dressed the wounds and applied an elastic compression dressing over his head, with holes for his eyes, nose, and mouth.

Once the Propofol wore off and the patient breathed on his own, Travis carefully removed the breathing tube. He timed it so the patient was awake enough to do his own breathing, but asleep enough so he wasn't in pain. Either way, when he pulled the tube, there'd be no going back.

The surgery could not have gone better. They used the operating room as a recovery room. Rolf applied ice to control bleeding and swelling. Travis gave small doses of Fentanyl through the IV whenever the heart rate or blood pressure started to climb. An hour after surgery, Mohammed sat in a recliner, his face hidden under the compression dressing for the next week, accepting well wishes from his advisors and council.

"Great job, Rolf," Travis said, still hoping for a miracle reprieve.

Rolf had removed his operating mask. He shrugged his shoulders, shook his head, and then turned his attention back to Mohammed. Haleema dabbed blood from the tip of Mohammed's nose with a gauze sponge. She also glanced at Travis, but mouthed nothing. She looked only sad. Once surgery was over, she'd be on the first jet back to Dubai with her money. It was the last time she would see Travis.

They heard scuffling outside the door before an out-of-breath guard in street clothes burst into the operating room and whispered something to one of the advisors, who then leaned close to Mohammed and whispered. Even with all of the dressings covering his face, Mohammed could not hide his sadness. His shoulders slouched. The room grew silent except for the beeping heart monitor. Mohammed motioned Rolf to his side.

"I've just received bad news about your father," said Mohammed, still slurring his words a little from the anesthesia.

"What do you mean?" said Rolf.

"I'm so sorry, but I've just learned that Ahmed Omar El-Hashem, your father, was killed two nights ago."

"What? How could this happen, Mohammed? This can't be!" Tears ran down Rolf's cheeks. He looked at the courier, who nodded back.

"The Americans bombed one of our villages and massacred all the men, women, and children while they slept. I'm told there were no survivors," said Mohammed. "I'd just left that madrassa that very morning. They were good people and good soldiers. In the short time I spent with your father, I saw the greatness in him. Just as I've seen in every El-Hashem and just like I see in you, Dr. Marques. Your father was proud of you and what you were doing for jihad. I'm truly sorry for your loss."

Rolf slumped to the floor, sitting cross-legged with his face buried in his weary hands, sobbing.

"We'll never forget the success and sacrifice of those brave soldiers and families," said Mohammed, with a hand resting on Rolf's head. "No Americans can be trusted," he said, and pointed a shaky finger at Travis. "This son of a bitch most of all."

They all turned their death stares toward him.

"We're through with this one. Let's see what this American spy is hiding. Search him!"

18

Chitral, Pakistan

The room filled quickly with curious Taliban fighters bored by three days of standing around, drawn in by the ruckus. Two guards seized Travis while a third buried his fist in his gut. Travis's legs gave out. They kept slugging until he drooped like a passed-out drunk.

With each blow, the intensity grew until the noise snapped Rolf out of his detached fog. Any surgeon worth a damn maintained control of his operating room at all times, especially when the shit hit the fan. They held Travis by the hair. His mouth hung open, dripping bloody drool. Two teeth were gone. His nose twisted awkwardly to the side. Rolf jumped up and, after a nod from Mohammed, stepped between the guards and Travis, held his hands up, and demanded silence.

The heart monitor beeped along with Travis's gasps and groans. Rolf ordered several men to follow him across the hall and fingered the crates Travis had packed. While they searched, he returned and pointed out where they should start searching in the operating room.

"Well, how's it feel now?" Rolf spoke down to Travis. "The more you've tried not to be an American, the more you've become just like them, you two-faced, lying son-of-a bitch. I hope your SEAL brother didn't have anything to do with killing my father."

Travis tried to lift his head to say something.

"Save it! There's nothing more you can say," said Rolf. "Just lie there and say your prayers."

Mohammed eased back in the recliner, his face masked, while Rolf reapplied the ice. His blood pressure bumped up from the commotion, and his nose started bleeding.

They spoke softly, consoling one another. Rolf explained what the next several days of recovery entailed. Mohammed comforted Rolf about his father and started getting himself worked up again. He yelled at Travis. Rolf gave another dose of painkiller. Mohammed's eyes closed briefly, his blood pressure came down, and the bleeding stopped.

"Pathrai! Pathrai!" one of the men who'd gone through Travis's medicine bag yelled. He held up a small black microchip, the size of a penny, he'd found sealed in a cigarette wrapper. Everyone in the OR stopped. Mohammed's eyes opened, and he sat up.

"What is it?" asked Rolf.

They jerked Travis back to his feet. When Travis saw them hold up the transmitter, all hope drained. His face turned white.

The proud finder of the transmitter handed it to an officer, who in turn held it out for Mohammed to inspect.

"Now do you believe me, Doctor? He's a spy, and this is a CIA tracking device. He and his secret agent brother used you to get to me and the security council," Mohammed said to Rolf. Mohammed flipped the pathrai on the floor, and a field officer smashed it with his rifle butt.

"We must go quickly," Mohammed ordered. "I don't think even the Americans would blow up a hospital, but they know where we are."

Commanders yelled. Several men ran to carry out their orders. One of the guards slammed his rifle into Travis's stomach, doubling him over onto the cold linoleum.

"Search him quickly! Then bring him. This piece of shit may still be of use," yelled Mohammed, towering over Travis.

With an advisor supporting each arm and Rolf at Mohammed's side, they threw a blanket around his shoulders and hurried him outside into the cool air and into a black sedan.

The guards tied Travis's hands behind his back and threw a blanket over his head. He stumbled along, and they shoved him up into a truck full of Taliban foot soldiers that did what they did best. Kick and punish. He fell to the floor and curled into the fetal position. His gut and face had had enough.

Four Toyota pickup trucks with fifty-caliber machine guns mounted above their cabs led the convoy, followed by the sedans and trucks. They raced through the dusty streets to the outskirts of town. The entire convoy pulled inside a cavernous armory building. They reorganized and, moments later, drove back out in four identical three vehicle convoys, headed in four different directions.

Mohammed, the security council, Rolf, and Travis vanished into the Chitral night.

19

The Catacombs, Afghanistan

Travis's tracking signal hadn't moved for three days.

"Gunner, your brother's signal went dead fifteen minutes ago," said Wade, the intel watch commander.

"You're shitting me?"

"I wish I were." Wade shook his head, but did not take his eyes off the screen.

"What do you make of it?" asked Jack, as he hastily took a seat, breathing hard. A satellite feed zoomed in on a mountainous region, then coned down on Chitral and so on, until Jack and Wade could make out buildings, trucks, and individual people.

"Satellite just came over his position in Chitral about the time we lost the signal. His transmitter was still at this hospital." Wade pointed with a laser.

"Local word is there's a sewer leak, and all patients and staff were evacuated several days ago," Wade said. "Doesn't look like a cleanup crew to me. An awful lot of military trucks and firepower to fix a leaky pipe, wouldn't you say?"

"Any of your people in the area?" asked Jack.

"Chitral is a fanatic city. Jihad central infected with wackos. Of course we have a contact there. We're the CIA." Wade puffed his chest. "He confirms the sewer leak. His wife heard someone

who helped with the evacuation talking about the awful smell.
He can't get anywhere near the place. The Taliban has taken
over. Something's going on in there besides a leaky pipe."

"So my little brother disappeared in the middle of that?
Fuck!" cursed Jack. "Wish I knew what other wack jobs are in
there and what they're doing. Travis led us right to them, and
all we can do is watch." Jack slammed both fists on the desk.

"Look," said Wade. "They're moving out."

Heat signals glowed from every car hood and exhaust pipe.
Jack clearly saw people walking and running from the hospital
and jumping into vehicles. He could not make out faces, but
the detail was pretty good from fifty miles in space.

Jack sighed and rubbed his scalp stubble when they shoved a
blanket-covered, stooped-over man with hands tied behind his
back into a truck. "Bet that's Travis. They must have discovered
that fucking beacon, and now they're going take him and run
for the hills." Wade and Jack looked at each other. "He's alive.
But for how long?"

Since they were kids, Travis was always running off, losing
his way and needing Jack to guide him back. He was like a lost
puppy, and it had always infuriated him. Now Jack felt nothing
but sadness as he thought of his baby brother in that truck full
of dirt bags.

The satellite tracked the caravan though the city and into a
large armory building on the outskirts, near the Chitral River.
All hope of tracking and rescuing Travis from certain death
disappeared a few minutes later when the convoy reappeared,
split up into four smaller convoys, and vanished into the Swat
Valley hell.

Wade and Jack turned quiet and pale as they imagined what
sick and twisted way the Taliban would use Travis to bolster
support for jihad. Would he have a private execution? Would
he be tortured first, as the Taliban were so fond of? Or would
he have a public beheading, filmed for Al Jazeera, like Keeler's?

Jack was not someone easily rattled. The SEALs had trained
him well. He stayed calm in the direst circumstances. But when

Travis's truck disappeared from the satellite picture, Jack felt like the night he panicked trying to save his mom. She knew she was going to die and there was nothing he could do. Travis must have felt like he was about to die too. Every fiber of Jack's being told him that it was not the last time he would see Travis, but he had seen too many hostage rescues gone bad.

He remembered something Grandpa Joe had said: "In you are natural powers. You already possess everything necessary to become great. Let the spirits guide you." He needed to stay calm and focused on using every resource, Sioux and American, to rescue Travis before it was too late.

20

Northern Tribal Area, Pakistan

A key rattled in a lock. A hinge squeaked. Then silence. Not the lonely silence of Travis's condo in Dubai, but the crowded silence of someone sneaking around, trying to be quiet, but not doing a very good job of it. Travis had heard a rooster crow and a goat bleat earlier. He lay on a pile of burlap grain sacks, bound hand and foot, and gagged with a coarse piece of hemp rope. Every time he moved his head, the rope sawed deeper into the corners of his mouth. The room smelled like cornmeal and animal manure. Early morning sunlight filtered through the slats of the corncrib wall, highlighting his dismal predicament.

The door inched open, and two hillbilly-looking guards stumbled in. Travis recoiled into the fetal position. They mumbled and giggled stupidly, as each took another long, sloppy pull from a brown whiskey bottle. Smoke trailed behind the cigarettes dangling from the corners of their mouths.

They eyeballed the American spy and took another swig. Travis understood nothing they said, but from the tone of their taunts, he knew he was in trouble.

They grabbed him under each armpit, jerked him off the floor, and dropped him onto a chair. One pulled out his bayonet and held it close enough for Travis to smell steel. The guard licked the filthy blade like it was a Popsicle. Travis tried to turn away, but the gag cut deeper. He remained face to face with the creature from hell.

Native Americans did not have the concept of hell until the Jesuit missionaries arrived. Indians heard the voice of the Great Spirit everywhere, in the chirping of birds, the silence of stones, and the sweet breathing of flowers. The spirit of the deceased went to live with Wakantanka, where the weather was ideal and animals plentiful. Sioux, Cheyenne, Apache, and whitey all ended up in the same wonderful place. The missionaries introduced hell as a place where bad people and heathens went to be tormented by Satan. Satan stood face to face with Travis and smelled horrible.

With one swipe, the guard cut the rope binding Travis's ankles. His mouth was an inch from Travis's nose when he belched a smoky, alcoholic cloud that sent Travis into a coughing spasm. Both drunks laughed. They murmured back and forth. Pulled him to his feet. Walked him around behind the chair. Bent him over so his chest rested on the chair back. They kicked his feet apart, ripped his shirt-back in two, and pulled it up over his shoulders. Their knife tips jabbed him randomly up and down his spine. Not deep enough to cut, just deep enough to terrify. He flinched and twisted with each poke, until the chair and Travis toppled over. They kicked him first. Then pulled him and the chair upright again. They bent him over the chair, slipped a noose over his head, and tied the other end around the front chair legs.

A knife in the side and bleeding to death at the hands of two Taliban perverts. That's what Jack had predicted. Why hadn't he listened?

"Fuck you, you son of a bitch!" Travis tried to yell as loud as he could, but the gag swallowed most of it. He didn't have anything to lose, or so he thought.

Suddenly, the knife slipped beneath Travis's belt and, with one quick wrist flick, the belt was cut, thrown aside, and his pants jerked down to his ankles. He tried to squirm away, but two hands held his shoulders firmly down on the chair. The other kicked Travis's feet as wide apart as his pants would allow.

They tore his underwear off and threw them aside. The cold steel blade poked and prodded his dangling balls from behind. A calloused hand spread his cheeks. Dug around. They took another chug to kill the bottle and tossed it.

He heard a zipper go down. Travis froze. His ass tensed. He didn't dare move. He could barely breathe. They started pawing. He squeezed with all his might. He felt something warm.

"Oh God!" he pleaded.

"What the hell's going on in here?" Travis heard Rolf say. The hands released his ass and shoulders.

"Wait your turn outside," said the guard. He waved the knife at Rolf.

"I need to question him, you ignorant bastards," Rolf said. "Now pull his pants up and get the hell out of here!"

They held their ground and stared down Rolf till he blinked. As the one wiped his bayonet blade on his pants, he said, "Out of respect to Mohammed and your father, Ahmed, we'll do as you say . . . this time. But we don't take orders from you."

"You'd do well to remember whom you're talking to," said Rolf as he got in their faces. "The El-Hashem's given the orders, and you'll do what you're told. If you have a problem with that, maybe we should ask Mohammed. I hear he's good with a hatchet."

The guards made a wobbly attempt to stand at attention and salute. "No, sir. We got no problems."

"What's that smell? You boys been drinking?" asked Rolf.

"No, sir. No, sir," said the drunks. "We were just going to have a little fun. You know."

"No, I don't fucking know," said Rolf. "Now get the hell out of here before I change my mind."

As they shuffled out, Rolf loosened the noose. Travis pulled up his pants and untied his gag and wrist restraints. He straightened up slowly, holding his pants with one hand. Drying tears with the other. Travis sat on the chair.

"I'm sorry, Rolf. I'm sorry about your father. I'm sorry for everything," said Travis. He sobbed. "I was scared. I knew this was a bad idea."

"The only bad idea was that tracker, transmitter, whatever the fuck it was. If it weren't for that . . ." Rolf turned up his hands. "But that's not how it went down, is it? You got caught, and you're in some deep shit now. You think this was bad? Just wait." He flipped Travis's shirttail. "Lying is what got you into this shit, so you might as well tell the truth. You don't have to die, if you cooperate. Are you a spy? Is it like they said, you've been setting me up all along?"

"I'm the same guy I've always been," said Travis. "I'm no spy, for God's sake.

"Then why did you have a transmitter? Where'd you get it?" asked Rolf.

"I was worried for . . ."

"Cut the bullshit, Travis. Where'd you get it? The CIA? Your brother?"

"I didn't tell anyone," said Travis. "My brother gave me that transmitter years ago. I didn't even know if it worked."

"And I'm supposed to believe that? How fucking stupid do you think I am?" asked Rolf. "All those years, it's funny you never mentioned you have a brother." Rolf towered over Travis. He had pulled out a knife of his own.

"Jack's been an asshole most of his life. Our parents died when we were kids. Our grandpa raised us. We haven't spoken in years, except for my grandpa's funeral five years ago." Travis looked away, out the open shed door at a goat. "He gave me that transmitter at the funeral. His wife worried about me after flunking out of rehab and losing my license."

"Where'd he get it?" asked Rolf.

"I don't know. I've kept it locked up in my safe. I never intended to get you in trouble. I won't tell anyone, I promise. Please, Rolf. I just want to go home."

"Just stop right there," said Rolf. "We know your brother is a SEAL, and you're giving me some horseshit story. You still don't get it, do you? I'm not the one in trouble, Travis."

Travis slumped in his chair, chin on his chest.

"You Americans killed my father. We'll retaliate by killing an American. Maybe lots of Americans. Either way, you're fucked," said Rolf. "If you don't start squawking, they'll cut you up," said Rolf. "You know they will. Jihad is everything to them. They'll do things to you, you can't even imagine."

21

The Catacombs, Afghanistan

Jack, Wade, and Preacher drank the dregs of a scalded pot of coffee, gritty from hours on the hot plate. They eavesdropped on their two "patients" playing a game of chess beside Ahmed's hospital bed in their make-believe Taliban hospital room. Everyone, Ahmed's son Rolf, Mohammed, the American government, everyone thought Ahmed was dead, except the three men conducting his interrogation.

Chess was not considered *haram* by any but the most conservative Islamic clerics. Games of luck, like cards and dominoes, were reprehensible because they led to gambling, but chess was not forbidden because it developed skill and fighting strategies.

Ahmed was trussed up in layers upon layers of medical gauze and propped up on a couple of lumpy pillows. He used a straightened coat hanger to scratch an itch inside his body cast.

"It looks like Ahmed-the-bomber is recovering nicely," said Jack. "You boys did a real bang-up job. Hate to see him struggle with that itch, though. Maybe I should help him out. You know, fluff his pillow. Shove that wire up his ass."

Wade smiled. "It's not your style to kill them with kindness, Jack."

"An eye for an eye. Right, Preacher?"

"I know you're worried about your brother, Jack. Let's see what we can squeeze from this Taliban turd my way," Preacher said, pointing at the screen. "They switched the IVs over about thirty minutes ago and have been opening the stopcock on the alcohol mixture. He's starting to loosen up, jabbering a little more, and getting that shit-eating grin we know so well. He's about three sheets in the wind. Let's listen in."

Jack and Wade sat to watch the monitor. Preacher said, "Go" into a microphone. The actor patients tapped their earphones hidden under their turbans, left their chess game, and sat on the floor next to Ahmed's bed.

"Your brother, Mullah El-Hashem, would've been proud of you, Ahmed. First you led an attack on the CIA and captured their leader. Then you crushed the infidels when they attacked Mohammed's madrassa. You defeated the Americans twice in two days. Praises to Allah," said one of the actor patients as he raised his gowned arms to the sky.

"What'd you say?" asked Ahmed, trying to sit up, drool rolling out the corner of his mouth. He even smelled like alcohol. "I must have gone into shock. The last thing I remember is an explosion in my room after we killed the American spy and the Americans attacked. We won?"

"Won? You annihilated them. Killed them all."

"It's coming back to me. I put bullets right between their eyes. The American bastards deserved it. Bring them on. I'll kill them all."

"Yeah! Yeah!" the two patients cheered and jabbed each other on the shoulders.

Ahmed smiled, and then ground his knuckles into his eye sockets. "I can't see shit! Everything is spinning." Then his arms flopped back onto the bed like dead fish. His legs rocked in the plaster monstrosity stretching from his hips to toes. Half his body was wrapped in cement.

"Are you okay?" They turned the IV up another notch. "Your family is anxious to see you. But it'd be far too dangerous for them to travel here. We'll take you to them. It's incredible that even after Mullah El-Hashem is gone, his legacy lives on in you."

"I won't ever run and hide from the Americans." Ahmed said, clenching his fist high. "We must go to my family in Chitral. But how will I get there with all of this?" Ahmed said, pointing an unsteady finger at his casts.

Jack sat up straight. "Chitral. Now we're getting somewhere, Preach. That's where Travis disappeared. Keep it coming."

The "patients" did not need prompting. They knew where to go. "Yes. It's all arranged. They're sending a special ambulance to take you to Chitral. You'll get a hero's welcome."

Ahmed started getting tipsier and the Versed insured he would never remember any of their conversation. So they pressed on.

"I don't have any fucking idea where they'll fucking take me," said Ahmed. "I've never been to Chitral before." His head flopped forward, and his chin bounced off his chest. He struggled to lift it back up. His eyes were half open and bloodshot.

"Give me a cigarette," Ahmed ordered. "I need a smoke."

One of the "patients" made sure the oxygen was turned off, then cuffed a smoke out of his robe pocket and lit a match while Ahmed inhaled deeply. The smoke triggered a choking spasm ending with him hacking a grey wad on the floor.

After he regained his breath, Ahmed continued, "It'll be good to see Mullah Mohammed Abdul again. He knew my brother. He's the only one I trust. And you want to know a little secret? Come over here." Ahmed tapped the side of his bed. They scooted over. "It'll be an El-Hashem family reunion. My only son, Rolf, is in Chitral, too. It's been years since I've seen him. We'll most certainly celebrate!"

"Holy shit!" Preacher said, looking back at Jack with a nod. "And you thought it wouldn't work."

"Pretty fucking amazing," said Wade.

It was as if Jack bit into four jalapenos at once. His brain was on fire. Ahmed and Rolf were father and son? What did that mean? He was on his feet, focusing on every word that came from Ahmed's mouth.

An actor continued, "Yes, let's all celebrate. We must get you to your family as soon as possible. Your son Rolf is there, too? He must be a great El-Hashem warrior like his father and uncle."

"Yes, yes. I mean no, no. He's a famous plastic surgeon from Dubai. He supports our cause in his own way. He isn't a soldier, but he is brave and brilliant and gifted."

"Well, of course he is," said one of the patients. "You must be proud that your son's a jihadist. And he waits for you in Chitral, too." Ahmed looked close to passing out, like a drunken sailor telling his life's story to a complete stranger and best friend.

"He's not waiting." Ahmed struggled to sit up, but his legs weighed a ton, and he quit. "He's part of the new Age of the Crescent! The Grand Jihad! He changed the identities of all twelve members of the security council with plastic surgery. The Americans will never see it coming." Ahmed passed out in a drunken stupor.

"That kicked his ass better than I could've, Preach," said Jack. "I can't believe Travis is mixed up in this. The head of their security council is that crazy fuck, Mullah Mohammed Abdul."

"Yeah, he's been a tough son of a bitch to pin down," said Wade.

"Isn't he the one who named his hatchet?" asked Jack.

"The one and only," said Wade

"What about this Grand Jihad and Age of the Crescent?"

"It's just started popping on some intercepts. This is the first solid intel we've had."

"I'm positive Travis had no idea his surgeon buddy was an El-Hashem," said Jack.

"No one suspects your brother is a jihad sympathizer," said Wade. "They trapped him and used him. Now we've got to get him out before . . ."

"I'm not going to let that happen," said Jack. "Keep squeezing that little worm. Wade can start bringing in local sources to see who knows what. Someone will talk, if the price is right. I'm not going to sit here and wait for those son of a bitches to do to Travis what they did to Keeler. Not on my life."

CHAPTER

22

Northern Tribal Area, Pakistan

Travis struggled to breathe, gasping in only a portion of the oxygen his body craved. He heard voices. He tried screaming for help, but couldn't. He shivered. His head pounded. He strained to move his arms and legs. They would not budge. Bright lights blinded him as he fought to open his eyes. He faded back into an unconsciousness delirium.

The nightmare of being awake while a surgeon's scalpel sliced through his chest had awakened Travis in a cold sweat before. He'd watched his anesthesiologist, who looked like Travis's identical twin, draw up Fentanyl. Hidden from view behind the ether screen, his twin injected the narcotic into his own vein instead of putting it into the patient's IV. His twin's eyes rolled back, he smiled, put his head down on the anesthesia machine, and passed out while surgery continued.

As Travis watched his own surgery, he realized he was paralyzed, but his twin had forgotten to turn on the anesthesia gas. He was wide awake. He heard and felt everything, but couldn't tell them to stop. The pain was incredible.

The surgeon, a Rolf look-alike, made a twelve-inch incision, down to the bone, then used a saw to crack Travis's chest. After he cranked the rib-spreader open to make space, the surgeon reached in, wrapped his hand around Travis's beating heart and started to pull.

139

All the nurses in the OR laughed as Rolf tried to rip Travis's heart out. He was dying, and everyone thought it was hilarious.

Travis woke from his nightmare drowning in a freezing liquid. He sputtered and wheezed back to consciousness. Travis gulped air through a cloth gag ripping at the raw corners of his mouth. His arms and legs were bound together behind his back. His ribs burned and stabbed each time he tried to breathe.

Travis turned away from the water, but still couldn't get a breath. His nose was plugged with mud and blood. The panic of suffocating cast him into a mortal flop, like a fish out of water. He had to move. He needed air.

The water stopped. The noises morphed into voices screaming something he couldn't understand, but in a familiar tongue. He recoiled further into the fetal position as something, maybe a boot or fist, smashed his broken ribs. He tried opening his eyes to anticipate the next blow, but he was too late.

A coarse hand jerked him up by the hair to prop him against the dirt wall. Sitting, he got a deeper breath and glimpse of his black-eyed tormentors. He wasn't sure if it was his living hell or if he'd finally gone over to the other side.

Someone laughed and spit in his face. Another kick in the ribs. He was no different than the cave rats his captors used for sport. First they'd down some rot-gut, then snap their captured rats' hind legs and wager cigarettes to see which one could drag itself across the finish line first.

Win or lose, the rats all received the same reward. They were stomped, skinned, and roasted for dinner. Travis knew he could not win against the intoxicating power a man feels when he tortured a defenseless creature. Kicking a dog. Squashing a bug. Whatever they wanted to do, they did, and nobody could stop them.

Satisfied the prisoner was still alive, they slipped the black hood back over Travis's head. A parting jab to his shoulder with a rifle butt sent him toppling back over onto the dirt floor. Their murmuring and laughing vanished when the heavy door closed.

Travis fought to control his breathing and panic. His chest heaved, and he overrode his instinct to take deep breaths. Quicker, shallower breaths would serve him better. The wet hood sucked against his nose with each breath like a plastic bag. Scant air flowed around his blood and mud-caked gag.

By pushing against the floor with his left elbow, he wedged himself back up onto his knees. He let his head hang, chin to chest, and shook back and forth until the hood fell to the ground, uncovering his eyes. The cool air flowed more easily and, with that, his fear of dying receded. Blood dripped to the floor instead of gagging the back of his throat.

The cell was made of dirt and rock. Bars of steel held a solid oak door together. Beams wedged into each corner of the room prevented cave-ins. A naked light bulb burned about five feet up from the floor in a pocket hewn out of the rock and dirt. Dust hung in the musty air. It smelled like Grandpa Joe's root cellar.

The trap door with the horseshoe handle pulled up out of the kitchen floor of Grandpa Joe's depression-era farmhouse, a faded clapboard house with second story dormers and a large screened-in porch. Travis and Jack went down the ladder to the root cellar to fetch onions, potatoes, or a jar of canned tomatoes or huckleberry jam. The walls and floor were dirt. A light bulb turned on with a pull string. The wooden shelves were stocked with enough homegrown food to get through to the next summer.

Travis spooked easily. He hated climbing down into that black hole. One time Jack hid down there all afternoon so that when Travis lifted the door to get something for dinner, Jack screamed and grabbed him. Travis cursed Jack and kicked while Jack and Grandpa Joe laughed. It was the last time Travis touched that handle. It still made his stomach jump just thinking about it.

He heard voices and footsteps approaching the door. Too terrified to move, he cowered where he was as the door swung in, waiting for another whipping.

A guard more sinister than the last two stepped into the light, revealing a rotten-toothed smile. His right hand slid under his robe. He paused momentarily, and then whipped out a twelve-inch knife, waving its sawtooth edge inches from Travis's chin.

A second guard came in and plopped a wooden chair down in the middle of the tomb. They grabbed Travis by the arms and swung him onto the chair. The one with the knife went around behind Travis and started untying the gag while the one in front started rubbing his groin and thrusting his hips.

Travis closed his eyes and flashed back to the corncrib. He started to hyperventilate. He didn't want to see or know. He just wanted to go home. He closed his eyes and waited for the sound of a zipper.

Instead, he heard heavy footsteps coming down the cavern, and both guards immediately ceased their foreplay as they grumbled something and smacked Travis on the back of the head. They took positions outside the door. With the gag off, Travis spit blood and gasped for air.

"Well, well, well. I can come back if you boys are busy," Rolf said to the guards, and they both laughed.

"Rolf," Travis said, but he was barely audible. He cleared his voice and again said, "What's going on? Where are we?"

"It's not we anymore. There's you, and there's me," said Rolf. "From where I stand, it looks like you're fucked."

"But why?" asked Travis. "I came to this shithole to help these barbarians and you, and it's been one nightmare after another. I've done everything you asked. Won't you please help me?"

"Just stop right there," said Rolf. "My father is dead because of you, your Navy SEAL brother, and every other American infidel in our land. You're not fooling anybody except yourself if you think you're getting out of here alive."

Tears spilled down Travis's filthy cheeks, and he sobbed.

"That device was not some businessmen's toy," said Rolf. "You know it, and we know it. You've been helping the Zionists all along to try and kill Mullah Mohammed and the rest of the security council. You're the number one enemy of jihad. But your plan has failed. We're still alive. The device is destroyed, and the surgery we did to change the identity of the security council was a huge success. The Americans will never find them or you."

"But you're not like them," pleaded Travis.

"Just shut the fuck up," said Rolf.

More steps echoed off the cavern walls. As each one grew closer, Travis's anxiety level notched higher and higher. Finally the walking stopped. A grinding noise started, metal on stone, around and around. Travis vaguely remembered the sound from his past, but could not place it. It was hard to look directly at Rolf with the light behind him. But when Rolf stepped aside, Mohammed faced Travis, honing his hatchet's razor edge on a stone. He shaved his thumbnail. Studied the blade as light reflected off its polished surface into Travis's eyes. Mohammed smiled. "How would you like it, Mr. Gunn?"

Travis barely recognized Mohammed. He looked nothing like his old self. The scar on his neck was gone. Everything was different. Travis tried to look away, but Mohammed grabbed his chin.

"I want names, and I want them now, or I'll invite my students back in to carve you up like a wild pig." Mohammed pointed at two rusty shackles hanging from the mud wall about shoulder high and two more ankle shackles lying in the dirt. Mohammed's eyes twitched. He held up the hatchet. "Either way, my friend Dard here wins."

Mohammed let go of Travis's chin.

"You know what Dard means, right?" Mohammed's teeth flashed through his black beard when he hissed. "Pain, Mr. Gunn. Pain. Now what's it going to be, the truth or blood?"

Travis was in panic mode.

Mohammed rubbed his neck where his scar had been. He suddenly turned and slammed the hatchet into the chair between Travis's legs. The force nearly splintered the seat in two. Travis pushed away and the chair fell back against the wall. The guards pushed him back up toward Mohammed.

"We can film you telling us the truth about who you really are, or film your last moments naked and chained to a dirt wall," Mohammed said, pointing at the two guards. "Is that what you want? To have the whole world see you being raped and killed on television?"

Rolf pulled a video camera from his shoulder bag.

Travis looked back and forth like a trapped animal—at the guards, the camera, Rolf. Mohammed, the hatchet. The guard with the knife moved in first. The lens cap was off, and the green light was on. He had nothing but bad options left. His mind went blank.

"Okay. Okay. I'll tell you everything. But first I need a drink," said Travis.

One of the guards handed him a half-full bottle of cloudy water while the other tacked a jihad flag into the dirt wall behind Travis. They slid Travis and his chair back against the wall, facing the camera. One guard stood on either side, the big knife clearly in the picture, pointing at Travis's neck.

"Your name?"

"Travis Gunn. I want to say—"

A rifle butt knocked him off his chair, hands and feet still bound. Travis lay motionless for a minute before coming out of the fog. When they saw him twitch, they picked him back up and sat him on the chair. He wobbled, leaned forward, and threw up. After another minute, he sat back up and looked at the camera.

"Good stuff, Mr. Gunn. Now, if you will please just answer the questions," said Mohammed. "Are you an American doctor?"

"Yes," said Travis.

"Look at the camera. Did you recently go on a secret trip to help Mullah Mohammed Abdul, the Taliban leader?" asked Mohammed.

"Yes, I did."

"Why did you do that? Are you a traitor?" asked Mohammed.

"I . . . I don't know," said Travis.

"What's your brother's name?" asked Mohammed.

"Jack, Jack Gunn," said Travis.

"And what does Jack, Jack Gunn do?"

"He's in the Navy," said Travis.

"In the Navy," mocked Mohammed. "And what does he do in the Navy?"

"He's a Navy SEAL who hunts and kills ignorant bast—"

Another gun butt slammed into Travis's solar plexus, knocking the wind out of him. The chair fell over again, and it seemed like an eternity before he took a breath.

The guards taunted Travis and landed a few easy kicks to the gut.

Mohammed dropped to a knee. "Do you know the secret to chopping off the head of a snake? I mean, you can't just take a half-hearted whack at it."

Mohammed held the cutting edge where Travis could examine it closely.

"No, to get a clean cut, you have to focus every muscle on the tip."

Mohammed raised the hatchet and slammed it into the dirt with a thud, right next to Travis's head.

They sat him back up and duct-taped him to the chair.

"So you admit you're a liar and a spy, Mr. Gunn," said Mohammed. "Your brother gave you the tracking device so they could drop bombs on our innocent women and children. What has Pakistan ever done to the United States of America? We're defending our homeland from American crusaders who want to annihilate all Muslims."

The camera zoomed in on Travis. He spit out a couple more teeth and a mouthful of blood. Dried blood mixed with dirt smeared his face. His right eye was swollen shut. He breathed like he was sprinting for his life.

"Your country and brother have abandoned you. You've failed everybody. Your plan is fucked," said Mohammed. "What'll it be? Life or death?"

Name, rank, and serial number. Jack probably wouldn't even give them that. His only brother and all Travis ever did was screw things up. Even the trip to Afghanistan was supposed to somehow be him doing the right thing, and he had screwed it up, too. They had not failed him. He had failed them. He was going to die. He deserved to die. What'd Jack say? Let the last thing be the best thing he ever did.

Travis stared into the camera. He glared at Mohammed, Rolf, the two guards, and back at the camera. He yelled, "You can all go straight to hell!"

A final blow crushed his skull, and the lights went out.

23

The Catacombs, Afghanistan

Jack hadn't left the Catacombs since Travis disappeared off the grid. They continued to milk the prisoner. While the information helped connect the dots of who's who in the Taliban and Al Qaeda, they weren't any closer to tracking down Mullah Mohammed Abdul, Dr. Rolf Marques Omar El-Hashem, or Travis.

A week had passed. With each passing day, Jack's mood festered like a volcano.

The CIA information specialists continuously monitored Al Jazeera and other sites broadcasting English-interpreted, real-time segments from Arab TV and news. They also monitored a host of other web sites and chat rooms thought to be Taliban and Al Qaeda linked.

There hadn't been a word muttered about Travis or any American doctor being taken hostage. So when a posting about Travis popped up on a top-secret, CIA-Taliban link, no one was happier than Wade and he immediately sent someone to wake Jack.

The Sentinel drones had loitered over Chitral, Pakistan, and the surrounding mountains continuously, since Travis's disappearance. While the smaller and older Predator fired the Hellfire missile, the more powerful Reaper and Sentinel drones carried five-hundred pound laser-guided bombs. They were outfitted with million-dollar, full-motion video cameras that could see day or night. The pilots back at Creech Air Force Base were convinced it was just a matter of time before they found their man. But an early winter storm with a fifty-thousand foot ceiling moved into the Kush Mountains, and they pulled the drones off target and back to base.

Travis was all alone again. Probably beaten to unconsciousness, hopelessly imprisoned inside a mountain in the wild no man's land of northern Pakistan. Rolf had been using Travis all along. Mohammed destroyed his one link to Jack, the tracking chip. No one knew where Travis was. No one was on his way to save him.

Jack slid his ID into the slot to Wade's room. The light above turned from red to green. He rushed in, as he slid his ID badge back in his pocket.

"What do you got?" Jack asked, sleep and stress still creasing his aging face.

"Fifteen minutes ago this flash file posted to you specifically on a link we set up for high-priority communications and negotiations."

"Who did?" asked Jack. He rubbed his stubble. "What?"

"It's pretty eerie, I'll admit," said Wade. "I've no fucking idea, but we're checking into it. We don't know how they found you, but they sent this."

It was a surreal horror for Jack to see Travis, his one and only brother, beaten and tortured by Mohammed in some Taliban torture chamber. Agent Keeler, Act Two. Imagining the fear and panic Travis must have gone through, made Jack as dispirited as he had ever felt. Travis had endured far more than his share of pain. Jack knew Travis had lost all hope until this last chance to redeem himself came along. The worst part was Jack encouraged him to go. He shoved Travis over the edge without a second thought.

"I liked how Travis told them to fuck off right before they whacked him," said Wade.

"He knew they'd cream him. Did you see the look on his face? He was like, 'Suck my dick,'" said Jack.

"He looked crazy."

"He looked like he knew exactly what he was doing. If he was going down for the final count, he was going out with a bang. Fuck the Taliban."

Jack had seen plenty of times how brutal the Taliban were. In the name of Islam, they committed atrocities far worse than the beheadings he'd witnessed in Serbia. Far worse than the American public could know. In fact, America would never believe Jack if he showed live video with Walter Cronkite narrating. The things they saw seemed unfathomable in today's age. People couldn't get away with it, much less do it publicly. Yet they did. The videos his team confiscated on raids of terrorist camps proved what animals they were. The video stayed locked up in a safe.

The fundamentalists employed ancient punishments from the Qur'an to enforce a vigilante-style justice on their women. The Hadd crimes included sex outside of marriage, adultery, or drinking alcohol. Punishment for Hadd crimes included flogging, stoning, amputation, exile, honor killings, or execution. Thousands of women worldwide were murdered annually in the name of family honor.

In the 1990s, fanatics paraded accused women into the Kabul National Soccer Stadium on Saturday afternoons. The charges were read, and the sanctimonious male crowd cheered as the beheadings and stonings were immediately carried out. The women's heads were jabbed on tall, wooden spikes and displayed in public places as a warning for not obeying the Taliban's laws. Jack had the video.

In a different video, after a man accused his wife of cheating, thugs jumped out of a car and shot her in the head, point-blank. Another showed a group of Islamic extremists stoning a guilty woman to death in front of her own children. But those videos were G-rated compared to some.

Jack fished a wintergreen antacid out of his pocket and crunched. The cougar inside him growled each time he exhaled, clawing at his stomach lining. The second-hand clock on the wall ticked. He stared at the video screen.

"All we had to do was put two and two together. Ahmed and Rolf are father and son. What the hell. How'd the CI-fucking-A miss that one?" he cursed.

How many lives had his fuckups cost? A lot more than Travis ever had. Jack had made heat-of-the-battle decisions that got men killed. Sometimes, men were going to die no matter what. Other times, they died because Jack made the wrong call. Swimming the Konar River at the peak of monsoon season, at night. Bad call. Sending a squad into a firefight when he should have known the weather would shut down air support. Lost some friends that night. Not stopping his mom and dad's argument— maybe they wouldn't have died in the accident. There were more. Jack conked himself on the side of the head with his fist.

When the scene finally ended and the gun butt smashed into Travis's head, knocking him to the ground unconscious and motionless, it was all the confirmation Jack needed. Finally, he had someone to kill. He just needed to find the bastards.

The video concluded with an ultimatum. Two pairs of hands rolled Travis onto his back. The video zoomed in on a knife sliding back and forth across his throat, deep enough to draw blood.

The voice on the video said, "This American spy will end up like all the rest. Naker and Munkar, the angels of death, will be interrogating him in hell soon enough. It's demanded in the Qur'an, Surah 2:190-193." Then he quoted the Qur'an:

> *Fight those who fight you along Allah's way.*
> *Kill them wherever you may catch them.*
> *Fight back. Such is the reward for disbelievers.*
> *Fight them until there are no more.*

The screen went black.

"Crazy sons of bitches," cursed Jack.

"I'm sorry," said Wade. "That's the most misunderstood passage in the Qur'an. They use it to . . ."

"Who gives a shit about the Qur'an?" Jack screamed. "They're a bunch of crazy, murdering, sons of bitches."

"Well at least we know Travis is alive," said Wade. "He's better off than Keeler."

"Are you deaf? The CIA hasn't done jack shit to help Travis. When are you going to fucking do something?"

Wade clicked his pen open and closed, as fast as he could for a full minute, and stared off like he had not heard a word Jack said. Different night, same story. Travis was a dead man, that much was certain.

Jack watched the video play again as he scratched his head. "Wait a minute. Wait one fucking minute," said Jack. "No one outside of here knows Ahmed is still alive, right?"

"We've kept a tight lid on it." Wade sat up and stopped clicking, mildly interested.

"Mohammed and Rolf don't know we've got Ahmed or they would've said so," said Jack.

"What difference does it make?" asked Wade.

"They've got someone I want." Jack tapped the screen, pointing at Travis sprawled on the floor with the knife at his throat. Jack turned and studied the Catacomb closed-circuit loop of Ahmed lying in his hospital bed, smoking. "And we've got someone they want. It's essentially a family matter," said Jack. "Letting Ahmed go free isn't exactly ideal, but if that's what it takes to get Travis back, so be it. Besides, Ahmed shouldn't be too hard to find with all the information we've sponged from him."

They watched the video again, going back and forth between the two screens, silently working through scenarios at the speed of light. Jack froze the video on the last frame.

"We might be able to work something out, but it's got to be done completely off the books," said Jack. "The President of the United States doesn't negotiate with terrorists."

"Yeah, right. We need to deep six that video before the press gets a hold of it."

"Go on," Jack said.

"We'll need a close-up of Ahmed. Once they see that, they'll be all ears," said Wade.

"You start working out the logistics of a prisoner swap," Jack said, "and make it quick. By the looks of Travis, he needs medical attention. Can we get authorization?"

"I'll run it by the station chief."

"What are you waiting for?" asked Jack.

Wade was already on the phone.

24

Northern Tribal Area, Pakistan

Travis breathed out a sigh of relief when he heard voices approaching his cell door again, beating or no beating.

For twenty-four hours he'd been tied up like a ball of twine. Pissing his pants. Lying in his own mud. Pain racking every bone. Drifting from one delusion to the next.

He wondered if they'd be back to wring the truth out of him, chop him to bits, or would they simply walk away and leave him there to die, confined to his lonely, dark grave? Jack would never find him. He'd simply vanish. His empty grave, next to his parents, marked by a headstone bearing his name and a giant question mark. Here lies the spirit of Travis Gunn, a disappointment to those who knew him.

From what he'd seen though, he could not imagine they'd walk away and miss out on the fun of punishing him to death.

A feeling had calmed Travis that his mother's spirit was there, watching over her baby. He'd tried being the keeper of his father's spirit after their deaths, but his spirit was dark. He was a drunk and carouser, and Travis had to let him and his condemning energy go. His mother was an angel. She always treated Travis differently than Jack. Jack was all Indian. He could take care of himself.

She had watched the accident that killed Travis's cousin

destroy him. One moment, he was a carefree six-year-old, catching frogs and riding ponies. The next, he was in their medicine man's sweat lodge, and his life revolved around pipe ceremonies, fasting, and isolation. The innocent, happy-go-lucky little boy who used to follow his big brother everywhere was suddenly unwelcome, and unforgiven. She heard the women's whispers. She knew some would never forget, which made her want to shield him all the more. A momma bear protecting her cub. Travis had never put it together, but her mom's name was Grandma Bear Nose. Protecting her Travis-cub was part of her spirit.

To become a twenty-first-century healer, maybe even a doctor, became his vision. He secretly wanted to find a cure for the broken spirit. He tried every native remedy and incantation. He read books. He tried alcohol, drugs, and therapy. He even tried God. He had some fun, experienced great sorrow, and learned a great many things about himself, but never healed his broken heart.

In the dark and isolation of his tomb, he felt like he was in the sweat lodge. He smelled the perfumed air of burning sage and steam from sage water poured over hot lava rocks. Immersed in the darkness in a strange country, sensory deprived, thoughts from deep within surfacing, Travis felt at peace. He didn't know if it was Jesus or Grandpa Joe, Jack or his Mom. The old spirits stirred his soul. His instincts were awakening. Just in time to die.

Travis started to cry again. Tears dripped off his cheek, plinking into a tiny pool in the dust. An angel as radiant as the Dubai sunrise appeared overhead and scooped Travis up like a newborn, cradled him in her arms, and kissed his tears away. She sang, "Don't cry, my baby. Momma still loves you. Momma still loves you."

The angel glowed brighter and brighter. Travis tried to shield his eyes, but his hands were still tied.

His cell door had opened, and someone shined a flashlight in his eyes.

The guards kicked him in the ribs to flip him over and cut

off his wrist and ankle restraints. "Get up! Get up!" they yelled. He rolled onto his knees and they jerked him up by his armpits. His angel vanished.

They shoved him out the door. He walked for the first time in days, stumbled, and fell against the cave wall. He scrambled back to his feet and started walking before they kicked him again. They prodded him down a short, dimly lit corridor, past a maze of side tunnels, around a corner into a rocky cavern, which had other side tunnels.

A bowl of water and his clothes lay on a small rug where he was allowed to clean himself and change. He ate a heavenly meal of fried bread, boiled mutton, and goat's milk. He lit a Marlboro from a pack on the ground. His hands were shaking so badly, he had to hold the match with both hands.

Tobacco had been a part of Travis's life since before he could remember. To Grandpa Joe, nothing had been more sacred than the family pipe. He'd taught, "The pipe symbolizes our prayers. The smoke becomes our words. The fire is like the sun, the source of life. Tobacco connects the two worlds because its roots grow deep into the earth, and its smoke rises high into the heavens.

"The white man puts up fences. The pipe tears down fences. The pipe, when smoked in the right way, sitting in a circle, dissolves barriers and brings peace."

Travis felt cold and exhausted, but it was the bloodthirsty stares from a room full of Taliban henchmen that made him cringe. Each cough made his ribs stab, but he hadn't had a smoke in days and, for all he knew, it might be his last.

Travis chain-smoked his way through half a pack, lighting the next one with the cigarette he had just finished. They escorted him down a different corridor where the air was fresher and smelled of pine. A generator reverberated loudly off the rock walls. Black power cables ran along the floor and under a door they passed through.

A rough-hewn plank table and two sofas woven from aspen saplings, twine, and straw furnished the room. Two days of lying in the dirt made sitting up a wonderfully odd sensation. Like the first time going outdoors after being sick in bed for a week. Any hints of pleasure vanished when Rolf walked in and set his laptop on the table.

"Enjoy your smoke?" asked Rolf.

Travis said nothing and looked straight ahead.

"It seems this brother of yours is a bit more formidable than you." Rolf smiled at the guards and gave a nod. Travis glanced over both shoulders to anticipate the next sucker punch. "Relax. You're among friends."

Travis didn't see a machete or jihad flag. But a movie camera on a tripod stood off in a corner next to a couple aluminum suitcases. Why would they feed me bread and milk if they were going to kill me? He was confused.

Rolf turned the computer around so Travis could see the screen. He started the video. Travis heard Jack's voice coming from the computer. It was like a bucket of cold water reviving his life.

Jack spoke on the video: "You know who the man on the screen is. I know who he is. This will be the last time you'll ever see Ahmed Omar El-Hashem alive, unless you do exactly as I say. Believe me when I say that nothing would give me greater pleasure than to put a bullet right between his eyes. You do not want to fuck with me."

Rolf paused the video.

"If you haven't figured it out by now, the man your brother is holding captive is my father," Rolf said through clenched teeth. "We thought he was dead, but Allah has saved him. An interesting dilemma presents itself. Your brother may be resourceful, but he's as much a fool as you. He's willing to swap my father for you."

Travis perked up.

Rolf continued. "And just when we were ready to martyr you, to teach the infidels a lesson. Now, we can trade your worthless-piece-of-shit hide for the life of my father."

Travis timidly held up his hand.

"What now?" asked Rolf.

"So you're saying my brother is going to exchange your father for me?" His voice still scratchy from being gagged all week.

"Obviously, your brother doesn't know you like I do. What a disappointment he's in for."

"When? How?" Travis kept his eyes down.

"None of your fucking business." Rolf turned on the video camera. "Now, sit up and say cheese. One fucking sound and we'll send you back in a box."

25

The Catacombs, Afghanistan

The CIA's back-channel link with the Taliban worked. Fifteen minutes after Jack and Wade sent out the video of a living, breathing Ahmed, the video of Travis disappeared without a trace.

"Looks like they want to play ball," Jack said. There was little chance any American government or media types had seen the video, which was the critical first step. Wade's programmers had infected it with a virus before sending it back.

Keeping the whole operation in-house was the only way to keep it from turning into a headline-grabbing, political free-for-all. Rescuing an American doctor from the Taliban counted for votes. Jack could not let that happen. If he lost control, his brother was dead.

For the next twenty-four hours, Jack or Wade checked for new mail every five minutes. Nothing. They had the computers and links checked. Still nothing. All they could do was wait.

Jack spent hours grunting and sweating in the Catacomb's gym while he formulated a game plan. He benched, squatted, jerked, pulled, and crunched until he could barely breathe or move. He recovered, and did it again, always with an eye and ear to the news feeds on the flat screens. There'd been nothing about an American physician being held prisoner and tortured by the Taliban. Their luck was holding.

Jack jawed with Preacher while watching their VIP (very important prisoner) from the observation room. The patient recovered nicely from his blast injuries and was anxious for the other two prisoners to reunite him with his son, Rolf.

"Our dream is still possible after all," drooled Ahmed.

"What dream?" asked a "patient."

"The day is coming when America will be defeated. I don't mean America will be defeated in Afghanistan. I mean America will be destroyed in America. The Grand Jihad is in place. It can't be stopped."

"He's so juiced, all he talks about is the Grand Jihad and Mohammed and killing Americans," Preacher said. "His brain's scrambled. He has no sense of normal."

"I keep replaying the video of Travis over and over in my mind. When they put that knife to his throat and beat him unconscious," Jack stopped to take a deep breath. "Give me the green light, and I'll put that little fucker out of his misery."

"Hold on, Chief," said Preacher. "What they did to Travis and Keeler is inexcusable. For you to go in there and carve him up would be worse. You'd be no better than them."

"Who the hell cares? He deserves it," said Jack. He quietly seethed for a minute, looking at the monitor. Not at Preacher.

"I know things that I can't explain," Jack said quietly, trying to relax. "Instincts or intuitions. I don't know. It's weird. I do know we'd be better off if that asshole was dead." Jack nodded toward Ahmed.

"No doubt," agreed Preacher. "But you're a smart man, Jack. Focus on getting Travis first. Ahmed's days are numbered."

A phone rang. The control room requested Jack get back to the intel shack ASAP.

When Jack walked in, Wade had a new video queued up.

"He's alive, Jack," said Wade. "It looks like Travis recovered from his head bashing. Doesn't look too bad either, except for some missing teeth."

"Thank God," was all Jack could say as he collapsed in the chair to watch the video.

"I can't make anything out of the surroundings. Just another generic Kush Mountain shithole," said Wade. "They included a message full of the usual rah rah Taliban bullshit, but in the end, they agreed to your proposed prisoner swap. The Taliban and us both have proof of life, so what's next?"

"What the hell is with these aluminum suitcases? They look like the ones we found near Keeler during that raid."

"No traces of any explosives on the ones you brought in. Obviously something's going on. Maybe part of this 'Grand Jihad,'" said Wade.

"Stay on it." Jack pulled a map out of his back pocket, and spread it out on the desk. "I've been studying the region around Chitral. Sixty miles south-by-southwest of Chitral, on the border sits Arandu, Pakistan, and Barikowt, Afghanistan. The Konar River separates them with a three-hundred-yard-long bridge spanning it. Your boys have an outstation in Barikowt where we could stage Ghost Team. There's plenty of Pak Mill on the Pakistan side of the river. They're kissing cousins with Al Qaeda and the Taliban, so this Mullah Mohammed should be cool with it. He'll have plenty of protection." Jack traced the road from Chitral to Arandu with his finger. "Give me one clear shot and I'll put this Mullah fucking Mohammed in the bag," said Jack.

"Save us all a lot of trouble. I'll give you five bucks for that shot."

Jack pointed back at Chitral on the map. "It's going to take a couple of days to come down out of their hideout and transport Travis to Arandu. How about a sundown swap, day after tomorrow? That'll give us time to get our own prisoner and Ghost Team up to Barikowt."

Wade said, "That whole area's an inbred, cesspool-mixing Taliban, and Al Qaeda, Uzbekistani guerillas, plus foreign intelligence agencies and their endless supplies of money. It's a nightmare. The CIA just waits for the nutbags to kill each other, then we come in to see what we can learn."

"I don't give a shit about any of that." Jack rubbed his

forehead, eyes closed. "Soon as I get my brother back, you can nuke the whole fucking place. But one thing's for sure. I'm not about to let this murdering son of a bitch walk away free and clear. I've got a plan. A sick plan, even a pale face like you can appreciate," said Jack with a devilish wink.

26

Bagram to Barikowt, Afghanistan

The Chinook landed inside the CIA's secure corner of Bagram Air Field, the busiest Air Force base in the Afghan theater, picked up Jack and Ahmed, and was gone inside sixty seconds. All base personnel were so focused on the breakneck pace of their jobs, it was easy to get in and out without being noticed.

Civilians and military personnel did not have to be rocket scientists to figure out that snooping around the CIA would land them on a peacekeeping mission in Korangal or some other haji village where Americans died quickly and violently. They stayed alive by minding their own business. The CIA did what it wanted.

As the bird went airborne again, Jack stuffed Ahmed into his seat and strapped his waist to the bulkhead, cinching the webbing extra tight. Ahmed's body cast had been replaced by a knee-high walking cast on one leg. His hands were zip-tied together.

"We wouldn't want him to fall down and get hurt, now would we?" Jack said to his reunited Ghost Team, who still looked primed to rip the prisoner's head off. If looks could kill.

Sarge had his snout jammed into Ahmed's crotch, ready to chomp his balls off with a single command. Ahmed clamped his legs together, slamming Sarge's head. Sarge growled and nuzzled in farther. He was always hungry.

"Okay, ladies, ready to get back to work?" asked Jack.

They gave him the one-finger salute. They were bored after sitting around for a week and willing to do anything.

Jack snapped a pair of noise-cancelling earphones over Ahmed's black hood.

"Remember, this one's on the down low, boys," said Jack. "It's only us, this helo, and CIA drones. No Air Force. No Strike Eagle. No Warthog. Nobody can know, not even our own government, or we're screwed."

Jack patted Sarge on the shoulder. "You hungry, boy?" Sarge drooled on the PUC's crotch and growled.

The helo banked away from the sunset toward the shadowy peaks to the northeast. The pilot went to full throttle. The turbo shaft engines roared. They needed maximum altitude to avoid haji and his RPGs hiding on mountain ridges along the way up the Konar River valley, hoping for a lucky shot.

Jack leaned toward the team and shouted, "I'm not about to let a bunch of assholes get my brother killed. This asshole's son is the guy holding Travis captive. We've arranged a prisoner swap, day after tomorrow."

"Now you're talking, Gunner," said Dewey. "Let's nail the bastards."

"We're heading back up to the outstation at Barikowt. You remember that shithole." Death stares burned holes through his Kevlar. "It's the chance we've been waiting for to even the score."

"Fucking A," one of the men said.

Jack pinched Ahmed's neck until he winced. "The last time you boys saw this prick he was a hurting machine. His justice should've been a double tap, and any one of you would have been happy to oblige him."

Dewey said something to Sarge. Sarge bit down on Ahmed's wrist and twisted. Ahmed screamed. Dewey backhanded the hooded screamer, and then grabbed him by the throat. Blood dripped onto Dewey's hand from under the hood. The rest of the men cheered, but Jack stopped him.

"Fuck him, Jack. Let the dog eat him," said Dewey. He still had Ahmed's throat in his grip.

"Sorry guys," said Jack. He pushed Dewey a little harder until he and Sarge sat back down. The prisoner thrashed in his restraints. Jack grabbed him by the throat and squeezed until the whimpering stopped. When Jack let go, the prisoner collapsed forward and buried his head on his knees. He started in on his *Allah Akbars* again.

"Shut the fuck up," yelled Dewey and kicked him in the shin.

The prisoner said nothing after that.

"Thankfully we kept this piece of shit alive." Jack eased back into his web seat and let out a big sigh. We've learned a great deal. Like this asshole's an El-Hashem who's rapidly working his way up the Taliban chain of command."

"I don't think Sarge's eaten any El Hashem yet. How about it, Jack?" asked Dewey.

"Shut the fuck up, Dewey." Jack looked around. "We're still not throwing him out, and we're not feeding him to Sarge. If this mission goes as planned, we'll be flying back to Jalalabad tomorrow with Travis. If it doesn't, then too fucking bad for haji."

"That's more like it," said Dewey.

"All I care about is getting my brother back alive. By sundown tomorrow, we'll be trading this sack of shit for Travis," said Jack. "Once we get him back, it'll be bad juju for this one. He'd better enjoy his little taste of freedom because, when this is over, we'll crucify him!"

They all said, "Fucking A," and nodded.

There was only one route to Barikowt: one hundred eighty miles up the Konar River valley by air. Flying was the only chance Americans had of arriving in one piece. The last fifty miles of the so-called highway from Asadabad to Barikowt was an IED alley. A pot-holed gravel road that teetered on mountainous knife ridges where top speed was five miles per hour. Granite walls rose straight up, towering over one side of the road and falling off a five-thousand-foot cliff on the other. There was no room to turn off or turn around.

As Ghost Team flew up the valley, Taliban campfires flickered in the darkness below like hundreds of fireflies. Easy to see, impossible to catch.

Infrared strobes marked the landing zone inside the CIA base. The end of the line. Another mile up the Konar River and they would have crossed into Pakistan. They hovered briefly, and then put down behind the twenty-foot high, solid mud brick walls crowned with razor wire. There was no hiding the CIA's presence in the area.

The agency's Sentinel drone was up watching local Pak Mill movement on the other side of the river. As the team deplaned, they were NODs down and weapons hot, searching for threats. Precautionary but necessary. Jack unstrapped Ahmed, removed his hood, and shoved him toward the open hatch. After Jack jumped out, he pulled Ahmed to his feet and hustled him through a door just off the courtyard.

"Sit," Jack ordered Ahmed, as he pointed to a metal chair. Ahmed sat. Sarge, still hoping for a nut-sack snack, growled and bared his teeth. Ahmed crossed his legs and started praying again.

"Jack 'Boom Boom' Gunn, you old son of a bitch," said Station Chief Drum. They shook hands.

"This place smells like a shithole, Drum. What you boys eating up here?" said Jack.

"Beans and jerky. What more does a growing boy need?"

"You might want to try a salad once in a while. You're starting to smell like a bean."

Drum laughed. "Yeah, and what's your excuse, Indian boy? You're redder than my favorite hemorrhoid."

"Same old Drum. Full of shit, as usual."

"What kind of trouble are you up here to perpetrate tonight?"

"A little international peacekeeping," said Jack. "You know, live and let live. I'm a changed man."

"Yeah, and I'm Santa Claus."

"We're strictly off-the-books," said Jack. "No operational orders or chain of command on this one. Twenty-four hours from now, we'll be gone, and you'll get back to spying on haji or jerking off. You know. Important CIA bullshit."

"Who's this asshole?" asked Drum, pointing at Ahmed. "Or don't I see him either?"

"Why he's the gold nugget," said Jack. "This sacred cow is the butcher who blew up the IED in Jalalabad and carved up Keeler for prime time Al Jazeera."

Drum sprung to his feet and pounced on Ahmed like a cat on a mouse. Before Jack pulled him off, Drum landed a few bone crushers and knocked Ahmed to the floor.

"That's for Keeler's family, you son of a bitch," snarled Drum. He spit in Ahmed's face.

"Easy does it, old buddy," Jack said. "You'll have to take a number. The TQ line is a mile long for this bastard. He'd already be celebrating in paradise; except there's something else I didn't tell you. His brother was Mullah El-Hashem."

"Oh, yeah? I see the resemblance," said Drum. "They both look like a couple of flaming assholes."

"He's nothing more than a bargaining chip now. Mohammed the Hatchet and this guy's son are holding an American doctor hostage. We're swapping them at sundown tomorrow on the bridge. There's something else."

"Do I want to know?" asked Drum.

"The doctor is my brother, Travis," said Jack.

"What the hell, Jack? How twisted is that?"

"They were ready to do their Al Jazeera slash-and-gash until they found out we had this El-Hashem progeny of theirs alive," said Jack. "You and me, we're after the same thing, Drum. We want to put a stop to the madness, and being so close to an El-Hashem seems like a good place to start."

They both stared at Ahmed and could not deny they wanted to cap him right there.

"I'm not going soft on you, but I need to get my brother out first. After that, there's not a place on earth this fucker can hide where I won't find him. Believe me. I know what I'm doing. Just have a little faith in old Boom Boom."

Before turning in, Jack called Nina. He was halfway around the world, when he needed to be home. She and Jake were all he had to fight for. And now Travis. Without them, his life was meaningless.

"How you feeling?" asked Jack.

"It's a hell of a way to lose weight."

"Still bad, huh?"

"I started shedding clumps of hair, so I hope you like the no-hair look. I had my head shaved yesterday, and bought some hats. Actually I kind of like the new look."

She was choking up. Jack gulped. She was not the crying type. He didn't know what to say. "I'm sure you look great, sweetie." Nina's straight black hair had hung to her mid-back. Jack couldn't remember her any other way. He struggled to get a mental picture. Nina was Nina, no matter what. Looks change, the person doesn't. Wrinkled as an eighty-year-old prune, she'd still jump-start Jack.

"Hair is very overrated. Aren't I the most handsome guy you know? Look at me."

"And you're so humble." Nina laughed and wiped away her tears. "That's why I love you."

"I love you too." Jack hung up before he lost it.

27

Chitral to Arandu, Pakistan

The beat-up Land Rover transporting Rolf and Travis to Arandu had no choice but to risk taking the main road. Going the back way would have taken days, and they had twelve hours. They followed the Shi Shi River through a maze of crumbling mountain-cliff roads and organ-jarring jungle weaves. The monsoons had recently finished. The width of the river varied from fifty yards to a half mile. The waters of the Shi Shi swirled death black at times and at others tumbled in a blue-white fury over rapids beyond classification. Their two-vehicle convoy side-winded back and forth, up and down the chunky, muddy roads, but they made Arandu by dusk the day before the exchange.

Darkness came early in Arandu, pierced by the Konar River and surrounded by the Himalayas. The town had no electricity, no running water, no phone service, and no law enforcement.

Arandu sat on a plateau, up off the Konar and downriver from where the Shi Shi emptied into it. The most noticeable structure in town was a five-story Saudi house sitting on the highest point in town, clearly visible from Barikowt on the other side of the river. The mansion was the obvious and only civilized place for Rolf and his security force to hold up. But Rolf had no intention of making them an easy mark for the Navy SEAL team to attack and kill before the swap.

Rolf's convoy set up shop in a leftover bunker from the 1980s Soviet invasion. It had a bird's eye view of Arandu, the river crossing, and Barikowt on the Afghanistan side. Plus, the Taliban had secretly armed the bunker with an old Soviet howitzer whose five-inch artillery rounds could reach the bridge, the CIA base, and beyond, if needed.

Not a word was spoken to Travis during the eight-hour drive to Arandu. He lay inside of the back seat of an old Land Rover. The seat padding had been cut away like a Travis-shaped cookie cutter. He was stuffed into the space with two security guards sitting on top of him so they'd ride at a normal height and look less suspicious, but still keep him hidden. No longer the focus of their attention, he felt more like baggage being dragged along. Heat from the exhaust pipe running along the bottom of the car burned his belly. Whiffs of cold air puffed under the seat through rusted holes in the bottom of the car. The hot and cold somehow balanced out. His hands and feet were bound again. His chin crooked to his chest for eight hours, stretching every nerve in his spinal cord to its snapping point. But worst of all were the two stinking haji asses sitting on top of him. Every bump, every turn they bounced and ground on him like two rank dirty diapers. His face was swollen. The gag cut his mouth. His cracked ribs killed. As miserable as he was, he had felt worse.

Travis was proud of himself for the first time in years. Maybe his entire life. So that's what it felt like to challenge a bully. To stand tall in the face of certain death. And he'd done it of his own free will. Nobody had guilted him into telling Rolf to fuck off and have his head bashed in. He had figured it out on his own. Jack should have seen that. He would have been damn proud.

When they finally stopped moving and pulled him out of the SUV seat, they were in the cold, dark bunker, sweetened by the aroma of roasting meat, most likely lamb. After what he'd been through, it smelled like heaven.

He wobbled on rubbery legs. His fingers tingled as the feeling returned. Every time he coughed, the gag cut in farther.

Dry blood caked his chin. He looked like hell, but he felt alive. The cobwebs of his mind were clearing. The Zuya started talking to his spirit again. He studied his surroundings in a whole new light. He looked for potential weapons, weaknesses in his enemy, and routes of escape. Anything to use against Rolf.

"Sit."

Travis pressed his back against the bunker wall and slowly lowered himself until he sat Indian style.

Rolf and the other soldiers ate dinner by a single candlelight, leaning or sitting wherever they found a spot. Travis guessed they were coming up with a plan for the prisoner exchange. The looks they cast Travis's way had scared the shit out of him two weeks earlier. Times had changed. He had taken to staring back at them until they blinked and looked away. Exerting his will on the stupid bastards.

"What do you think you're doing? You think this is some sort of game?" said Rolf. He got up.

Travis said nothing, but stared at Rolf with eyes full of contempt.

"You have no idea what I'm capable of." Rolf wound up to kick Travis in the head. Travis kept staring. Sat up straighter and stuck out his jaw. Rolf swung his foot, then pulled it back right before contact with Travis's ear. "Fuck you," he yelled. "Put the hood back on him."

Travis didn't move. He didn't lower his head to make it easier. He closed his eyes and started moaning something, like a chant or mantra. He swayed back and forth slightly in an ancient rhythm, like grasses blowing in a prairie wind. It seemed like the sounds were coming from the earth. A deep mournful plea. He replaced the moans with words, like first humming a song, and then singing the words. They were in a language unknown to Rolf. They were in Sioux.

"Shut up. Shut the hell up."

Travis chanted louder.

"Shut him up," Rolf said, looking toward the guards. He stomped out of the bunker.

A guard matter-of-factly walked over, took his rifle, and slammed the butt end into center mass of Travis's black hood. He toppled over again, thankfully silent with another concussion.

The guard shrugged his shoulders, and went back to finish his meal.

Rolf peeked around the corner, and watched Travis have a grand mal seizure. Travis flopped like a fish out of water, choking and gurgling on his own saliva. The guards enjoyed the entertainment. Rolf rejoined the guards around the fire after kicking Travis in the guts for old times' sake. "Where's your brother now, asshole?"

28

Barikowt, Afghanistan

The morning call to prayer woke Jack at 0530. The muezzin's tinny chants blasted from loudspeakers nailed to poles and rooftops throughout Arandu and Barikowt. Both sides of the river belonged to Allah.

Jack used to curse the wailing wake-up call, after all the barbarism and cruelty he'd witnessed in the name of Allah. There had been missions where he observed despicable men doing things in plain view most Americans could not fathom. His job was to watch and listen, shoot video, and take pictures of suspected terrorists but maintain cover. Do not engage the enemy.

He'd seen Taliban and Al Qaeda men do horrible, unspeakable things to other men, women, and especially boys. There was a saying among Taliban men; others too: women are for procreation and little boys are for recreation. The cries for help and mercy hadn't seemed to bother any of the fundamentalist perverts as they enjoyed sodomizing their future jihadists.

He eventually realized the morning call was a plea for Muslim men to stop the insanity and listen to God in the quiet of a new day. *Allah Akbar* or "God is great." Instead, they seemed to think it meant, "Hurry, hurry, time's wasting. It's time to get up and fight for Allah."

Today's the day, Jack thought as he rolled out of the rack and headed for the nearest coffee pot. Sipping his first heavenly cup of coffee, he watched the CIA's uniformed Indigenous Force soldiers kneeling in the courtyard with their foreheads touching the ground, praying. Drum showed up for his coffee, too.

"Looks like your indig numbers are staying up. No deserters?" asked Jack.

"We move them a long way from home once they sign on. It would be suicide to try to leave. There's nowhere to go in Barikowt," said Drum. "Plus, they've got it pretty damn good. We feed them, clothe them, and pay them a thousand dollars a month. We also pay generously to the tribal leaders and warlords for information and cooperation."

"Fucking CIA has all the money."

"You have no idea. Follow me." Drum led Jack to a platinum-colored safe in another room with a blast-proof door, electronic keypad, and a three-spoked handle. Jack sipped his coffee while Drum unlocked it. When the door swung open, an interior light clicked on.

Jack choked on his coffee, scalding the roof of his mouth, when he saw what was inside. "Each bale contains one hundred thousand dollars. We hand these out like sugar cubes. Those forty bales will be gone in a month."

"Holy shit," Jack said. "You Ivy League brain wizards know they use it to buy more guns, right?" said Jack. "We're paying them to kill us. How fucking idiotic is that?"

"Not all of them. We buy cooperation instead of beating it out of them like the Russians did in the 80s. The money makes their lives better," said Drum as he took a sip of coffee.

"I thought we were here to stop terrorism, not make them fucking millionaires."

"I'm just following orders. Talk to the White House if you want answers."

The muezzin's chants stopped and the men got to their feet. "Got any Afghan nationals up here?" asked Jack

"No Afghani guns over here, but plenty of Pak Mill hanging around on the Arandu side," said Drum. "Too many for you to go over and try any kind of sneak and peek, if that's what you're thinking. Pak Mill, Al Qaeda, or Taliban, they're all inbred anyway. One big Taliban hillbilly orgy, dueling banjos and all. Besides, if we're doing this on the down low with no Storm to cover our asses, so Arandu is a no-go, anyway."

"Check," said Jack. "We're here for the peace and tranquility that I read about in your travel brochure."

"Sounds good to me," said Drum.

"Let's get some chow and contact our zealot friends," said Jack. "I need proof that Travis's still alive before we go waltzing out on that bridge tonight."

After breakfast, Jack, Drum, and the team took the short drive through Barikowt to the bridge. They headed north on the dirt road cutting across the foothills leading down to the Konar River, two hundred yards to the east. Rock walls and terraced fields were bare, except for brown, twisted vines and scrub. The meager crops had been harvested and stashed for the long winter.

On the outskirts, at the north end of town, lay an ancient ruin of a fortress besieged by Alexander the Great in 330 B.C. Excavation stopped with the Taliban reign of terror, but at least the Taliban hadn't dynamited it like they had the Buddhas of Bamyan in 2001. They had no concept or care of anything except jihad, jihad, jihad. They'd destroy the entire civilized world and send it back to the dark ages for jihad. For Allah. That's the insanity Jack battled nightly.

They drove down off the Barikowt terrace, across a small bridge, and north again past a few more compounds just ten feet above the shores. Local men waded in the torrid current, snagging trees as they floated by, or hauling out logs trapped in their backwater snares. For those dirt-poor peasants, selling firewood pulled from the river was their sole means of providing for their families. Everyone needed firewood for heat and cooking.

The convoy pulled around the final curve and off the side of the road, just short of the two-lane bridge.

The water ran dark, deep, and fast. Like most rivers, it had a mesmerizing rhythm. The river had swallowed one of Jack's SEALs the year before. In the swirls and eddies, they still saw his scowling face. Jack and Drum knew they would not have any swimmers wet for the swap. The river was still too fast and dangerous. A footbridge crossed the river about two hundred yards downstream and would come in handy if someone went for a swim.

"Looks like this'll be a straightforward play. No big muscle-flexing, shove-it-up-your-ass, helicopter hovering show of force. My club-footed friend and I will take a stroll, and I'll come back with Travis. We'll get back on our bird and blow. I don't want this to be so much as a blip on the screen for some snoop back at Bagram or Langley."

"Just a couple of ghosts passing in the night, eh, Jack?" said Drum with a nod. "We'll have our drone up and keep a fix on the bastards afterwards. Sooner or later, they'll lead us back to the Big Kahuna."

The Bridge, Afghanistan

Jack, Drum, and Ghost Team were at the bridge an hour before sunset, and shut it down. The men fanned out to find cover in case a firefight broke out. Jack used binoculars to scan the opposite bank for any sign of the convoy and Travis.

The longer they kept him waiting, the more agitated he got. Fuck this. Fuck that. He tried Rolf's phone every few minutes. No answer. He paced up and down the bridge. There was no calming Jack down when he got worked up. Just stay out of his way.

He leaned over the guardrail, stared into the water, and took a deep breath. He raised his head to the mountains and listened. It was a peaceful yet tormented place, much like Jack's Montana reservation. He heard Grandpa Joe's spirit remind him: "In you are natural powers. You already possess everything necessary to become great." He closed his eyes and moaned an Indian war cry to himself.

When he opened his eyes and looked into the swirls of the Konar River ten feet below, he saw a fifteen-foot crocodile sawtoothing back and forth, just below the surface. Its yellow eyes broke the surface and stared up into Jack's for what seemed like eternity. It opened its mouth wide, snapped its killer jaws shut, then slid back into the darkness.

The crocodile was the keeper of all knowledge. He was a symbol of creation and destruction, furious and calculating. It alerted Jack to trust his animal instincts, be smart, and attack relentlessly.

Jack did not feel great, but he realized it was a great moment. His defining moment. Trust the spirits, trust his training, trust his men and be brave. He stood erect and walked down the bridge to Drum. Out of his go-bag he pulled his face paint and smeared the broken arrows on his cheeks. He was good to go.

Five minutes after sundown, the lift gate went up and two trucks rumbled down to the water's edge. Thirty men quickly spread out on the far banks. Even though it had been five years, he recognized his little brother immediately. Thank God he was alive. A wave of anger flooded Jack when one of the guards shoved Travis to his knees. Watching low lifes abuse Travis right in front of him was grounds for an ass kicking in Jack's book. He had never felt like that during an operation. But then again, he had never been saving his own flesh and blood. Calm immediately returned and Jack locked down his doubts. He was the crocodile.

Travis walked head down, hands roped together, surrounded by hajis. He'd lost a lot of weight, but he was alive. That was all that mattered. A shorter, unarmed, weaselly looking guy shoved Travis toward the bridge. Had to be Rolf, Ahmed's son. Jack zeroed in on Rolf's face. Thought of the beating video of Travis. Killing Rolf would be his pleasure. He did not see Mohammed anywhere. Not unexpected, but Jack would have to wait to collect his five dollars from Drum.

An unarmed Pak Mill soldier trotted across the bridge from the far side and patted down Jack and Ahmed, while one of Drum's indig soldiers ran across to the Pakistan side and did the same to Travis and Rolf.

Even with frost in the air, Jack wore only desert camo pants and a sand-colored T-shirt. No MOLLE pack loaded with grenades. No rifle, no knife, no helmet, no bulletproof vest, no tricks up his sleeve. Just him. Jack "Raging Bull" Gunn with a belly full of butterflies stirring a gut full of coffee. He squeezed the cougar totem in his pocket, and reverted back to what he did best—got his kill on.

After the searchers had given the all clear, Jack gave the okay for them to hand a CIA secure-link radio handset and pair of binoculars to Rolf on the other side of the river.

"I assume I'm speaking to Rolf, the son of this worthless piece of shit, Ahmed," Jack said into his radio.

"And I assume I'm speaking to the man, if you want to call him that, who practically got his brother killed to further his own career," said Rolf.

"Save it, asshole. The only thing that matters now is that everybody stays nice and calm," said Jack. "Do as I say and you'll go home in one piece. Try anything cute, you and your murdering sick fuck of a dad goes for a swim. Do you understand or should I draw you a picture?"

"Drawing pictures should be right up your alley," said Rolf.

"Look, I kill shitbags like you just to get warmed up. So unless there's something else?"

"How do I know your men won't shoot us once you've got your brother?" asked Rolf.

"How do I know you won't blow the bridge? What do you want, a fucking contract?" said Jack into the radio. "You've got my word, that's how you know. Let's dispense with the horseshit and get this done before dark."

There was a pause as the earth breathed. A chilling breeze followed the river downstream. Darkness shaded them, but the sun-tipped peaks held fast to the last moments of day.

Rolf started walking up the far side of the bridge with Travis.

"Shirts open! Hand's up!" Jack yelled into the radio as he and Ahmed started walking. He wanted to get to the crown of the bridge first. Jack kept a firm grip on Ahmed's arm and pulled him along, keeping the other hand with the radio up where all could see it.

Jack assessed Rolf for any physical threats as they got closer. He immediately marked the doctor as a cream puff. Soft on the outside and pudding on the inside. One snarl by Jack and he would probably shit his pants.

A quick glance toward Travis told Jack he was trying hard to keep it together. But he limped pretty badly. His lip had been cut, and one eye was swollen shut.

Jack's clamped onto Ahmed's arm like a pit bull and jerked him closer. Ahmed stumbled on his casted leg, and then recovered, mumbling something in Pashto.

"Shut up," Jack said. He kept Ahmed between him and Rolf in case someone on the far side got any stupid ideas. There were plenty of Pak Mill and Taliban guns pointed in his direction. But there were an equal number of guns pointed back at them from Jack's side, and his guys were the best shots in the world. He didn't worry, as long as he got Travis off the bridge quickly and kept Rolf and Ahmed between him and the Taliban shooters.

Jack never wanted to kill anyone more than the candy ass, son of a bitch who'd nearly killed Travis, and mocked him, Jack "Boom Boom" Gunn. He was as lethal as any man alive and could easily think of twenty different ways to kill Rolf with his bare hands.

The four figures finally came together in the dark over the pulsing Konar River. They faced one another momentarily before Jack, without a word, gave Ahmed a shove toward Rolf, and grabbed for Travis's arm. He gave Travis a bear hug, and then untied his hands.

"You okay?" asked Jack

"I am now," said Travis.

Jack pulled Travis past him and let go, pointing him toward the friendly side of the bridge, and said, "Get off this bridge as fast as you can. I'll be right behind you."

Jack turned back to see Rolf release his dad from a hug and say something as he pointed at the leg cast. Rolf put his father's arm around his neck, grabbed around his waist, and started to help him limp toward the far side of the river.

"Hold it, you two," yelled Jack.

They sped up.

"I will find you. And when I do, I'll drag you two, along with Mohammed and his little gang of perverts, out of whatever rathole you're hiding in, and teach you a fucking lesson."

Drum chirped from the radio, "Come on, Jack. You got what you came for. Now get the hell off that bridge."

"On my signal," Jack growled. He started backing away from the middle of the bridge like the wolf in retreat. To his surprise, Travis had limped back out onto the bridge and stepped up beside him. Jack looked him in the eye. Travis looked clear, strong, resolute, and had painted broken arrows on his cheeks, too. He slid Jack a handgun. They nodded, stood shoulder to shoulder, and looked to the far side of the river again. "You're up, little brother. You've earned it." He handed Travis the radio.

"I'll be right beside my brother the day you eat a bullet," Travis said to Rolf. "And you can tell that to fucking Mohammed too. You have fucking fucked with the wrong family, the wrong people. If it takes a hundred years, you will suffer like I did. Ever hear of a Badal, asshole?"

"Someone get me a gun," said Rolf. "I want to shut this fucker up for good." A Badal was the ultimate Pakistani insult. A blood war challenge.

All their guns were aimed at Jack and Travis, who stood just beyond the crest of the bridge, silhouetted by floodlights. Rolf's gunmen waited for the signal to shoot, but Rolf kept his hand up.

"I declare my own Badal on you and your whole fucking El-Hashem family," yelled Travis. Blood trickled from the corners of his mouth. "For the thousands you've killed, you'll pay. I promise we'll never stop until we hunt you down and bleed every last one of you."

Rolf raised his hand higher.

Travis thrust his arms high like a victorious gladiator and bellowed a mighty Sioux war cry, which echoed through the surrounding canyons and streets.

Everyone on both sides of the river paused. Then Rolf dropped his hand.

All thirty Taliban guns opened fire.

30

Barikowt to Jalalabad, Afghanistan

Jack grabbed Travis and dove back from the crest of the bridge, shielding him as best he could. He emptied the pistol Travis had snuck him, on terrorist gun flashes. Concrete chips kicked up all around, but his instincts kept them moving when he wanted to curl up in a ball. With only a T-shirt on, the shards cut deep.

Drum and the SEALs opened fire. The floodlight went first, and then three of Rolf's bodyguards were blown backwards, their heads bursting like watermelons dropped from a mountaintop. Rounds rocketed through the sixty caliber's white-hot barrel, strafing the Pakistani shoreline. Three bodyguards pulled Rolf and Ahmed up off the ground and into a government SUV, which escaped back up the hill to Arandu.

An enormous blast from the Arandu compound, like a close-range Fourth of July firework, jerked Jack's head around. He knew the sound was big trouble. Jack and Travis rolled onto all fours and scrambled down the bridge as fast as they could go, keeping their heads below the rail. The first five-inch Howitzer shell hit just short of the bridge. The explosion knocked the Gunn brothers off their feet, like getting hit by a water cannon. They were both out cold.

Drum and Dewey sprinted out onto the bridge, grabbed them under the arms and dragged them the rest of the way, just as the Howitzer fired again. This time their aim was right on. The bridge heaved up in the center, and then caved into the Konar River. Another round obliterated the pedestrian bridge down river. The CIA helicopter fired a missile from the Afghan side. Its fiery tail crossed the river and found its target, putting an end to the WWII heavy gun.

Jack and Travis sprawled out on the gravel off the end of the bridge. Jack was breathing hard, and had a pulse. The PJs held smelling salts under his nose. One whiff and he stormed back to consciousness like an old angry bear, swatting his paws, growling, and sitting up. He threw up.

"Easy does it, sailor. Relax and let me check you over," said the PJ. He checked Jack's pupils with a flashlight. Jack was bleeding from both ears.

"What?"

"How many fingers do you see?"

"Fuck you, Doc."

"Fuck you, Jack. Now how many fingers do you see?"

"Two dammit. I'm fine." Doc's voice sounded like he was talking underwater to Jack. Jack wiped blood from his eyes. "How's Travis?"

"Pretty beat up," said Dewey. "I'll go check."

Twenty holes ripped Jack's pants, and his shirt was saturated with blood, but no bullet wounds. The PJs plucked out concrete fragments with forceps. The jagged lacerations needed stitches, but compression dressings were good enough until they got back to the compound. They cleaned Jack's face off and stuck Steri-Strips on his left eyebrow and cheek.

"Enough. Enough. You'd think I was dying or something," Jack said. "Where's that little brother of mine?"

Drum stepped back.

"Well, if you aren't the ugliest son of a bitch I've ever seen." Jack grabbed Travis and gave him another bear hug, lifting him off the ground.

"Take it easy, Jack. You don't want to pop him," said Drum.

When Jack put him down, they were both groaning and laughing at the same time. Broken ribs and fresh lacerations hurt like hell, but they kept squeezing one another anyway.

"Are you alright?" asked Travis. "You look terrible."

"Look in a mirror." Jack felt the bandages on his face. "You look like you fell out of the ugly tree and hit every branch on the way down."

"I never thought I'd get the chance to say it but, it's damn good to see you, Jack."

"Who do you think you are? Fucking superman or something? You were in the clear. Why'd you come back out on the bridge?"

"I'll be damned if I was going to let my big brother have all the fun," said Travis. "At that point, live or die, I really didn't give a shit."

"And now you, I mean we, are going after them? I thought you were a live-and-let-live kind of guy."

"I can tell you firsthand, they're all insane."

"That's what I tried to tell you," said Jack. "The arrows look good."

"Just like the old days, except we're not playing cowboys and Indians anymore. Those guys are crazy and need to be stopped."

"Badal? Isn't that Sioux for Warpath?" said Jack with a hint of sarcasm.

"I think it means you fucked with the wrong family and now we're gonna shove it up your ass," said Travis as he gave another war cry. Jack joined him. The guys on Ghost Team turned to look. It put a smile on their faces. It looked like things were finally going to get crazy.

It was a once-in-a-lifetime moment for the entire team. Usually, when they were done, the team would pack up, go home, eat, sleep, and go out again, without ever hearing so much as a thank you. Their satisfaction came from killing lots of bad guys and not getting killed.

They would savor Travis's rescue later, but first they needed to convoy back to the CIA base where their ride back down the Konar River valley was warming up. Ghost Team loaded up and got Travis secured. Jack and Drum took one last look across the river at the glowing Pak Mill compound in Arandu, flames shooting out of the cave where the howitzer burned.

"No FKIAs and a few less hajis to worry about, plus my brother's alive," said Jack. "Not too bad, Drum."

"Not bad at all." Drum checked out the patchwork of dressings covering Jack. "You've looked better, though." His face soured. "Now maybe you won't be such a pain in my ass."

"Nothing against the CIA and your luxurious accommodations, but we're eager to get home and celebrate," said Jack as the team climbed onboard.

"I don't blame them. In fact, I wish I were going with you," said Drum, as he turned to Travis. "If everyone had a brother like Boom Boom here, the world would be a safer place." Drum reached into the helo to shake Travis's hand.

"Thank you, sir. Thank you and your men for everything," said Travis.

"Oh, and by the way," said Drum, "If anyone asks, I never saw or heard a thing. Now get the hell out of here. We'll keep an eye on the sky and let you know if we find anything."

Tension did not ease up until they had climbed off the bird onto terra firma and into their own hooch back at Jalalabad. They peeled off and stowed gear, cleaned their weapons, inspected and maintained their equipment, and re-supplied to be grab-and-go ready. No room for cutting corners or getting lazy.

Jack and Travis got over to sickbay, where Jack got stitched up. Normally, he would not have allowed the corpsman to use local anesthetic. Being sewn up without local made him feel alive. "Pain is weakness leaving the body," he liked to brag. But with twenty-plus lacerations, he felt plenty alive. He took all the numbing medicine he could get.

After they were cleared, Jack and Travis retreated to Jack's hooch.

"I can't imagine the hell you've been through," said Jack. "You must've lost thirty pounds. How about a hot shower and some good old American chow?"

"Sounds great, but I've something I want to get off my chest first." They eased into a couple of nylon fold-up chairs. "I just want to say I'm sorry for everything." Jack tried to interrupt, but Travis held up his hand. "Believe me, these last few weeks, I've had a lot of time to think about why I'm alive. I've always wondered why our cousin died and not me. I'm sure that's what everyone else thought, too."

"Forget all that bullshit," said Jack. "Today you proved you're one tough son of a bitch."

Travis stared at the ground for a minute before continuing. "I know I've embarrassed you and Nina, too. Doing the right thing's always been so automatic for you."

"Look, Travis. If anyone's a fuckup, it's me." Jack cleared the lump in his throat. "Besides Nina and Jake, we're all the family each other's got. If anyone's dropped the ball, it's me. One phone call and I practically got you killed."

"That call was the best thing that ever happened to me. What Rolf and Mohammed did to me wasn't your fault. What is your fault is that I feel alive for the first time in years," said Travis. "I can't wait to hear your story, as Grandpa Joe used to say, but how about that hot shower first."

"Sounds good to me, too," said Jack as he got up. They threw an arm over each other's shoulders as if they were kids again and had just won a championship baseball game. After getting cleaned up, they had platefuls of pancakes, eggs, bacon, hash browns, and milk. Jack burned through his stack while Travis picked at his. "Not that hungry. It might take a day or two to get my stomach working again."

Jack poured a couple of cups of coffee, spiking each one with a shot of Jack Daniels, a Ghost Team tradition. "Not sure if this will help, but here's to you," said Jack. They raised an eyebrow to each other, clinked their mugs together, and sipped.

"How can you keep doing this? I mean, how can you be normal after what we've seen?" asked Travis.

"I started having nightmares, mainly of Nina and Jake. Then the faces of our forefathers, who were slaughtered by the white man invaders of Sioux territory. I mean there are a lot of similarities. I felt so sorry for the kids here, that I started bringing candy along to give them. I loved to make them smile."

Jack went quiet for a moment, thinking of little Jake.

"I had to get over that in a hurry," said Jack. "One friend stepped on a mine and lost both legs. Four teammates were crushed when an IED dropped a house on them. A booby-trapped door killed another agency friend. There've been many more, where wives and kids back home lost daddies. Sometimes it was women and kids who pulled the trigger."

"How'd you keep from going crazy?" asked Travis.

"I had to toughen up. I realized everyone over here is a threat—women, children, teenage boys, old men. They'll use anybody. I cried the first time I held a four-year-old boy who'd been blown to bits because he walked home the wrong way. I don't cry anymore," said Jack. "I know it's not what Grandpa Joe or the elders would want."

"Grandpa Joe was never in Afghanistan and Pakistan."

"Maybe not, but plenty of our women and children were massacred by the whites. It was never our way."

"I can't imagine," said Travis. "How can you go back home and live a normal life?"

"I don't. I can't," said Jack. "I'm hard-wired. I can't stop being who I am. Anyone wearing a robe is a threat, here or there."

"My God! I had no idea," said Travis. "How does it end? You can't do this forever."

"This is all I know how to do. It's simple. Kill or be killed," said Jack. "I'll keep killing them until haji gets lucky and kills me. Grandpa Joe raised me to be the warrior and you the healer. As a warrior, I welcome death."

"It's not worth dying for, Jack. You got to get out," said Travis.

They each took another swig of Jack Coffee.

"There are only two things I am afraid of, Travis. I have nightmares of Nina and Jake being taken hostage from our home. I turn on Al Jazeera, and I see Nina and Jake kneeling in front of a giant, black-hooded executioner. I always wake up right before the blade strike. I'm afraid of being too late to save Nina and Jake.

"The other is dying of old age. I was bred to be a Sioux warrior. My greatest honor would be to die on the field of battle. Not as a demented, crippled Indian in some nursing home, shitting my diaper and drooling all over myself. I plan on living up to my name, Raging Bull."

Travis added another shot of whiskey and a splash of coffee to their cups and said, "I propose a toast. Here's to the Brothers Gunn. That we find hope and forgiveness."

"Here, here," said Jack as they both sipped. "I also want to propose a toast." He lifted his mug. "Now that the Brothers Gunn have been reunited, we swear to never give up on each other again. We stick together come hell or high water. The tribe is back."

They drank again, basking in the dream that their most haunting sins could be forgiven and forgotten.

For Jack, a wraith trapped and tormented by memories too horrific to believe, the invitation to cross back into the light of honor and hope seemed a misty blur just beyond reach. Hope that there was still good in the world, and he could be a part of it. "Hope," Jack whispered, rubbing his eyes.

A SEAL stuck his head around the doorway of Jack's hooch. "Jack, they need you in the radio shack."

"Come on, Travis." They got up gingerly and shuffled to the shack. Even breathing hurt.

"Hey, Jack, I've got Drum on the line," said the radioman.

"What do you got, Drum?" asked Jack.

"I'm pretty sure your guys just flew north out of here on a

Pak Mill gunship. Our drone saw your guy with the cast and his son climb on board. Our guess is they're heading back up to Chitral. The tracker signal is loud and clear."

"Looks like leaving those two alive may yield the El-Hashem mother lode yet," said Jack. "Better get a drone over Chitral."

"Roger that."

"You a fisherman, Drum?" asked Jack.

"I was when I had a life," said Drum.

"Well, just imagine you and I are in Canada, fishing, and the granddaddy of all walleyes takes the bait," said Jack. "I'm just playing with this big son of a bitch, letting a little line out, and just when he thinks he's in the clear, I'm gonna set the hook and nail the bastard. He'll never know what hit him."

31

Jalalabad, Afghanistan

"Congratulations on getting your brother back alive, Jack. The drinks are on you the next time I see you," said Wade on the radio.

"Count on it, bro. Anyone at headquarters catch wind of it?" asked Jack.

"Nobody's saying anything if they did."

Jack saw Wade shrug on his webcam image and asked, "How's our little plan working?"

"Just like we thought," said Wade. "We watched Rolf push Ahmed into the hospital in a wheelchair on the drone-cam. The same Chitral hospital where they caught Travis with the first one. How ironic is that? They must have found the tracker in his cast right away, because they weren't there more than thirty minutes before they hobbled back out, minus the cast, and took off by land.

"Excellent!" said Jack. "What about the second one?"

"It's working like a charm! The signal's five star. Easy to track," said Wade.

"Where are they now?" asked Jack.

"They took off like a bat out of hell at the same time as an early season snowstorm set in. We had to pull off, but nailed the signal down later with a satellite to a compound on the northern edge of Chitral," said Wade. "We've pulled headquarters back in. Sentinel's up keeping a sharp eye on the whole area. Too early in the morning for much movement yet, but we've got assets over the area to nail them quick if we get confirmation and good fidelity video. There's been a hiccup in the upper atmosphere, but it's passing and should clear by this afternoon. Video won't be much good till then."

"Roger that. Keep us posted," said Jack.

Travis sat next to Jack in Ghost Team's hooch and said, "Another tracker? Are you shitting me? Don't you have any better spy shit than that? The little bastard almost got me killed. They've already found two of them."

"Relax, Travis. They found the one they were supposed to find. They'll never find the other one, unless they open Ahmed back up."

"What?" asked Travis. "You hid one in his food?"

"No, we didn't make him swallow it. Give us a little fucking credit," said Jack.

"Before we turned Ahmed loose, one of our CIA friends knocked him out, stuck a new tracking beacon inside his belly wound, and sewed him back up."

"And he'll lead you right to the security council reunion, the mother lode, without knowing it?" asked Travis.

"That's the plan."

"That, my brother, is sick. I love it!" said Travis. "How'll you know when or where?"

"The same way we followed you to that hospital," said Jack. "Drones, planes, satellites. We won't lose them this time unless they go gopher on us."

"How can you be sure?" asked Travis.

"You'll see for yourself once this storm blows out. You'll be able to count the hairs on their asses," said Jack. "If we get a little lucky, we'll drop a bunker-buster on the bastards before they split up to the four corners of the globe to do their Grand Jihad. You're welcome to hitch a ride as an observer."

Travis seemed shocked. "What?"

"We'll have to haul ass if this thing goes down, and it might be some hairy shit, but you've got more invested in this than anyone," said Jack. "Plus, you'd be valuable to help identify the security council. You're the only one who saw them after Rolf changed their identities."

"I never saw any of them after the dressings came off, so I'm not sure how much help I'd be. But if I can help, I'm in. I want to see this through to the end."

"That a boy. Ever shoot one of these?" Jack handed Travis his assault rifle. Travis fumbled with it for a couple of seconds and handed it back.

"Things make me nervous," said Travis.

"Let's get you over to the range and learn how to use one." Jack motioned for Travis to follow. "If you're going to run with the big dogs, you got to know how to bite."

"Are you sure you're up for it, Jack? You look like you should be in a hospital instead of gearing up for a mission."

"I'm fine, but there's something I need to tell you before we go any farther."

The tone of Jack's voice erased the smile off Travis's face.

"Nina has had breast cancer for two months." Travis looked like he'd been cold cocked. He staggered and took a seat. "She had the double mastectomy and started chemo a month ago. It was stage three, into the lymph nodes."

"Shit, Jack. I'm so sorry. How's she doing?"

"You doctors know more about this cancer shit than me. Her hair fell out and her blood counts are low. Is stage three bad?"

"Well, it's not good, but she still has a great chance of beating it."

"What kind of chance? And don't give me some bullshit answer. I want the truth," said Jack. He sat down too.

"I've known Nina since we were kids too, and it breaks my heart. She's the healthy one of the family, eating right and exercising. It doesn't make sense." Tears streamed down Travis's cheeks.

They both sat silently for the longest time, slumping under the weight of Nina's cancer.

Jack broke the silence. "There's something I need you to do, Travis. Something for me."

"What? Anything, Jack. You name it."

"You're the only family Nina and I have. And we're damn glad you're alive. Anyway, uh, uh . . ."

"What is it Jack. I'll do whatever you say."

"You know in my line of work, there's a better than fifty-fifty chance that I won't make it to see Jake graduate. And there's a chance Nina won't either. I want you to take Jake if both of us are gone."

Travis was absolutely speechless. He felt like he had a hood over his head again and he couldn't breathe. He let it sink in for a minute, and said the only thing he could: "You and Nina aren't going anywhere, Jack. The three of us will be sitting around a powwow campfire in Montana twenty years from now, telling stories about the good old days." His voice got quiet and shaky. "But it would be my honor to take care of little Jakey if you and Nina can't. It would be my honor, brother."

Travis stood and shook Jack's hand, and hugged the big bear. When Jack backed away, tears filled his bloodshot eyes, too.

By mid-afternoon, the clouds blew out, and the skies over the terrorists' compound in Chitral, Pakistan, cleared. The surveillance satellites got a good view of the season's first coating of snow and ice sticking to every tree branch and needle. The citizens of Chitral were lured outside by the warm sun and snowy masterpiece.

The pilots at Creech AFB had Sentinel's high-definition video camera focused perfectly, orbiting the compound four miles straight up. The copilot running the camera almost shit his pants when he saw a tall man wearing a black robe and headscarf. The man walked out into the courtyard, using a staff.

The intelligence community had a library of surveillance tapes of Mullah Mohammed Abdul walking along mountain trails or through villages. The technician knew immediately whom he was watching. He was surrounded by other robed and turbaned men carrying weapons, presumably his deputies and security council.

The copilot double-checked to make sure the signal was being seen back at JOC at Bagram. Colonel Richards, the in-country Air Force commander at JOC, Wade in the Catacombs, and Jack and Travis in Jalalabad, all watched and realized it was that once-in-a-lifetime opportunity to change the course of history. But how long would the window stay open?

"Looks like they've got the whole fucking El-Hashem family together," said Jack. "There must be twenty or thirty."

"I don't feel sorry for any of them," said Travis. "Rolf made his choice. Fuck him." They both listened in on the communication channel.

"This is Colonel Richards, commander of JOC at the moment. I'm authorizing the immediate destruction of that Taliban compound, and I want eyes on the ground ASAP."

The F-15 Strike Fighter patrolled sixty miles away, over the Afghan-Pakistani border. They received their tasking orders in less than sixty seconds. The target's GPS coordinates from Sentinel were programmed directly into the two-thousand-pound JDAMs.

Within minutes, the supersonic F-15 reached the launch point, lobbed the two bombs toward the target five miles away, and bugged out. What made the JDAM the weapon of choice was that, regardless of weather conditions or time of day, the bomb would fly to the exact GPS coordinates. Two JDAMs would destroy any compound, guaranteed. Less than eight minutes after Colonel Richards gave the order, the courtyard and main buildings were swallowed by two white-hot expanding bull's-eyes.

32

Chitral, Pakistan

Ghost Team's Chinook was airborne and burning northeast, back up the Konar and Shi Shi River valleys, within minutes of the JDAMs strike. Black Hawks flanked the CH-47 and, higher up, the Storm formed up and joined them for the dangerous broad daylight helo assault into Pakistan.

Back channel diplomatic calls were probably being made, but no matter what, the mission was a go. No one in the region had the power or insanity to try to stop them. A delay of any kind was unacceptable. They needed boots on the ground.

"Listen up," said Jack into his mouthpiece. "Thanks to Preacher, we sent our VIP back home yesterday with a little piece of Americana. You didn't think I was done, did you?"

Devilish smiles, the only smiles SEALs seemed to have, spread across their usually stony faces.

"We tracked our dodo bird right back to where Mullah Mohammed Abdul and his tribe of Islamic El-Hashem perverts were flocking up, getting ready to fly the coop," said Jack. "Minutes ago, our United States Air Force shoved two JDAMs up their ass. We're flying balls to the wall, right up to the bombsite. We'll do our SSE, verify the EKIAs, and get the hell out. It's close enough to the city and Pak Mill headquarters that there'll be plenty of looky-loos and pissed off hajis, so watch your six."

194

Jack glanced at Travis, strapped in next to him. "You look like an honest-to-goodness warrior, Travis." Jack rapped him in his chest plate with his gloved knuckles. Travis and Jack both had painted on their broken arrows.

Even Travis looked intimidating all geared up, carrying an assault rifle. He had seen the security council's faces in the operating room, and would be valuable in identifying them. Regardless, he and Jack were on the warpath and had personal business with Mohammed, Ahmed, and Rolf.

It wasn't unusual to have observers on ops. More often the observers were Afghan special forces, trying to learn to do what SEALs did, which ended up being more of a babysitting job than anything. Plus, they couldn't be trusted. Green-on-blue attacks where the Afghan soldier or police officer opened fire on NATO forces became more and more common. But Jack called the shots as far as Ghost Team operations, and if he wanted Travis along, Travis was along. No question. Besides, Travis wasn't going to shoot him in the back.

"This is a little over-the-top." Travis was out of breath, and his eyes were twitching. "It's like I'm in the middle of some crazy video game. I don't know how you can do this without having a heart attack."

Travis looked around at each SEAL, preparing to do whatever it took, including dying for one another. They acted like they were commuting to a nine-to-five job instead of going where no one else dared.

Travis turned and looked Jack in the eye. "I'm a doctor, not a warrior, brother. I think I'll just stay right here. You'll have enough to worry about without having to babysit me. If you need me to jump out and ID somebody, I'm good to go."

Travis bit his lip before continuing. "If Mom, Dad, or Grandpa Joe could see you now, they'd be prouder than hell." He slapped a heavy hand on Jack's shoulder.

Jack didn't say anything. Didn't even hear Travis. He had his kill on. He was focused. It was go-time.

Over the compound, the storm of A-10s, AC-130s, manned ISRs, and Strike Eagles were joined by the EA-6 Jammers to keep the Taliban from using their hand-held radios and walkie-talkies to organize themselves for a counterattack.

The Helo Assault Force circled wide of Chitral and approached from the north. Black smoke rose from the destroyed Taliban complex that was a half-mile from any neighbors. Easy to spot.

A section of the twenty-foot-high north wall, big enough to drive a tank through, was blown out. The southern wall stood intact. Most of the central buildings were a pile of grey, smoldering rubble, but several of the peripheral ones were partially standing.

The Black Hawks began a slow orbit of the surrounding area, two hundred feet in the air. The ominous black silhouette of the chopper with its loaded missile pods was clear invitation to the locals. Stick your heads up, please.

Once the Black Hawks secured the perimeter, the Chinook pounded in and put down in the middle of ground zero. Jack and the team quickly deployed while Travis stayed strapped in his seat.

"Get our SSE done before the shit hits the fan," yelled Jack.

SSE at bombsites was some of the most gruesome destruction on earth, much like a plane crash site. There weren't dead people lying everywhere. There were parts of dead people lying everywhere. As if everyone had swallowed a grenade and blown themselves to bits. Even Ghost Team needed a few seconds to adjust to the grisly scene.

"Not going to need you Travis. Nothing left to identify," said Jack.

Someone started taking pictures while Jack combed through the carnage. He found part of a person in a black robe, but the head was missing. Mullah Mohammed was the only person they tracked who wore black robes. Next to him were other EKIAs, whom Jack figured were Rolf and Ahmed, but who could tell?

"Looks like we hit one out of the park, boys," said Jack. "It's a complete vaporization of Hatchet Mohammed and his whole fucking Grand Jihad. I've got what looks like the Big Kahuna, but he's not all here anymore. The fingers are torched. I'll bring both arms. Clip a finger from every arm. The FBI can sort it out later. I want a couple men to SSE the perimeter structures. Take the dog."

After five minutes of intense SSE, everyone's Peltors started squawking about a Pak Mill garrison approaching from the south. The Black Hawks slid over the compound, kicking up dust and rocks, to take up station over the south wall.

"Wrap it up. This isn't the time or place to tangle with these bastards," said Jack.

The Black Hawks started to take on small-arms fire. Jack and the rest of the assaulters ran to the south wall.

Automatic gunfire erupted from behind, and Jack yelled for Ghost Team to take cover. He started oozing again from old and new wounds. ISR confirmed there were four hajis hunkered behind the partially destroyed north wall.

One of the Black Hawks broke formation to line up its twenty-millimeter cannons for the kill. Jack recognized the rocket-blast sound of an RPG being fired outside the north wall. In the next instant, the hovering million-dollar Black Hawk and crew exploded and crashed outside the compound in a giant fireball.

Immediately, another RPG was fired. In a surreal, slow-motion instant, Jack turned to watch the fiery tail of the rocket-propelled grenade race across the compound, five feet off the ground. He screamed, "No!" but the grenade plunged into the guts of their Chinook and exploded. Jack ran across the courtyard, screaming, holding up his hands to get it to stop. Travis was in there, where Jack told him to stay.

The helicopter rotor blades zinged past in jagged pieces. Secondary explosions knocked Jack backwards. A chunk of something bounced off Jack's helmet. He lay on the frozen battleground, staring up at black smoke and blue sky. A firefight between the SEALs and Pak Mill on the south wall raged on. Another RPG exploded somewhere nearby.

Someone yelled, "Jack!"

Jack snapped out of his concussion fog, crawled to his feet, and stumbled to the burning pile with one hand up to block his face from the searing heat. He yelled, "Travis! Travis!" It was a good thing Jack carried Cat medicine. The number of times he had come back to this life from the other were mounting. He had used his nine lives up long ago.

One of the other Black Hawks put down, and two crewmembers came running with fire extinguishers, but the fire burned and burned. More extinguishers were exhausted, and after several minutes, they'd knocked the fire down enough to reach the charred remains of the pilot and crew strapped in their seats. Travis wasn't in his seat.

Jack was frantic. He scrambled over the piles of debris surrounding the helicopter's remains, pawing at everything, burning or not, screaming, "Travis! Travis!" At one point, he leaned over and puked.

Someone yelled for Jack. Travis lay face down on the far side of a broken wall. They turned him over. He breathed. He opened his eyes when Jack lifted his head and called his name. He smiled. "Did we get 'em?"

"You're going to give me a fucking heart attack, little brother," said Jack.

"It was the weirdest thing, like slow motion. Something in my head, a voice warned me to get out. Get out fast. So I yelled at the pilots, unstrapped and dove. Then I was flying, no, make that cartwheeling, through fire and smoke. I was in the air long enough to make a deal with God. If I lived, I would change. I would start listening to him. I'm still here looking at your ugly mug, so he must have taken my deal."

"Saving your ass is getting to be a full time job." Jack smiled and kissed Travis on the forehead. "Are you hurt?"

"It's pretty bad in my low back and left hip. I can't move."

The PJs went to work, putting on a neck collar, and strapping Travis to a spine board. Jack's team retrieved the remains of the Army crew from the first downed Black Hawk after the four haji shooters were wasted with a missile.

Ghost Team's survival instincts took over with the Pak Mill a hundred yards from the south wall and pushing hard to gain control of the compound. They crammed on board the three remaining Black Hawks, and lifted off to the north while the A-10 Warthog came in to fly cover.

The Hog, also known as Shredder, strafed the south and north walls of the compound with its forty-millimeter Gatling gun, firing four thousand rounds per minute. The Pak Mill stopped in their tracks and waited to give the invaders and their death machine space to escape.

Jack collapsed onto the floor of the helo next to Travis's stretcher. Between old and new wounds, he was exhausted. Travis got morphine. The helo smelled like a rendering factory where they roasted dead horses, pigs, and cows into dog food or glue. Except their dead were Army heroes and bags of blown-to-bits haji body parts, the DNA evidence.

It was a great day for the free world. Two-thousand pounders, right on target, had wiped out the Taliban Security Council, Mohammed, Ahmed, and Rolf. It was a sad day for six Army families back in the States who'd just lost loved ones. It was both for the Gunn brothers.

33

Jalalabad, Afghanistan

When Al Jazeera broadcast photos of the smoldering remains of two American helicopters in the middle of an obliterated compound deep into Pakistan, the worldwide media went berserk. Photos of terrorists posing in front of the helicopter carcasses, one of them defiantly hoisting an RPG launcher, were on news magazine covers everywhere.

The Taliban claimed the bombsite had been a school and, since the brutal attack was carried out in broad daylight, hundreds of children were killed. Footage of a burqa-clad mother kneeling in the rubble, clutching her limp child and wailing while other mothers frantically searched and screamed for their missing children was gut-wrenching.

The newscast led off with "How could the U.S. make such an unforgivable mistake?" Public opinion for the war on terror soured instantly.

Once the camera crews were escorted back to the airport, the weeping women and children were bused back to their homes. Taliban supporters dug through the collapsed buildings, hoping to find survivors trapped below ground. Even if there were no survivors, the crawl spaces were where any stored ammunition and weapons would be found. Someone would want revenge. Someone always wanted revenge.

At a White House briefing, the press secretary read a statement: "A high level Taliban meeting was taking place at the compound. It was not a school, as reported. No women or children were killed. The attack was a war-zone operation, based upon irrefutable evidence that Mullah Mohammed Abdul and his security council were present at the meeting.

"As the leader of the Taliban, Mullah Mohammed Abdul conspired to kill thousands of innocent people worldwide. He was on the verge of initiating a new level of violence worldwide in what he called the Grand Jihad. Citizens of the world should rest easier knowing that the Taliban leadership has been eliminated, and Mullah Mohammed Abdul has been killed. As a precautionary measure against retaliation, the Department of Homeland Security has elevated the national threat level."

Most were dubious of the White House's version of the story. The image of the Pakistani mother mourning over her dead baby had served its purpose, but verification was easy for the news services to obtain, if they cared to report the truth. Hundreds of military personnel were connected with supporting the Chitral bombing mission. They had family back in the states that worried about them, and families trusted their own flesh and blood far more than their government or the news services. So when the families started to privately confirm the official story, the scent of blood faded, and the media backed off.

Ghost Team was ordered to stand down until everything blew over. They'd paid a steep price, but accomplished their mission. With the Taliban leadership wiped out, their job was done. Corralling and controlling the leaderless Taliban terrorists was the ground force's responsibility.

The terrorist's arms, fingers, and other body parts were turned over to the FBI. After they were photographed, cataloged, and packed in coolers, the macabre evidence was shipped to Bagram for ASAP blood typing, fingerprinting, and DNA analysis.

Jack was watching the CNN re-broadcast when he was called to the intel shack at their Jalalabad base. Jaz had heloed down from Bagram and was waiting for him, in her desert camo uniform.

"I hear your brother's quite the hero . . . and single. If he's anything like you, I'd like to meet him," said Jaz.

"Then you're in luck, Lieutenant, because he's nothing like me."

"You're both alive. That's a start."

"He's headed stateside to get his back fixed."

"Will he walk again?"

"What's with all the questions? You getting lonely up there?"

"You're jealous."

"Jealous! Of what?"

"Another Gunn stealing your spotlight."

"Listen, Jaz. Travis can have it. Give me a cold, black night in a target-rich compound and I'll be happy," said Jack.

"If you're done with the small talk, we've got business to discuss," said Jaz.

"I didn't . . . You started . . ." Jack heard Jaz laugh and hated being manipulated. "What's up?"

"I know your team is headed stateside, but I have something I need you to watch and tell me what you think."

"Roger that," said Jack. He centered himself in front of the monitor and Jaz rolled the video as she narrated. "You'll recognize the Chitral compound. This is t-minus sixty seconds. We count three men leaving in a car just before impact. It's impossible to ID them, since we had pulled back to monitor the attack. Nothing on the car either. One of them's carrying something. Looks like a briefcase." The car quickly disappeared off screen, immediately followed by the double detonation. "The drone pilots fulfilled their primary mission, but when they tried to reacquire the car, not surprisingly, no luck."

"It's an aluminum suitcase, just like the other ones we've found."

"What do you make of that?"

"Not sure yet. What about the second tracker we stuck in Ahmed?" asked Jack.

"It's off the grid."

"So who and what were in that car? We know it wasn't Ahmed if the tracker's dead. Rolf would have stayed close, so they're probably both in the bag of goodies we sent you. We had a black robe at the scene too, so my guess is Mohammed is toast, too. I have no fucking idea who that might be. Maybe the pizza guy."

"Whoever they are, they should go to the casino," said Jaz. "By the time you get back to Nina and Jake, we should have a list of dead. But, put this out of your mind. You go home to your wife and son where you belong. They need you more than we do. But first, introduce me to your brother."

It wasn't like Jack to mix work and family, but when Jaz mentioned Nina and Jake, he could think of nothing but home. He wanted to take care of them. He was nervous of how he'd react when he saw Nina with no hair. Then Travis's face popped into that same vision, and a smile pinched at the corners of Jack's mouth. Never in twenty some years had Travis been around. And sober. Once Travis got healed and Nina cured, things were going to be different. A whole new life waited. Jack was ready to begin.

34

Norfolk, Virginia, United States

"How bad is it?" asked Nina. She sat next to Travis's hospital bed, a couple hours after his back surgery. Dried blood caked the corners of his mouth where the scabs must have broken open when they put him asleep. He swished some ice water to clear his cotton mouth, and then swallowed. He still looked drugged. Six-year-old Jake sat on Jack's lap, a little too rambunctious to run free on a surgical floor.

"I've got a whole new pain scale after what I went through. These people can't imagine what a ten is really like," said Travis. He fell silent, distant. Stared at the ceiling. "The nightmares are something I'm going to have to live with, I guess." The wall clock ticked. An ambulance siren shut down as it approached the emergency room, seven stories below.

As quickly as he left, he returned. "How are you doing, Nina? I was shocked when Jack told me."

"There's good and bad days." She stretched her legs in the hospital vinyl recliner. The clock ticked. "It's great having Jack back. We really, really missed him."

"Thanks for sharing him," said Travis. He managed a morphine-induced smile. "Boom Boom." Nina and Jack both laughed. "Did he tell you? We're a team again."

"Is that right? A team of what?"

"We haven't exactly figured that out. Why? You want to join?" asked Travis.

"I already have one baby. I don't know if I can handle two more."

"My legs better get with the program or you'll have me to stroller around. But, never mind that. I'm blown away by how great you look."

"Same old Travis the Charmer. Thanks, anyway," said Nina.

"No, I mean it. It's great to see you and Jake."

"Get some rest. We'll come back tomorrow."

The three of them looked like they'd been thrown through a windshield. Cuts, scabs, stitches, bruises, circles under their eyes. Nina looked the best, and she wasn't great. They had moaned and groaned as they reminisced their childhood and what Travis had missed over the years. They were done with the old regrets, guilts, and grudges. They agreed they had wasted a good portion of their lives under the weight of the past. Everyone made mistakes. It was time to move on.

Jack hung back to have a word with Travis before they left.

Since returning from Afghanistan, Jack had been doing some digging. Trying to wrap his arms around the Grand Jihad. What had they been planning?

Forensic data from the FBI had started to paint a picture, but there were lots of questions. One of the fingers Ghost Team clipped at the Chitral bombsite showed signs of advanced radiation damage, enough that it was still evident after being blown to bits and incinerated. The FBI put the DNA fingerprint through FBI, CIA, and NSA databases, and got nothing. The Pakistan government got a positive match though. His name was Mustafa Abdul.

Pakistan had the fourth-largest nuclear weapons arsenal in the world, with over four hundred warheads. At their primary research facility in Kahuta, twenty thousand centrifuges cranked out yellow cake, twenty-four hours a day. Yellow cake was turned into enough highly enriched uranium, plutonium, and tritium to create fifty new weapons a year.

The Taliban attacked these and other facilities weekly, desperate to steal a bomb. One nuke would be a game changer. They professed that Pakistan was run by a bunch of gutless puppets that cared more about lining their pockets with American gold than following Allah's command to Jihad. Maybe they were. The mullahs had made inroads into the political hierarchy, but not enough to get control. If they could overthrow the government, they would control its nukes. Pakistan's armies would become Islam's armies.

Mustafa Abdul was a shift supervisor at Kahuta. When two hundred fifty pounds of uranium disappeared over a year ago, he ran the investigation. The uranium was never found. Mustafa disappeared and was presumed dead.

"Have you ever seen this man?" Jack held a picture in front of Travis. Stamped in the border were the words "U.S. Customs."

"I don't think . . . no wait. That looks like the guy we did surgery on last year in Pakistan. I was scared shi—"

"That's what I thought. He was Mustafa Abdul, the brother of Mohammed the Hatchet." Travis shuddered at hearing Mohammed's name. Before Travis could ask, Jack continued. "We killed him at Chitral along with Mohammed, so don't worry about it and get some rest. We'll talk more later."

U.S. Customs had searched their backlogs for Mustafa. He made several trips to the U.S. on a false passport, remade with his new face. Different cities, but always ones known to financially support jihad. He received cargo shipments from container ships docking in Charleston, South Carolina. All U.S. ports of call scanned cargo for nukes, but Jack knew there were ways to shield nuclear material so radiation detectors wouldn't catch it. He hoped Mustafa hadn't known, too. Judging by the degree of radiation damage to his fingers, Jack was nervous.

Jack shivered when he felt the jihad spider crawling on his neck. Its claws dug deeper than a gun spider. A picture formed in his mind of what Mohammed, Ahmed, and Rolf had been planning before they were killed. He headed for an urgent meeting with his boss at Ghost Team's base.

35

Virginia Beach, Virginia, United States

"Congratulations, Chief Gunn, and welcome home," said Lieutenant Commander Winfield as they shook. "Grab a cup."

"Thank you, sir," Jack said, and sat in the office chair, wearing a black skull-and-crossbones T-shirt, blue jeans, and his wraparound sunglasses squeezing the folds of his shaved head. The stitches were gone, and scabs healed anywhere his coppery skin showed. He took a sip. "You officers get all the good shit. Not the swill we drink, sir."

"That's not the only perk, but I can't tell you or I'd have to . . ."

They both smiled, wondering who'd win.

"I appreciate your coming in on such a short notice," said Winfield. "There're a few things we need to discuss."

"Yes, sir," said Jack.

"First, get me up to speed on how Travis's doing."

"Travis is in the spine unit at NTRC. He had surgery. Says the nurses are angels."

"That's great news," said Winfield. "You should be proud. He's quite a warrior in his own right."

"Yes, sir. Thank you, sir."

"And how's Nina doing, Jack? I hear the wives have been looking in on her."

"She's a fighter, sir. Taking it one day at a time."

"My wife and I pray she returns to good health. Please give her our best."

"I will, sir."

"Thirdly, the president sends his congratulations to you and your Ghost Team for the masterful job you did to both rescue your brother and wipe out their Leadership Council. Off the record, he approves of how you negotiate with terrorists. Your vision, flexibility, and flair for carrying out your game plan with deadly force and precision have rightfully earned you a place in our Hall of Fame. You're truly in a league of your own. One of the best Ghost Team has ever seen."

"Thank you, sir," said Jack. "I'm just doing my job. I may piss a few people off, but my teammates and missions are all that matter to me. We're happy to answer the bell when no one else will."

"Well, that's something I'd like to talk to you about," said Winfield. "Doc says we need to pull you out of line and get these concussions checked out."

"Negative, sir. A little time off and I'll be fine. What's up?"

"We take this kinda thing seriously, Jack. You and I, we're in this for the long haul."

"I'm good to go, sir. Doc worries too much."

"Jack." Winfield took a sip of coffee, set the cup down deliberately on its coaster and looked Jack in the eyes. "You're like a son. Better than any I've ever had the honor to command. I'm not saying you're done; just it's time to reevaluate how to use you best. I need to keep you around for a long time."

"I don't like the sound of that, sir." Jack got up out of his chair.

Winfield clicked his computer mouse a couple of times and studied something on the screen, shielded from Jack.

"I've thought about retiring, sir, but I'm not sure," said Jack. "There's still a lot of work to be done."

"Take a step back for a minute and look at the bigger picture," said Winfield.

Jack stood at Winfield's second-story office window looking out over the SEAL marina. Sunlight glinted off dark water. Seagulls sunbathed on the weathered pilings. A zodiac loaded with a team of divers headed out to the main channel.

"There'll always be bad guys to chase. You've certainly

WARPATH **209**

done your share, and you should feel proud. But say you were promoted to Chief Warrant Officer." Winfield raised his bushy eyebrows and smiled.

"A warrant officer, sir? No shit?" said Jack as he sat back down. "Move up to management. Get the good stuff." Jack held up his coffee cup. He knew what kind of pay raise it meant.

"That's right, Jack, a warrant officer. You'd be able to oversee the training and execution of missions and take a bigger role in shaping Ghost Team's future in the war on terror. Think of it like you'd have your finger on a thousand triggers."

"A warrant officer," Jack said again. "When I started the teams, I had the option to be an officer, but I chose to stay enlisted," said Jack. "To be with the real men, uh, no offense, sir."

"None taken, Jack." Winfield smiled.

"This warrant officer thing's caught me a little off guard," said Jack. "I do like the image of pulling a thousand triggers from here in Virginia. You're right—even without Mullah Mohammed Abdul, there's always going to be a surplus of fucking wack jobs running around wreaking havoc."

"That's something else I need to talk to you about," said Winfield.

"What do you mean, sir?" Jack put down his coffee and sat up. He didn't like the tone in Winfield's voice.

"We've gotten the FBI report back from the DNA analysis. They confirm we've wiped out most of the cards in the deck."

"I heard, sir."

"Funny thing about DNA identification, though. It's one hundred percent accurate." Winfield looked Jack straight in the eye. "Those arms you sent back from the bombsite weren't Mohammed's."

"What? They had to be!" said Jack defensively.

"The DNA was similar, but not a complete match—only about fifty percent," said Winfield. "We believe it was one of his brothers. Maybe this Mustafa Abdul we've ID'd. We're checking to see how many brothers Mullah Mohammed Abdul had."

"What about all the other evidence?" asked Jack.

"Not there. Mohammed wasn't one of the EKIAs. Neither were Ahmed or Rolf El-Hashem. I'm sorry."

The jihad spider dug its claws deeper into Jack's neck. "What? Sir, I saw the video right before the bomb hit. I was there," said Jack.

"I saw it, too, Jack. We know we killed everyone on the security council and then some. Mohammed, Ahmed, and Rolf must have been the three we saw escape in the car right before impact," Winfield said.

"What about the tracker Preacher stuck in Ahmed's gut?" asked Jack. "We checked. It was off the grid."

"Funny you should ask," said Winfield. "That's the first thing I asked, too. I initiated a global search through the NSA. In the last hour, the satellites tracked it to a Yemeni container ship off the coast of Oman, halfway between Karachi and Yemen. They'll enter the Gulf of Aden in a day and potentially make land in two to three days, depending on the weather."

Jack sat forward, gripping the chair arms.

"Those waters are as crowded and unfriendly as hell," said Winfield. "To make matters worse, it seems that part of their plan involves Somali pirates. There've been at least a dozen raids on ships in the Internationally Recommended Transit Corridor off the Horn of Africa in the last twenty-four hours. We're rapidly becoming bogged down, dealing with a hijacked Belgian-flagged ship and hostage situation along with a swarm of pirates. We've got very few available assets in the area close enough to help."

"Good! Blow the fuckers to kingdom come!" said Jack.

"That's not all. We've been sitting on a report that there was a breach of protocol at Pakistan's Kahuta Nuclear Research Facility," said Winfield. "Two hundred fifty pounds of uranium disappeared about a year ago, and they still can't account for it."

"I read the report."

"It looks like it was an inside job by one of Mohammed's brothers, Mustafa Abdul." He took a deep breath and sighed. "We've got to assume the uranium is part of this Grand Jihad with our terrorist trio."

"We had to have blown a giant hole in his Grand Jihad," said Jack. "Travis and Rolf did surgery to change the security council and Mohammed's identity, like they did to Mustafa a year ago. But now they're all dead, except for Mohammed. How's he going to carry out their plan with just Ahmed and Rolf? They didn't have surgery."

"Good question."

"Well, I'll be a son-of-a bitch," said Jack. "This changes everything."

"How do you mean, Jack?"

"It's personal, sir." Jack looked around the office at the pictures of some of the SEAL greats from the past, men who also lived in the shadows. "When Travis and I stood shoulder to shoulder on that bridge over the Konar River, and declared war on Hatchet Mullah and his Grand Jihad, I meant it. Those three did things to Travis, and Keeler, that can't be forgotten. And now you're telling me that Mohammed and his plans are still alive, possibly with nukes."

"All I'm saying, Jack, is Mullah Mohammed Abdul, Rolf, and Ahmed *may* be alive," said Winfield. "That's why it makes perfect sense for you to take the promotion and work with all of the resources here at Little Creek to capture the nukes and end this fight. You can engineer your Badal from right here and sleep at home with your family."

Nina, Jake, Travis. They all flashed through his brain. He'd just gotten home two days earlier. Travis was in the hospital. Nina was fighting for her life. They were all three banged up. Blue Team was standing by, fresh and ready to go. An office chair already had Jack's name on it. No one would blame him for taking a seat. But that's not who he was. Nina and Travis would agree.

"It may make perfect sense to you, sir, but that's not how I see this playing out," said Jack. "The boys and I have some unfinished business. I can have no peace as long as those sons of bitches are alive."

"I need to follow the advice of the doctors, Jack. I'll have Blue Team take this mission."

"That's bullshit, sir, and you know it. You're going to have to shoot me, because I am going to finish the job I started." Jack breathed hard, stood hands on hips, looking like a bull ready to charge.

"Dammit, Jack. You can be a stubborn son of a bitch." Winfield studied Jack, long and hard, over the top of his glasses. "Against medical advice, I'll give you this last go. I need my best man on the job."

"Thank you, sir." Jack took a seat. "I owe you one."

"We'll talk about that when you get back," said Winfield, with a sigh. "It looks like a boat drop is the best option. Putting you boys in a sub and sneaking you in underwater would take too long. If they reach land, we're screwed. The thought of nukes in the hands of those three is unspeakable. We could blow them out of the water, but chancing a nuclear detonation in the Middle East could initiate retaliatory strikes."

"Good. Maybe they'd all kill each other," said Jack. "Save me the trouble."

"Or," Winfield said, and turned his computer screen to show Jack a map of the Gulf of Aden, "the nukes could sink to the bottom of the ocean, which would be a catastrophe of a different color. Trying to run a recovery mission would be treacherous in those waters."

"Executing a boat drop sounds right on, sir. We've trained for it. We're ready to get wet after playing in sand," said Jack. "I'll get the team together and give them the news. We'll be wheels up in eight hours. Thank you, sir."

In the parking lot, Jack sent a text message:

> *Good news!*
> *We're back on the warpath.*
> *Meet me at hooch ASAP.*

Jack pulled his shades down and revved up his black Harley Davidson. He rumbled past the guard post and gunned it down General Booth Boulevard to say a couple of quick goodbyes.

Travis about swallowed his tongue when he heard the three were alive. His blood pressure went through the roof.

"I'm the one who declared war on those fuckers. Why should you get to have all the fun?" said Travis.

"Don't worry. I'll see the job gets done the old-fashioned way this time. Up close and personal."

"Even if I'm not with you, my spirit will be with you, brother," said Travis as he calmed himself down. "Close your eyes and give me your hand." Jack did. Travis held Jack's meaty hands for a moment, and then placed a feather from his pillow into Jack's palm. "It's as close as I can get to an eagle feather."

"Thanks, bro. It means a lot."

"Fly high and strong, and don't worry. Nina, Jake, and I will watch after one another." Travis pulled Jack down to the hospital bed to give him a hug. Then he took his fingers and traced broken arrows on his cheeks. Jack smiled confidently, did the same, and left.

Nina was devastated at the thought of Jack leaving already. Blindsided by the Navy, again, she said. An unexpected sucker punch. He had not even unpacked yet. He knew it would be hard on Nina, so he forgot to mention the desk job promotion. She expected, no, she deserved, at least a month after he returned from a long deployment. "Why did it always have to be Jack?" she asked. "Why couldn't he let someone else handle it?"

Jack said nothing.

Nina said she knew Jack, and loved him for being the guy he was. He had to go. She wanted him to go. If anyone could get the job done, it was her Jack. And she was proud of it. As much as she hated saying goodbye, she gave him a hug and kiss as she walked him to his Harley. In his rearview mirror, he watched her disappear into the distance.

Arabian Sea

"We've just cleared Saudi airspace, Chief Gunn. One hour to bingo."

"What time is it?" asked Jack, disoriented from eighteen hours of jet whine, no windows, and nine hours of time change.

"2200."

"Hit the lights, Staff Sergeant," said Jack. "Time to get this party started."

"Roger that. It's going to ride a little rough from here on in. Pretty good nor'easter blowing," said the Staff Sergeant.

"Nor'easter? Where you from, son?" asked Jack.

"Maine, Chief."

"Have you ever done a boat drop before?"

"In training sure, but not for real. Not like this."

"It's a piece a cake. Just another day at the office," said Jack.

Dewey walked up and stretched his back. "Man, I'm getting too old for this shit. How're you doing, Gunner? Get any sleep?"

"Could these bastards be any bigger? Must take a shoe horn to wedge 'em in here," said Jack. "Eighteen hours on a metal deck. My head's killing me."

"Vicodin didn't work again, huh?" asked Dewey. "When's the last time you got a good night's sleep?"

"Long enough I can't remember. Too much shit going on."

"What's new?"

"There's Travis, this maniac with the nukes, and Nina fighting for her life. My mind's going a thousand miles an hour."

He really had put home out of his mind as they hauled ass to intercept Mohammed before he reached Yemen. He formed a plan of attack, communicated with Winfield about the latest intel, and shot the shit with his team.

"How's the girl doing?" asked Dewey.

"She worries me, like she knows something, but won't tell me." Jack's shoulders drooped.

"She's a tough cookie," said Dewey.

"When we get back, I'll use some leave and take them on a real vacation."

"I can't even remember what a vacation's like," said Dewey.

"Jakey would be in heaven at Disney World. One thing I've learned is next year never comes, Dewey, especially in our line of work."

Jack chomped on a protein bar and washed it down with some hot coffee.

He looked at Dewey and said, "What am I fucking talking about? *Tomorrow* may never come. When we get home, we're taking our families to Disney World. No more excuses. Let's end this tonight and go home."

Jack and Dewey shook on it, and filled up with fresh brew. Two microwaves cranked out hot sausage, egg, and cheese biscuits to go along with oranges, apples, yogurt, milk, and OJ.

While the team ate, Jack briefed them.

"Here's what we've got," said Jack. "For those of you just joining us, the three terrorists we're after killed CIA, SEAL, and Army personnel, and almost killed my brother."

Jack let it sink in while he scarfed half a biscuit in one bite.

"They're making a run for Yemen on the container ship we've been tracking. We believe they're carrying two hundred fifty pounds of stolen Pakistani highly enriched uranium and are planning to use it for their Grand Jihad."

Everyone groaned. One mention of HEU meant wearing

chemical, biological, and radiation gear, which meant sweating like a pig. It was bulky, hot, and cramped the style of SEALs.

Jack wolfed the other half of his biscuit and inhaled a carton of milk. "You're a pretty good cook, Staff Sergeant. There's nothing like sausage and coffee in the morning. Keep 'em coming."

Staff Sergeant smiled and popped twelve more biscuits in the microwave.

"Somali pirates are raising all kinds of hell in the area, so most of our assets are busy," said Jack. "But the USS Ronald Reagan has lent a hand. Their Prowlers have been jamming all communications from the target ship. Their radio and Internet access are mysteriously down," said Jack. "There's no Storm out here to cover us, just two Black Hawks from the Reagan, so we're on our own again."

The men gave him the look that said, "Do we look like we give a shit?" and kept shoveling in the food.

After Jack finished the briefing, everyone continued eating and bullshitting, two things they never stopped doing. SEALs could put away enormous amounts of food. Once, Nina invited three of Jack's teammates for a Thanksgiving dinner. She stayed out of the way as they devoured a twenty-pound turkey, potatoes and gravy, scalloped corn, two bowls of stuffing, and two pies.

"The Prowlers are out there jamming. You know what they say?" asked Jack. "If you want peace, prepare for war." Jack scanned the eyes of the other nineteen SEALs, eight SWCCs, and four EOD specialists. "We've been in the sand too long. Time to get wet."

"Hey Jack. What do you think?" Jack turned to find the whole team smearing broken arrows on their cheeks. He growled. "Let's go kick some haji ass."

The Arabian Sea never varied much from sixty-eight degrees Fahrenheit, which wasn't the Arctic Ocean, but it was cold enough. The jumpers donned cold weather poly-pro and fleece warmies under their wet suits. They slipped their neoprene booties through the loops of their swim fins and velcroed the flipper-ends up to the top of their shins so they would not flop around in the air.

Over their wet suit hoods, they pulled on goggles and waterproof NODs. They strapped on their parachutes and stowed a radio and pistol inside a dry bag, in case the boat went down. All the rest of their war toys were stowed in the boat's dry bags.

The two Scarab cigarette boats stuffed in the eighty-eight-foot-long cargo hold had the ancient look of a knight's battle ax with futuristic carbon fiber and Kevlar skin stretched over its foam-core hull, a M134 mini gun, and three outboard motors.

Balancing the water missiles on pallets, hauling them halfway around the planet, and parachuting them into a foreign ocean from 5,000 feet still amazed Jack.

Dewey checked Boat Two while Jack climbed into Boat One, along with the SWCCs. Their weapons, boarding poles, and grappling-hook ladders were stowed with their CBR suits and hand-held radiation detectors. The EOD had an additional tub of gear for dealing with the uranium.

"Chief Gunn," called the jumpmaster.

"What's up, Staff Sergeant?"

"Better get your men up front. Five minutes to bingo. Boats and SWCCs go first. We'll pull a loop and drop you and your men off on the next go round. They'll have the boats de-rigged and be ready to get underway. You'll be landing five miles from the target vessel."

"Sounds excellent, Staff Sergeant." Jack climbed down and joined his men.

The lights went to UV, and the ramp at the rear of the cargo hold opened to the dark, stormy night. The jet's cruising speed of five hundred and fifteen miles per hour had slowly decreased to one hundred miles per hour and 5,000 feet altitude. The jumpmaster released the small pilot parachute that trailed a hundred feet behind. The line snapped tight as a bowstring. Grooves in Boats One and Two's custom pallets were locked into the plane's slotted deck rails.

The jumpmaster counted down "three, two, one, bingo" and punched the green "go" button, which released another hundred feet of line and pilot chute number two.

After a split-second delay, the first Scarab-pallet was jerked down the ramp by the chutes, accelerating to seventy miles per hour in forty feet. Clear of the jet wash, four grey main chutes opened on cue. The boat swung beneath, and the pallets automatically jettisoned to the ocean below.

The boat's four crewmen ran single file and dove off the ramp bellyflop style, counted to four, and pulled. They located the IR beacon of their boat and aimed to land an arm's reach astern. A crewless boat in those waters would not last long.

Boat Two landed three miles from Boat One. The Globemaster III looped around. On the next pass, it dropped the two SEAL teams right on target and headed back to Virginia.

Once in the water, the SEALs' chutes filled with saltwater—instantly changing from friend to anchor. Jack struggled as the chute pulled him backwards and down, still partially catching air in the heavy winds and surge. He'd forgotten how schizophrenic the chutes could be. Keeping him alive one second. Taking his life the next. He finally released the harness and slipped both arms free. The parachute system disappeared below the angry surface.

Sight of the boats came and went, bobbing in the fifteen-foot swells. Jack and his swim buddy, Dewey, untaped their fins, located the boat, and started kicking. It'd been a while, but just like riding a bike, they sidestroked with ease, instinctively never more than six feet apart.

The Scarabs idled. The electronics were up and talking with Prowler. The men exchanged their wet suits and goggles for the grey CBR suits and hoods, plus air filters, helmets with NODs, and radiation detectors. Then the boats launched.

First, they stalked the container ship from behind, and then took a wide arcing path outside its radar detection circumference to race ahead, park, and wait. The Scarab's low radar signature, due to the use of radar-translucent Kevlar and radar-absorbent material, made the SEAL boats essentially invisible at night, a black hole. Like hiding in a dark closet and hearing footsteps pass.

The Panamax container ship passed within fifty feet. Their tossing and turning Scarab compared to the size of that ship made Jack feel like a gnat on a cow's ass. She was nine hundred and sixty-five feet long. She carried containers stacked in neat rows of twelve, from below the waterline to above the deck. Jack saw a deck crane boom, which meant she was a smaller Panamax, but still a moving behemoth.

The Scarabs crept through the ship's foamy wake, a shadow in its radar blind spot, and up her side. When a fully loaded, top-heavy Panamax rolled in heavy seas, it was amazing they did not tip over. The truth was, thousands of containers fell overboard every year. As the ship rocked back and forth, the containers, stacked to the rail above, hung over the SEALs' heads. The ship groaned. The lashing creaked. One snapped line and it was all over. They'd go to the bottom of the Arabian Sea crushed by 60,000 pounds of wax, tampons, or nuclear material.

"We didn't come to the middle of the ocean to eat a fucking box," said Jack. "Three, two, one, execute."

37

Panamax Container Ship on the Arabian Sea

The SEAL Scarab crept up the leeward side of the target ship to the lowest hook point. Shorter climb. Quicker boarding. The container ship cruised at seven knots, slowed by a howling crosswind. She listed over five degrees, bringing the handrail even closer to the water. The containers, too. With each roll of the ship, the tall stack of containers looked like they were coming over the side. At the last moment, they rolled away, one last time.

As the SEALs eased past her stern and up the starboard side, they slammed the door on the gale-force wind blowing from left to right. The heavy seas on the port side would have swamped them or split them in two against the ship's hull. The starboard side provided the only calm spot within a hundred miles of ocean. The Scarab's keel knifed silently through the seas, ten feet to the target ship's side. No chance of banging into her hull and alerting the oblivious crew.

Jack reached up with the boarding pole and quietly placed the grappling hook ladder over the rail, thirty feet above.

Wearing the CBR suit was a miserable, hot, sweaty exercise. The suit was constructed of a rubbery material that did not breathe. Not a speck of flesh was exposed, in case some terrorist unleashed nerve gas, HEU, or flesh-eating bacteria. Climbing a thirty-foot ladder up the side of a moving ship, seawater cascading over the deck from above, in the dark, in a CBR suit was a royal pain in the ass.

Jack went first, followed by Dewey and the rest of the team from Boat One, while Boat Two trailed. The boats switched places, and Two unloaded while One trailed. Someone from Two lost his grip and fell into the sea from ten feet up the side.

He popped up like a buoy marker. The SWCC in Boat One spotted his IR beacon and fished him out before he was sucked into the ship's vortex and eight-foot screws. It wasn't uncommon for someone to dump. It was a lot to keep straight. But it cost the swimmer a round at Boneshaker's the next time they were home.

"Listen up," said Jack. "Prowler reported a small boat leaving here an hour ago, heading for land. They're tracking it, just in case."

"What about the tracker?' asked Dewey.

"Prowler says it's still here," said Jack. "If you get a clean shot, take it. But until we know where the uranium is, use your Tasers. EOD will scan the topside containers for radiation."

Container ships did not usually have sentries or guards posted, which made them easy targets for Somali pirates. Typically there were thirty to forty men on board sleeping or working below deck in the engine room or kitchen. A rough night at sea gave them even more reason to stay off the deck. Things shifted. Men died. The sea collected her toll.

The freighters and tankers were steered by autopilot. There'd be one man in the pilothouse, maybe the captain, and no weapons. Surprise and scare the shit out of the helmsman, zip-tie them, gag and tape their mouths shut, and move on. Any troublemaker got a butt stroke, Taser, nut-crunch, or whatever worked.

When the helmsman saw the assault rifle laser dots circling his face and heart, he dropped his *Playboy*. He turned and saw Jack and Dewey dressed like two bug-eyed killer flies in their CBR suits. He threw both hands up and started shaking his head, screaming, "No! No!" Jack put a finger to his mouth. The helmsman kept pleading for his life. They gagged and zipped him.

Jack checked his handheld. Zero radiation detected. He killed the porno playing on the monitor. Paper wrappers and crushed coffee cups littered the corners. Three ashtrays. All overflowing. A half-eaten plate of something brown. Anything to break the monotony.

"Has EOD found anything?" he asked.

"Negative. Forward deck looks clean," EOD responded.

"Check. We'll kill the lights and start working our way down the superstructure. Muster in the pilothouse and catch up." Jack and Dewey stood at the top of the stairs leading from the pilothouse to the living quarters, galley, and engine rooms.

"Do you smell something, Gunner?" asked Dewey.

"Even with two air filters, it smells like a boat full of road kill. What you thinking?"

"I sure miss Sarge. He'd go right for the worst smell and dig in."

"Well then, what are you waiting for, Dog?" asked Jack.

Jack and Dewey worked their way down through the dark, combat-clearing each compartment like a well-oiled machine. They heard a noise behind them, maybe a groan or gasp. No spider on Jack's neck, though. They dropped to a knee and spun, NODs on, guns hot. No one there. They crept down the passageway and pressed their backs against the steel bulkhead on either side of the only remaining door. Jack's radiation detector still registered zip. He turned the knob. The door swung in. They were both glad for the CBR suits. They'd found the source of the stink.

In the grainy-green light of his NODs, Jack could see the decaying body of Ahmed the bomber. His head turned to the side. Mouth open. Swollen tongue hanging out. Not breathing. A stack of paper towels shoved in a gaping belly wound. His heat signal dim, compared to the man kneeling next to him, who sobbed and caressed his limp hand.

"Put your hands up," said Jack in English.

No change. Rolf had a bandana smeared with axel grease, tied over his mouth and nose to kill the smell of rotting flesh and diesel fuel.

"I said put your fucking hands up," said Jack.

Rolf stiffened. "What? Who are you?"

"I won't say it again, asshole!"

Rolf let go of his father's hand and stood in the rolling, pitch black. "My father's dead. Can't you respect that?"

"Well isn't that just too fucking bad, Rolf? Or is it Dr. Rolf Marques Omar El-Hashem? That's what happens in Badals. You didn't kill me when you had the chance, so you and your father are going to die."

"Gunn? You're supposed to be dead, you son of a bitch!" Rolf lunged across the dark void like a crazy man, to strangle the voice. But in two steps, collapsed to the deck as fifty thousand volts contracted every nerve and muscle. They heard one long groan as the air was wrung from his lungs. Jack held the Taser trigger for fifteen seconds.

Something fell from Rolf's hand. Jack picked up the camera-memory-card-sized tracker, still slimy with pus.

Rolf stayed curled up on the deck, weeping.

"Have any other bright ideas, Doctor?" Jack and Dewey did SSE of the compartment. One dead haji, still no radiation, and a ghoulish nightmare with water, blood, and pus everywhere. The deck was a slippery slide in the rocking ship.

Dewey got on the radio. "We found two . . . still missing Mohammed and the HEU."

Jack put his boot on Rolf's shoulder and pushed him over onto his back. "Hey, where's your buddy? Where's Mohammed?"

"Dead," said Rolf.

"Don't fuck with me, shit-for-brains. Where is he?" asked Jack.

Rolf looked at his father. "You put that tracker inside him, you son of a bitch. You killed him," said Rolf.

"I should've killed him. He deserved it. But we kept him alive and sent him back in exchange for Travis," said Jack.

"At least you've got your dumbfuck brother. I've got nothing."

Jack took a deep breath and pulled the trigger for another fifteen seconds. Rolf's back arched. A scream squeezed out of him. Jack felt nothing. He'd been tased as part of training. They all had. He'd been through a lot worse. The doctor probably hadn't.

"Travis's dead," said Jack. Travis had suffered enough at the hands of this son of a bitch. Rolf didn't deserve the satisfaction of knowing anything. In fact, it was time he got what he deserved.

"What? How?" Rolf stopped sniveling.

"How about I pull this trigger again while you think about it, douche bag," said Jack.

"You killed him, you son of a bitch, when you started shooting across that bridge," Dewey said. He saw Jack nodding and giving him a thumbs up.

"What do you care?" said Jack. "You and all your crazy, jihad fundamentalist, Taliban assholes got what you wanted. Now where's Mohammed? Where's the stolen uranium?"

"I don't know what you're talking about," said Rolf.

"Well, let me paint you a picture. Like you said, it's more my style." Jack drew his pistol, chambered a round, and jammed it into Rolf's temple, just above his ear.

"You're in way over your head, fuckface. You've got no idea what I'm capable of, but pulling this trigger will be the easiest decision I've ever made."

Rolf lay still in the rancid dark.

"We know the rest of the security council was killed in Chitral. We know Mohammed is on this ship. We know he's carrying two hundred fifty pounds of uranium stolen from Pakistan," said Jack. "If you ever want to see your wife and kids again, you'd better start talking. And I mean now!"

Rolf lay in the fetal position as the ship rolled from side to side. A wave of blood and water did, too. The deck vibrated from the engines below.

Jack leaned into the gun. "This is your last chance. Where's Mohammed? Five . . . four

. . . three . . . two . . . one."

Rolf held his hands up. "I'm not one of them. I don't believe the Grand Jihad will do anything except kill thousands of innocent people. If I tell you, will you let me go back to my family?"

"Don't you think your mullahs might find it a little odd if you showed up in Dubai doing surgery again?" asked Jack. "Either way, you're definitely fucked."

"So you're going to kill me?"

"That depends on you," said Jack. "You deserve a bullet between your eyes for what you did to Travis. And I'd love to do just that. But you tell us what we want to know, and we'll see what happens. Despite my gut instinct and better judgment, you *may* get a second chance."

Rolf prayed in the dark for fifteen seconds.

"Five . . . four . . ." Jack jammed the gun barrel into Rolf's skull. "Three . . . two . . . one."

"Okay. Stop. I'll tell you everything."

CHAPTER

38

Arabian Sea

The Black Hawk raced along at one hundred eighty miles per hour and fifty feet above the ocean toward the coast of Yemen.

Prowler tracked the target boat since it had left the container ship. It was still sixty nautical miles from shore, moving at twelve knots through heavy seas.

"Radiation or not, these CBR suits have got to go," Jack said. "I'm more concerned about a bullet or blast, than radiation contamination, and either way, I don't want to go to the bottom of the Arabian Sea dressed like a fucking cupcake."

"Roger that," said Dewey. He scanned the radar screen. "Target coming up on the port in five." Gusts mixed with sea spray buffeted Dewey in the open hatch.

"What do you think Nina would think of you playing King Kong, chasing a crazy jihadi halfway around the world?" asked Dewey.

Nina's face suddenly appeared, like switching channels on a TV. She'd worry, but she wouldn't want him to know. She knew one moment of doubt could be the difference between Jack sinking to the bottom of the ocean or coming home.

Everything Jack did was calculated. Yes, he was an extreme risk taker, but not a glory seeker. Medals didn't impress him. Men putting their lives on the line taking down bad guys impressed him. He and Nina attended many SEAL funerals. Pride and honor, not sadness or regret, were the overwhelming emotions. When Jack's turn to speak came, he liked to portray the fallen SEAL as Samson, holding up the pillars of the coliseum until it collected as many bad guys as possible, then pulling the whole place down, killing himself along with everybody else. He was proud to be a Sioux warrior. He was proud to be a Navy SEAL. Nina would understand. He changed the channel back.

"She'd want you and I to do what needs to be done to stop this crazy fucker."

"Just making sure, good buddy," said Dewey. "Suzy feels the same."

"We've got a visual," said the captain. "One man at the helm in the pilothouse. A second ducked below deck. It looks like that battered old trawler out of *Jaws*. They're slamming pretty good. Taking water over the bow. Don't think they can hear us."

"Roger that," said Jack.

"Wait. The helmsman just looked over his shoulder and yelled something. He went to full throttle. He's got an automatic rifle. He's bringing the boat around, but she's a handful. Has to keep both hands on the wheel. I'm backing off. What's the play, Jack?" asked the captain.

"I'm not as worried about radiation when we're sixty miles out to sea, especially when he's carrying a dirty bomb like the doctor said, not a nuclear warhead. Twenty pounds of Semtex is the bigger concern for your crew, captain," said Jack.

"Roger that."

Dirty bombs were a combination of HEU and Semtex, a plastic explosive that caused massive explosions and radioactive contamination. They were known as "weapons of mass disruption" because while the blast killed, the radiation contaminated a twenty-mile area for only five to ten years.

"Dewey, get on the mini gun," yelled Jack. "Take out the guy topside. As soon as he's down, come in from behind and get me over the afterdeck."

The captain dropped down to thirty feet so Dewey could fire across the bow, not into it. They did not want a premature detonation.

When Dewey pulled the trigger, the gun barrels spun, spitting out two hundred rounds in seconds, with a tracer every ten. The fire line sliced across the bridge. Electrical sparks fizzled. Windows shattered. The pilothouse crumpled like an old man with a broken hip. The target turned into a bloody mess and disappeared in the next swell that crashed across her bow.

The boat turned broadside in the swells and wind. It rocked violently from side to side. No one else came above deck.

"Get me on that boat," yelled Jack. He dropped out of the helo bay door. The rope slid through his hands until he'd rappelled ten feet below the belly. The tops of the swells lapped at his boots, the troughs fell fifteen feet below.

The helo slid sideways toward the boat.

"This is tricky as hell, Gunner. I don't know," said Dewey over the radio. "Maybe we should just blow the fucker."

"Damn it, Dewey. Stop screwing around. We don't even know if Mohammed's on there. Now get me on that boat!"

"Roger that," said Dewey. He made the sign of the cross.

The helo slid back over the surging boat, waiting for it to come to them. Jack's feet kicked the side of the boat when it rose to him on a swell. He jabbed a finger to Dewey to have the pilot move over. When the next swell rose, his feet hit a boat seat. On the next swell, Jack timed it and let go. He dropped five feet, rolling against the gunwale. He gave a thumbs up to Dewey.

"He's down. Let's pull back, Captain. We don't want to make the crazy son of a bitch nervous or he could blow his package," said Dewey.

Jack scrambled to his knees. Rifle hot. NODs on. The Black Hawk's IR floodlight did little to illuminate his situation from three hundred feet away. The boat was dead in the water, tossing this way and that. No steering. No direction.

He pulled his IR flashlight and crouch-crawled toward the open hatch below deck. It was like looking into a mineshaft.

"I know you're in there, you son of a bitch!" Jack yelled. "Come out with your hands up."

No sound. No movement. No blood.

Jack looked over his shoulder. Nothing, but a giant spider clawing at his neck.

"I'm going in," Jack said to Dewey.

"Roger that." Through his NODs and a hundred yards of ocean spray, Dewey could not see much.

Jack hugged the wall of the stairway and sidestepped down, scanning the dark from side to side. At the bottom, he heard a noise to the left and inched toward it. He looked around the doorjamb to the left. A split second, then back out. He looked to the right. Could not see anyone. Came back out. Took a breath. He went in low.

Jack sensed it too late. A hatchet slammed into his armored chest plate, splitting it, and knocking him backwards. His feet flew out from under, and he cracked his head on the stairs.

A deluge of seawater crashed down the stairs. Six inches of oily water sloshed around below deck. Smoke filled the cabin. An acidic electrical smell like smoldering tires mixed with diesel fumes. The clock was ticking.

The black-robed Mohammed towered over Jack. Mohammed hung onto the doorframe with his left hand. He swung Dard again for the killing blow.

The boat rocked hard. Mohammed missed and splintered the doorframe instead. The hatchet stuck. Mohammed lost his grip. He fell sideways against the bulkhead. He was underwater for a split second. The boat rolled back the other way. Mohammed scrambled to his feet. In the fading light from the sparks of the dying radio console, he saw Jack lunge and grab his hatchet.

Jack stood back up. He blocked the doorway. Rifle in his left hand. Hatchet in his right. One way in. One way out.

The boat crashed back and forth in the white caps. The

wind howled. More water came down the hatch. The bilge pumps were dead. Water kept rising. Mohammed frantically thrashed around in the black water, like he was searching for his drowning baby.

"Turn around and put your hands up," yelled Jack.

Mohammed kept sweeping the sloshing water, paying no attention.

"This thing's going to the bottom in two minutes, and you're going with it if you don't put your fucking hands up and turn around," Jack yelled. A bullet would get his attention. Jack shouldered his rifle. Aimed for his leg. Mohammed could still confess while he bled to death. Jack braced himself against the doorway.

Mohammed froze. He stood erect and turned around. One hand was up. The other held something. He'd found what he was looking for. Another way out.

He clutched the aluminum suitcase across his chest. In his left hand, Jack spotted a trigger connected by two wires to the bomb. Mohammed flipped on a below deck light switch. Nothing happened, just more sparks.

"I wouldn't do that if I were you, Mr. Gunn. Even if you shoot me, I'll manage to press this button. You'll be killing yourself and tens-of-thousands of infidels." Mohammed waved the trigger to make sure Jack saw. "I thought you were dead."

"Not hardly, asshole," said Jack.

"You're a hard son of a bitch to kill," said Mohammed.

"And you're a slippery son of a bitch whose time has come. Your Grand Jihad is over. Take a look around you. The only one who's going to die is you."

"And what'll you do to stop the other eleven bombs from going off on New Year's Eve? How'll you find them if you kill me?" asked Mohammed.

"You're the only one who knows where they are, numbnuts. Stop you and your Grand Jihad is finished. Dr. Marques told us everything," said Jack.

"That's bullshit!" screamed Mohammed.

Another wave crashed overboard. The boat rode lower and lower in the water. Jack slowly backed up the slimy stairs, one step at a time, while he kept his gun trained on Mohammed.

Mohammed stayed close.

"If it's such bullshit, then who've you been trying to e-mail or call every ten minutes for the last three days?"

"What?" Mohammed stammered. "What kind of fool do you take me for? Do you think I told that imbecile everything?" Mohammed laughed and wiped a stream of drool on his sleeve.

"You told him enough, you stupid fuck," said Jack. "At least he's smart enough to get out while he still could. You're done." Jack pulled off his NODs so Mohammed could see his eyes. Above his broad nose, and hooded under a heavy brow, glared his laser blue eyes. They were playing back every atrocity, every brutality, they'd witnessed, compliments of Mohammed.

"You'll never take me alive," said Mohammed.

"That's the whole idea of a Badal? To the death, you murderous fuck!" said Jack.

"Give me my hatchet back, or else." He held out the trigger. The suitcase was under his right arm.

"Fuck you!" Jack backed farther across the deck, feet wide apart, keeping his sights trained on Mohammed's eyes through the stinging salt spray. He braced against the side with his hatchet hand. "We may not have changed the world, but we spoiled your plans. I can live with that."

Jack teetered at the back of the boat, a hand on the gunwale for balance. Another wave crashed on top of them. She was filling up. Below deck, the water was thigh high. Mohammed backed down into the stairway once he saw the hovering chopper.

"So what's it going to be?" screamed Jack. "Are you going to drop that fucking suitcase, and tell us where the other bombs are hiding? You're not going to need it where you're going."

Mohammed kneeled in the doorway and smiled. The suitcase was under one arm and the trigger in the other. The wires stretched across his chest. He looked up. He mouthed, *"Allah Akbar, Allah Akbar."* Jack wasn't a lip-reader, but that one was easy.

Jack squarely faced Mohammed. He was twelve feet away. A perfect distance. He had one option and a split second to perfectly execute it. It had been a long time. He raised his right arm above his head and snapped it back down to horizontal. He released the handle with his palm extended, like shaking someone's hand. The hatchet rotated once and slammed into Mohammed's sternum. The blade buried to the hilt. Probably went right through his chest and hit the spine, severing the ascending aorta. It knocked him over backwards, down the steps, into the water below deck.

Jack was the toll collector, and Mohammed had finally paid up for Keeler, Travis, and a multitude of other atrocities.

The helicopter moved closer. Jack put his NODs back on. The only thing he could see at first was the hatchet handle and blood. Mohammed pushed back above water. He gasped. He looked down at his hatchet, like his best friend had betrayed him. He still clutched the suitcase. Another wave hit. The boat did not rock as much anymore. It was more water than boat. He pushed up farther with his trigger hand. He looked at Jack and smiled again. Water was up to his chest. Blood drooled out the corners of his mouth. *"Allah Akbar, Allah Akbar."*

"Sorry. No *Allah Akbar* for you," said Jack.

Mohammed pushed the trigger. Nothing happened. He pushed it again. Still nothing. He held the trigger in front of his fading eyes. The ends of the trigger wires dangled, connected to nothing. As Mohammed fell backward and went underwater, he saw the other ends of the wires buried in his chest, under the hatchet.

Jack sloshed below deck. More water followed. He put a foot on Mohammed's neck and snapped it down like he was kick-starting his Harley. He reached underwater, found the hatchet, and jerked it out of Mohammed's chest. He stuck the hatchet handle under his belt, like the good old days. He grabbed the suitcase and pulled, still holding Mohammed's neck with his foot. Mohammed's hand seemed frozen around the handle, but it too, let go. Water rose up to Jack's chest. A few more waves and she'd be gone.

Jack struggled back up the stairs.

"You gotta get out now, Gunner," said Dewey. "She's going down."

"I didn't get to do any SSE. There're probably clues to this whole Grand Jihad down there. I need to go back."

"Negative, sailor. You gotta let it go. You gotta get out of there now! We're dropping a line."

One wave, then another, flooded over the sides and down the stairs. Water started coming up between the deck boards where Jack stood. If he went back down, he might discover the plan for the Grand Jihad on the way to the bottom of the Arabian Sea, but he'd die right beside Mohammed. He did not want to spend eternity lying next to that son of a bitch. He wanted to die on the field of battle, but not that way. Not that day.

Jack grabbed the rope.

39

Norfolk, Virginia, United States

Travis used a walker to get from physical therapy back to his room. His T-shirt was soaked up the middle of his back. He grimaced each time he swung his left leg through, determined to walk again. He smelled the bouquet on his bedside table before he saw it. When he rounded the corner, he understood.

He had seen some beautiful women, but Jasmine Johnson beat them all. And it wasn't the flowers that made his hospital room smell like heaven. Her smile was so uninhibited, so genuine, Travis bit hook, line, and sinker.

"Sorry you have to see me like this," said Travis. He stood taller than the pain would allow, winced, and hunched back over.

"What? You in your skimpy, see-through gown. I can only imagine." She came to his side and helped him into bed.

"Wow, you smell good. Sure you don't want to climb in?" Travis lifted the sheet, jokingly. Hopefully.

"Now don't you wish," Jaz said in a low, sexy voice. "You need your rest,"

Travis shrank back into bed as reality set in. Jaz fluffed his pillows, and then sat on the side of his bed, resting her hand on his knee.

Travis felt the warmth of her hand through the sheets. Every hair on his body stood erect. "I'm glad you came," he said.

She arrived unannounced only two days earlier. Travis had been struggling with post-traumatic stress in the worst way. Even though he had survived, faces and voices tormented him asleep and awake. Alone in his room, even with the TV, he started sinking into the quicksand where he spent most of his life. He wanted to stay positive, but old and new demons dragged him down. Other than going to physical therapy twice a day, he had no future plans. The roller coaster had crested and his was headed down again.

When Jaz washed in, it was like an ocean breeze through Travis's misery. She had taken vacation from the CIA and returned from Bagram after the bombing at Chitral. Once Ghost Team stood down, she stood down. She had watched what Travis had gone through from her control center. She wasn't the type to take chances in her personal life. She'd been hurt before. But there was something about him she was drawn to. He'd been victimized so badly, yet been so brave. She decided to roll the dice and see where things went.

"What's this?" she asked, and picked up a Bible.

"The nurse pulled it out when she was looking for my watch. The old Gideon's Bible I've seen in my hotel room hundreds of times. Never opened it. Until now."

"And?" Jaz flipped through the pages, like she knew where she was going.

"I made a promise to God. Seeing that Bible was like him giving me a nudge." He told Jaz the story. "So what have I got to lose?" Travis shivered, desperately hoping it wasn't Jaz.

Jaz traced her finger across a page and read, "Love is patient. Love is kind. Love does not delight in evil, but rejoices with the truth."

Travis started to smile.

"It always protects, always trusts, always hopes, always perseveres. Love never fails." She took Travis's hand. "My daddy was a minister."

Tears came to Travis. He'd never met a woman like Jaz. Beautiful. Strong. Tender. Spiritual. "I was raised by Sioux holy men."

She leaned over and kissed Travis, catching him by surprise. Before he could react, she stood back up, and then leaned back over and gave him another long, warm, sumptuous kiss. She tasted more lovely than she smelled. "This is going to be interesting," she said with a smile.

Jaz stayed with Travis till lights out. Travis didn't want her to leave, but she did. When she came back early the next morning, she found him sweating and twitching. The dreams had been horrible. She stayed all day as they talked and laughed between his naps and PT sessions. The nurse found a foldout bed so she could spend the night. It was the first good night of sleep he'd had in years.

Jaz told him she had always dreamt of being a SEAL. Wanted to make the world a better place. Since women weren't allowed to be SEALs, she did the next best thing. She earned a degree from Berkeley in international studies with a minor in Arabic. The CIA snatched her up, paid her loans, and stuck her down their intelligence black hole. She'd finally gotten her wish. Jaz helped mission-plan for Jack's Ghost Team. She wasn't pulling the triggers, but she pointed their guns.

Travis was in love with the female version of Jack, which made him laugh. He was sure she had some Indian blood in her somewhere. She came to the hospital every day, walked the hallways with him, holding hands. The walks went outdoors, and got longer. They talked for hours. His legs got stronger over the days and weeks. Time flew.

Travis had no plans for the future. But his roller coaster was headed back up.

40

Orlando, Florida, United States

"Five . . . four . . . three . . . two . . . one . . . Happy New Year!"

"These are the best fireworks ever, Daddy."

Jack stretched back on the blanket, hands clasped behind his head. Nina rested her head on his chest. She wore a ball cap. Her cheeks were shallow. Her skin was pale. She'd never looked better. She pulled the blanket up around her neck.

"You're not carrying a beeper, right?" asked Nina.

"I'm all yours," said Jack.

"Thanks for Jakey. He's gone through a lot."

"What about you?"

"I'm cold."

Jack gave Nina a squeeze. Dewey, Suzy, and their family oohed and aahed on the next blanket.

"How long till the next round?" asked Jack.

"I don't want to think about it. Let just enjoy tonight."

They snuggled for the grand finale. Later, after the kids were tucked in, the four rendezvoused by the reggae pool bar. The beat of the music made Jack feel like they were having their own victory powwow. He'd been to plenty back in the day. Grown men sitting in a circle, pounding the drum, chanting high-pitched songs, stirring the primal energies. Stirring their spirits. There'd be dancing, sage, sweet grass smoke, and

237

plenty of eagle feathers. He remembered, and pulled Travis's pillow feather from his pocket.

"I checked. No attacks. No dirty bombs and no Grand Jihad. Happy New Year," said Jack. He handed Dewey the feather. They clinked their bottles of beer.

Jack's theory proved to be true. The uranium stolen from Pakistan by Mustafa had been converted into twelve dirty bombs. Each suitcase carried about twenty pounds of HEU and Semtex, just like Mohammed's. They figured twelve dirty bombs, because eleven members of the security council and Mohammed had their identity changed. Two hundred fifty pounds divided by twelve worked out. Jack suspected Mustafa had planted the other eleven suitcases in key cities around the world, like New York, Washington D.C., London, and Rome, over the past year. Once the security council split up, each member would have traveled uninhibited by customs to detonate their bomb. Since the security council was killed, Mohammed was forced to improvise. Activating sleeper cells were his only options. With a gun to his head, Rolf spilled the beans. Everything was to go down at the stroke of midnight on New Year's Eve. Since they had been jamming Mohammed's internet and phone, Jack figured it out before Mohammed activated the cells. Mission accomplished.

Partiers twirled noisemakers, blew horns, boozed, groped, and kissed while the New Year's euphoria lasted.

"Look at those idiots. They don't have a fucking clue," said Jack.

"And that's a good thing, Gunner. We kill bad guys so they can be idiots if they want. It's the American way," said Dewey.

"Well, God bless America," toasted Jack, rolling his eyes.

"You know, the helicopter video of you throwing that tomahawk is like something out of a dream. That'll make Ghost Team's top-ten best kills ever. I mean, who does that shit anymore? Next, you'll be chucking spears."

"Spears? I love spears," said Jack.

"You'll have to teach me some of your Indian tricks someday.

It might come in handy if haji gets his wish and blows us back to the seventh century."

They took a drink and stopped talking to listen to Nina. "So it's Jaz and Travis now. She's got him practically dancing."

"You sure she's not just pumping him?" asked Dewey's wife, Suzy.

"That'd be pretty heartless after what he went through. I don't think even the CIA is that cold."

"Who are you kidding?" said Jack. "But you don't need to worry about Jaz. She's good to go."

"It's just great to see him happy and sober," said Nina. "They got his doctor's license back, too. So who knows?"

"If anyone's earned it, he has," said Dewey. He drained his beer.

He and Jack went to the bar for another bucket of brews. "You really think there're eleven more bombs out there?"

"Definitely," said Jack. "Too bad Mohammed died before we got a chance to milk it out of him. But the mullahs know they exist, just not where. The suitcases will turn up sooner or later."

"We'll want to keep Rolf on a short leash," said Dewey.

"I don't think he'll be getting out of Guantanamo any time soon," said Jack. They clinked their glasses together. "And don't ever tell Travis that Rolf's alive. He's suffered enough."

"Amen to that." They walked back to their table.

"Why didn't you kill Rolf when you had the chance? The little fucker deserved it," asked Dewey.

"Damned if I know," said Jack.

"Are you going soft on me? He tried to kill both of you," said Dewey.

"I know where to find him," said Jack. "Something Travis said kept me from putting one right through his earhole."

"The whole mission was bizarre," said Dewey. "We started out tracking IED haji and ended up stopping the crazy fucks from blowing us all to kingdom come."

"I'm just glad it's over and Travis is okay."

"Are you okay, Gunner?" asked Dewey.

"Hell, yes! It's New Year's Eve. We saved the world!"

"I mean your concussions." Dewey tried saying out of the corner of his mouth.

"Keep it down man. Nina has enough to worry about."

"So you're good?"

"It's covered. Doc's on top of it," said Jack. They took a shot and slouched back in their chairs. Bottle rockets fizzed and popped over the hotel. The kids were sleeping and the wives were drinking. The music cranked up another notch.

"It doesn't get any better than this," said Dewey.

"Maybe it does. How about celebrating my promotion to warrant officer and head of Counterterrorism Task Force?"

"A warrant officer? No shit?" said Dewey. "Congratulations. That's why you're being so weird. You're a big-shot officer now."

"Winfield's offering, and I'm thinking," said Jack.

"Are you crazy? What's there to think about? Take it before he changes his mind," said Dewey. "Isn't it what you want? To stay home with Nina and Jake?"

"Of course, but I don't know if I'm ready to be a spectator instead of a gladiator." He flexed his beer arm.

"We're getting too old to be running around chasing haji pricks from here to hell and back. And your head could use a break, too," said Dewey. "And what about your swim buddy, sir?" He stood and did a half-assed salute. "Are you going to abandon him after all the times he's saved your ass?"

"You must be drunk, you stupid fuck. Who saved whose ass?"

"So we're done?" asked Dewey.

"That depends," said Jack. "I love pulling the trigger, completing the mission, the camaraderie of the guys."

"You want to go out on top, Gunner," said Dewey. "You're better at this shit than anyone. Head of the entire CTF, seriously? If haji so much as farts, you can take a dump on him with the push of a button."

"And if we get bored, we head downrange," said Jack.

"Now you're talking," said Dewey. "So you're taking the promotion?"

"What do you think?" said Jack.

"Here's to kicking ass, sir!"

They chugged the rest of their beers, threw down a shot of whiskey, and toasted, "God bless the Navy SEALs! Hooyah!"

Epilogue

A mile from where they'd watched the fireworks with 100,000 vacationers, a weathered shipping crate is buried deep in a warehouse for unclaimed freight. Locked inside is a suitcase. Inside the suitcase is twenty pounds of highly enriched uranium wrapped in lead, and twenty pounds of plastic explosives connected to a trigger. Lightly etched in the trigger is the number eleven.

The half-life of highly enriched uranium is seven hundred million years.

The End

About the Author

Dr. Richard Blomberg has practiced medicine in the land of 10,000 lakes for twenty years. He grew up in an Iowa farm town, the oldest of ten kids, before serving as a Navy corpsman during the Vietnam War. For generations, Richard's family has proudly served in the Army, Navy, Air Force, and Marines. Richard and Kim have five wonderful children, and by the grace of God, are still deeply in love after thirty-five years of marriage. Kim's Nakota relatives fought at the Battle of the Greasy Grass (Little Big Horn). Writing *Warpath* allowed Richard to honor Native Americans and those who have served in the military by creating Jack Gunn, a Native American Navy SEAL extraordinaire. *Warpath* is his first thriller.

Warpath

Order more books for your friends

Richard Blomberg

www.RichardBlomberg.com

Facebook: https://www.facebook.com/AuthorRichardBlomberg

Author's email: RichardBlombergJr@gmail.com

Publisher: SDP Publishing

Genre: Military Thriller

Also available in ebook format

TO PURCHASE:

Amazon.com, BarnesAndNoble.com, GoogleBooks, iBooks

SDPPublishingSolutions.com

 **SDP Publishing**

www.SDPPublishingSolutions.com

Contact us at: info@SDPPublishing.com

CPSIA information can be obtained
at www.ICGtesting.com
Printed in the USA
LVOW12s2304131116

512822LV00001BA/18/P